SERAFINA
and the
SEVEN
STARS

SERAFINA and the SEVEN STARS

ROBERT BEATTY

DISNEY · HYPERION

LOS ANGELES   NEW YORK

First Hardcover Edition, July 2019
First Paperback Edition, June 2020
10 9 8 7 6 5 4 3 2 1
FAC-021131-20120
Printed in the United States of America

This book is set in 11.16-pt Adobe Garamond Pro, Liam, Qilin/Fontspring;
Minister Std/Monotype
Designed by Phil Buchanan

Library of Congress Control Number for Hardcover Edition: 2019011186
ISBN 978-1-368-00960-7

Visit www.DisneyBooks.com

Biltmore Estate
Asheville, North Carolina
1900

Serafina raced through the forest, her sharp panther claws ripping into the leafy autumn ground, propelling her long, black-furred body through the underbrush. She scrambled up moss-covered rocky slopes and dashed through shaded meadows of swaying ferns, making her way swiftly home.

The sound of rapid footfalls charged up behind her.

She burst forward with new speed, leaping over the trunk of a fallen tree, then tearing through an open field.

But now two of them were on her, snarling as they lunged at her sides.

The first mountain lion pounced on her back with a ferocious growl and tumbled her to the ground. The second slammed into her head.

She spun on them with a hissing bite, pushing them away with her legs and swatting them repeatedly with her claws retracted, then broke free and ran.

You silly cats need to get out of here, she thought as she leapt the stream that marked the back side of Diana Hill. *We're getting too close to the house. You've got to go back.*

She surged forward, trying to put enough distance between her and her young half sister and half brother that they would finally return to the depths of the forest. But seeing her attempts to outrun them, they became more invigorated than ever. Her sister bounded ahead of her, growling playfully as she looked back at Serafina over her shoulder, challenging Serafina to chase her.

Slow down, Serafina thought as they reached the top of the hill. *You need to be careful here.*

But in that instant, the air exploded with the loud, wrenching sound of twisting metal, bending wire, and a mountain lion yowling in pain. Her sister had been running so fast that she never saw the wire fence in her path—didn't even know what a fence was—and slammed right into it. The terrified lion kicked and clawed, trying desperately to fight this strange, coiling attacker.

The other mountain lion circled his sister's flailing, wire-entangled body in agitation, but was utterly unable to help her.

Serafina's heart lurched in panic. She quickly shifted into human form and moved toward her struggling sister.

The more the young mountain lion fought against the wire, the more entangled she became.

Serafina grabbed the rat's nest of metal with her bare hands and tried to tear it away. But the lion kept fighting, pulling against the wires, scratching and biting and growling.

"Just stay still, cat. I'm trying to help you!" Serafina told her sister in exasperation, but as the entwined lion stared up at her with her golden eyes, Serafina knew her sister couldn't understand her.

"I told you we were done playing for the day," she said as she pulled and pried at the wire. "You shouldn't try to follow me home. We're too close to the house."

As she worked to free her sister, she glanced around to get her bearings. A short distance away, surrounded by the vine-wrapped stone columns of a small gazebo, stood Biltmore's Roman statue of Diana, goddess of the hunt, with a bow in one hand, a quiver of arrows on her back, and a deer standing at her side.

We're far too close, Serafina thought again as she struggled with a length of wire that had ensnared her sister's legs. Her brother and sister might get themselves into all sorts of trouble if they passed into the grounds of the mansion; the last thing she needed was for someone to spot a mountain lion running across Biltmore's lawn.

From this high position atop Diana Hill, Serafina could see Biltmore House below her, with its pale-gray limestone walls and leaded-glass windows gleaming in the light of the setting sun, the steeply slanted slate-blue rooftops piercing the sky, and the misty ranges of the Blue Ridge Mountains rising in the distance.

The house was a beautiful sight, tranquil and serene. But she didn't trust pleasant feelings. Or beauty. And she definitely couldn't cotton to the nerve-racking peace and quiet that had been slithering around the estate for the last several months. This mishap with her sister aside, nothing sinister had happened at Biltmore in a long time, but she hadn't been able to shake the feeling that it soon would.

She finally managed to get her sister out of most of the wires, but there was still a bad one wrapped around her front leg. The lion kept yanking her paw away at the worst possible moment, anxious to get free, but hindering Serafina's efforts.

"Just hold on, girl," Serafina said, stroking the lion's head. "I'm almost done."

There were small cuts on her sister's shoulders and legs, but Serafina wasn't sure how she could help her. She didn't have any bandages, and even if she did, there wasn't any way to keep them in place.

I need Braeden, she thought in frustration. *He would calm the lion and heal her wounds.*

But Braeden was gone. And the shock of it still throbbed in Serafina's heart. After all their struggles, fighting to stay together and to stay alive, they had been undone by a few words on a wretched piece of paper in a city far away. She had wanted him to stand up, to fight, to slash at his uncle's words.

But he couldn't fight it. He knew he *shouldn't* fight it.

And now she was once again alone.

As she wrenched the last of the twisted wire from her sister's leg, the lion rose to her feet and rubbed her whiskered face appreciatively against Serafina's cheek. And their brother came over and rubbed his shoulders against them as well.

It seemed as if maybe they were a little sorry for their rambunctiousness, and she was sorry, too. She should have stopped running sooner than she did and warned them of the dangers of the man-made world. Biltmore's groundskeepers must have put up the wire fence to protect the stand of small maple trees they had planted at the top of Diana Hill. The cubs were fullgrown now, but they were still young and inexperienced.

But as she was hugging her brother and sister, a shift in the breeze touched the bare skin on the back of her neck, and put a chill down her spine.

Startled, she turned and scanned the line of trees surrounding the distant house, looking for any sort of danger: a mysterious figure or encroaching enemy—anything that might signal that trouble was a-prowl.

She studied the balconies and towers of the house for unusual movement, and then the gate, the road, and the paths leading into the gardens.

Over the last few months, she had patrolled the grounds day and night, sleeping only when she had to, for her memories of her past battles never slept.

No, she told herself as she gazed down at the house and out across the mountains, she wasn't going to let any of this beauty and pleasantness fool her.

Something was wrong.

Something was *always* wrong at Biltmore.

Black cloaks and twisted staffs, shadowed sorcerers in the

murky night—she didn't know in what form it would come, but she was the Guardian of Biltmore Estate, and she knew she had to stay alert, or people were going to die.

When she heard a sound drifting through the forest from the north, goose bumps rose on her arms.

She tilted her head and listened.

The whispers of the wind moved through the boughs of the trees.

She didn't trust wind. Or trees.

In the months since her past battles, the slightest creak of a distant stick or the faint rustling of leaves had sent her into a twitch and a shifting glance. And now, as she stood on the hill and heard the sound of the whispering wind coming toward her, she wasn't sure whether it was truth or lie, but a crawling sensation crept up her sides.

Pulling a long breath in through her nose, she smelled something on the breeze, a trace of sulfur and charcoal that she hadn't smelled in a long time. It reminded her of death.

And then she began to hear the sound more clearly: the *clip-clop* of trotting hooves, a carriage coming up the Approach Road toward Biltmore.

The logical part of her human mind told her that not all carriages were filled with demons and murderers. But her lungs started sucking in air, as if they knew they would soon be needed.

This could be nothing, she tried to tell herself. *It could be a carriage full of kind and gracious gentlefolk coming for a pleasant visit.*

But her heart pounded in her chest.

The beauty. The forest. The wind.

She quickly turned to her brother and sister. "Now listen— get on out of here, right away! Run!"

For once, the two big cats did exactly what she told them, hightailing it into the cover of the forest.

Serafina ran to protect Biltmore even as a carriage and its team of horses came barreling through the main gate into the courtyard. Before she could even see who was inside, a second carriage came rolling in behind it, and then a third, until there were thirteen carriages in all, their drivers steering them straight toward the front doors of the house.

$\mathcal{S}$erafina reached the front terrace and ducked behind the stone railing just as the carriages came to a stop.

Still trying to catch her breath from the sprint to the house, and staying well hidden, she peered out.

The carriages were disgorging a flood of passengers into the courtyard.

Some of the women wore long city coats with sweeping, upturned collars, but most of the new arrivals, both the ladies and the gentlemen, wore brown tweed jackets, autumn gloves, and leather lace-up boots for hiking and shooting.

A dozen of Biltmore's footmen and other manservants hurried out to attend to the new arrivals, unloading their strapped leather luggage, their riding gear, and their shotguns and hunting rifles protected in long oak cases.

The smiling Mr. and Mrs. Vanderbilt stood in the archway of Biltmore's open doors, shaking the hands of the new guests as they came in, embracing many of them—friends and family and acquaintances new and old—inviting them into their home.

Her eyes searched the new arrivals one by one. *How will the intruder cloak himself this time?* she wondered as she studied them. *How will he twist himself into our lives?*

The happy smiles and soothing charm of laughter didn't deceive her. There was an enemy among them, a killer, a kidnapper, an arsonist, she was sure of it, or maybe a doppelgänger, a haint, or a wraith-in-the-night come to drink their souls. She felt it twisting tightly around her mind, strangling her thoughts.

One of the new strangers was a distinguished, silver-haired, finely dressed man who gazed around at the surrounding forest and mountains as if he'd been dropped off in the middle of the wildest and most uncivilized place he had ever seen.

Another was a broad-shouldered, barrel-chested man in a khaki jacket and heavy boots wearing a stern hunter's gaze, as if he was just about ready to shoot anything that moved.

"Be careful of those rifles!" he shouted at one of the footmen unloading the stack of cases from his carriage.

As the very last figure stepped out of the thirteenth carriage, Serafina's senses seethed with anticipation. She was sure this was going to be the villain. But it was a young, dark-haired girl, maybe fourteen years old, in a plain, clean gray dress, a journeying satchel over her shoulder, and a pair of brass binoculars in her hand.

The girl looked around the surrounding forest, as if checking the trees for species of birds she had not yet seen, and then gazed at the lions, carved from Italian rose marble, sitting on guard on each side of the house's great oaken doors. Finally, she lifted her eyes up toward the immensity of the house.

The girl's face filled with an expression of awe as she took in not just the mansion's grand size, but all the details of its facade. Serafina watched her gaze up in wonder at the hundreds of ornate carvings of gargoyles and mythical creatures that adorned the walls, gutters, and steeples of the house. And then the girl's face bloomed into a smile of delight as she spotted the statue of Joan of Arc, a beautiful warrior in full plate armor carrying her banner into battle, and beside her, the statue of the chain mail–clad St. Louis holding his cross and longsword.

As Serafina saw the excitement in the new girl's face, the fierceness that she had been feeling moments before began to fade. None of these people looked like treacherous killers. And none of them looked like murderous demons. It had just been her old fears come a-boiling up again.

You're such a flinchy-clawed scaredy-cat, she scolded herself. *This ain't nothin' but thirteen bushels of everyday folk.*

She crumpled down onto the floor behind the railing, pulling her knees to her chest in discouragement and hugging them, her muscles twitching against enemies of the mind that she could not see and could not fight but that forever battled her.

Over the last few months, when guests in the house tried to strike up a conversation with her, she found herself watching the shadows at the edge of the room. She often startled at the clink of a teacup or the crackle of a warm fire. If someone touched her arm or brushed her shoulder, she flinched.

She was supposedly the Guardian of Biltmore, but she and Braeden had defeated all of the estate's enemies, and no new enemies had appeared. She had thought when this time of peace finally came, she would bask in the glow of trouble-free days. But nothing glowed. It *burned*.

What good was a Chief Rat Catcher once all the rats were caught?

What use was a warrior once the war was fought?

What worth was loyalty to a friend who had taken the train north to a different world?

I should have known, she thought as she glanced through the railing at the arriving guests. *The carriages weren't carrying enemies. They were just Mr. and Mrs. Vanderbilt's friends and family coming for the fall hunting season.*

They had come not just for the shooting, which was a long tradition among the ladies and gentlemen of wealthy society, but for the formal-dress dinners in the Banquet Hall, the elegant lantern-lit evening parties in the Italian Garden, and the late-night games in the Billiard Room. What better way to celebrate their own prosperity, and the arrival of a new century, than with the renowned company of the Vanderbilts?

And they had come for another reason, too. The night before, while sneaking through the rooms of a couple who had already arrived, she had overheard them whispering about getting their first glimpse of Biltmore's smallest and most beloved new resident.

Serafina had been waiting just outside the nursery with Braeden, Mr. Vanderbilt, and the other friends and family members when little Miss Cornelia Vanderbilt came into the world, a tiny bundle of wriggling coos in the arms of her loving mother. Serafina had heard Baby Nell's first cry, and she had played with her in the nursery many times since. During the night, Serafina had often lain on the balcony outside the nursery window, looking out across the grounds, swishing her long black tail back and forth in a guardian's contentment, while Baby Nell slept safely inside. She remembered thinking that Cornelia was the first Vanderbilt to be born in the mountains of North Carolina. Did that make her and Cornelia sisters of a kind? What would she be like? How would she speak? How would she see the world? Would the Vanderbilts of the future become people of the Southern mountains?

All through the summer and autumn days there had been an air of tranquility at Biltmore, a sense of new beginnings. She knew she should be happy. Just as everyone else seemed to be. She enjoyed her life in the workshop with her pa and her life around Biltmore, but when she was supposed to be sleeping, she tossed and turned. When she was walking the grounds, a mere squirrel dashing out in front of her would drench her limbs with fear. Several times while patrolling the forests around the house she had shifted rapidly into panther form, sure that an attack was a split second away, only to find nothing but a babbling brook or wind in the trees.

And now Braeden was gone as well.

"Sit down," Mr. Vanderbilt had said to her and Braeden as they came into his office that dreadful day. "Braeden, you know that in the time since your parents passed away, you have become like a son to me. I love you with all my heart."

Braeden sat quietly beside her, unmoving, as if he knew there was nothing he could do about what was about to happen.

"Your father specified in his will," Mr. Vanderbilt continued, "that his children should attend the school that he and the other members of the Vanderbilt family have attended for generations. It is incumbent upon both of us to put our personal feelings aside and do our duty to fulfill your father's last wishes. I'm afraid the time has come for you to leave Biltmore and return to New York City."

Braeden's brows furrowed, and he wiped his eye with trembling fingers. He looked more somber than she'd ever seen him. But he lowered his head, slowly nodded, and said very softly, "I understand, Uncle."

And now she found herself hiding, crumpled up behind a railing, without him.

School? Of all the godforsaken, no-good places on earth, why did he have to go to *school?* What kind of aunt and uncle would do that to a *child?* What good would school do for him?

He was already one of the smartest people she knew! And if he absolutely had to go to school, why did he have to go to school so far away?

She hated it. She hated everything about it.

When the day came that Braeden had to leave for New York, she went to the train station with him and Mr. Vanderbilt. She remembered standing on the platform in front of Braeden, not sure what to say to him. And she could see that he didn't know what to say to her, either.

For the last year, they'd been together almost constantly, but it had all come to this bitter end.

How do you say good-bye?

With all the various passengers shouldering past them and climbing hurriedly into the massive, steam-hissing black machine, she and Braeden looked at each other, their gazes locked. They had defeated their darkest foes, but they could not defeat this.

"I'm going to miss you, Serafina," Braeden said, very quietly.

"I'm going to miss you, too," she said in return, her voice shaking.

There were so many things she wanted to tell him, so many memories she wanted to recall together, but all the thoughts gathering in her head got stuck in her throat and she couldn't speak.

As the train whistle blew, he seemed like he was going say something to her as well, like he wanted to say good-bye, but he just kept looking at her as if he was struggling to find the words. When the conductor hurried by, shouting, "Last call!

All aboard!" Braeden muttered, "I've got to go," then climbed the steps into the train car and disappeared.

Standing at Mr. Vanderbilt's side, she watched the train pull away, the low rumble of its boiling engine and thumping wheels churning in her body.

She did not move.

She did not scream.

But she felt the pound of it in her chest even now as she remembered watching the train roll down the long, clicking steel tracks, and disappear.

I'm not just useless, she thought. *I'm lost.*

After the new guests had all gone inside, and the last two footmen closed the front doors behind them, Serafina picked herself up and made her way to the far side of the house.

How do you say good-bye? she wondered. *And how do you live after you have?*

She walked alone onto the South Terrace, near the windows of the Library, with the view of the mountains in front of her, and the thick vines of wisteria growing in the lattice above her head.

As the sun set and night fell, she remembered the time Braeden had sat alone on this bench in the darkness, wrapped in his woolen blanket, recovering from his wounds, and looking out at the stars. She had walked up behind him as pale as moonlight and put her wisp-of-a-spirit hand on his shoulder.

It seemed so long ago.

"Now *you're* the ghost," she whispered.

She gazed out across the forested valley at the view of the Blue Ridge Mountains as the sky darkened. There were not yet any stars, but the brilliant dot of Venus was setting over the silhouette of Mount Pisgah on the western horizon. The bright ball of Jupiter gleamed above, followed by the tiny pinprick of Saturn, and then the reddish orb of Mars rising from the mountains in the east. It was a rare, blue glowing moment when she could see all four planets wheeling across the sky at once, as if spinning on a great invisible disk.

With Braeden gone, the planets had once again become her companions. And a few minutes later, thousands of stars began to fill the dark, moonless sky.

Once Venus had disappeared behind the mountain, it was Jupiter that burned the brightest and the longest, and she imagined that it was her long-lost friend. She tried to imagine his life in New York City. He had told her that there were so many electric lights there that it was hard to see the stars, but she imagined that he must be able to see Jupiter. *At least Jupiter,* she thought, looking up at the planet.

"Wherever you are, Braeden," she whispered, "stay bold!"

It was hard to imagine what her life at Biltmore was going to be like without him. He was not only her best friend, he was the only person in her life who knew who she truly was.

She still had her pa, who had found her in the forest when she was a baby, and who had loved her ever since, but even her beloved pa had never seen her in her true feline form like Braeden had. She'd been far too scared to tell her father anything about that.

Her pa was in charge of building and fixing the mechanical contraptions at Biltmore. He believed in tools and machines and iron things made by man, and in normal, everyday human beings, not strange and unnatural shape-shifting creatures of the night like her.

She loved to run with her feline brother and sister through the forest, but they were pure mountain lions, not catamount shape-shifters, so she couldn't strategize with them, sneak through the house with them, make secret plans, devise ingenious traps, kill demons, or do any of the things that normal friends did together.

After she and Braeden defeated their enemies months before, time had frayed, and the world gone slow. The days had become long, like feathery gray clouds with naught but murky shape stretched across the sky. And now that he was gone, it made it all the worse.

What worried her now was whether after all these months of peace at Biltmore she would still be able to distinguish a real threat from a startled jump. With her friend and ally gone, how would she gather and sort out the clues of a mystery? What would she be fighting for if there was no one at her side?

And on many nights, she missed her catamount mother, who had taught her so much of the forest and the mountains.

Her mother was a shape-shifter like her, but had been imprisoned in her feline form for so many years that even after Serafina had freed her, she was unable to fully rejoin the human world. She had gone off into the Black Mountains in search of new territory, more animal than human now.

Glancing through the windows into the Library, and down the long Tapestry Gallery, she saw the glow of the lamps and candles, and heard the mingling voices of the evening's revelry, with the women in their long, glittery dresses and the men in their black jackets and white ties, all smiles and grand hellos, sipping their champagne.

All this happiness here, she thought. *Is this my world now?*

But she knew there were other places out in the world that weren't as safe and protected as Biltmore. Earlier that summer she had gone to see her old friend Waysa, who lived in the Great Smoky Mountains, and she saw the plight of his Cherokee kindred, and many others as well, struggling through a violent attack on the forests there. Hordes of men with great steel saws and steam-powered winches were slashing down the ancient trees. She and Waysa had barely managed to escape. Was it right for her to stay here at Biltmore in this quiet, peaceful, empty place when she knew there were others who needed help?

Months before, there had been a frightening, soul-splintering time when she had shifted into mist and dust and other forms. But she had turned thirteen years old now, she had her feet on the ground, and all that was behind her.

But sometimes, late at night, when she was in her panther

form, it felt as if she might go out running through the forest and just keep going, like her mother had.

And sometimes, more and more when she was in her human form, it felt as if her senses and her brain, and even the core of her body, were changing in dark and primal ways, like she was becoming less human and more panther every day.

She knew it was the way of her solitary, feline kind to wander, to explore, but how could she just leave her home? How could she leave her pa? And what about her brother and sister living in the surrounding forest, and Mr. and Mrs. Vanderbilt, and little Baby Nell? She could never do it. Even if there was a way in her mind to say good-bye to the Vanderbilts, she knew in her heart she could never leave her pa. She had to stay in this lonely, empty place whether she belonged here or not.

As she was standing on the terrace, consumed in her thoughts, she heard the step of a foot in the gravel behind her. Startled, she spun around, her heart lurching as she raised her hands to defend herself.

She could see right away that there was indeed someone standing behind her.

But he wasn't attacking her.

He was just looking at her.

The hair on the back of her neck stood on end.

It wasn't a stranger.

She knew that what she thought she was seeing was impossible.

He seemed to be standing in front of her, his skin pale in the starlight, his tousle of brown hair more disheveled than usual, his brown eyes brighter than she remembered, and his face filled with tenderness. But there were dirty scuff marks on the shoulder of his jacket, the knees of his trousers were badly torn, and traces of crusted blood streaked his face.

Her heart shuddered in her chest as a terrible thought leapt into her mind.

Had there been a train wreck?

Was this his spirit coming back to say good-bye to her one last time before he left the living world for good?

Or had all her startled jumps and scaredy-cat fears finally shattered her mind?

She felt a slow aching dread filling her insides as she tried to open her mouth to speak. "Are . . ." she began to ask the apparition. "Are you real?"

Gazing at her with soft eyes, he gently asked, "Are you all right, Serafina?"

When she finally spoke, her words came out as a whisper. "Did something happen to the train?" she asked. "Are you actually here?"

"I'm here," Braeden said, nodding.

"But how? I saw you get on the train and it pulled away."

"I only made it as far as Tennessee," he said, shrugging a little, almost as if he was embarrassed.

"I don't under— What do you mean?"

"I was sitting on the train, thinking about everything, but I only made it as far as Tennessee, and then I couldn't take it anymore."

"What did you do?"

"I jumped off."

"*What?* How did you get back here?"

"My uncle gave me some money for my first semester at school, so I used it to buy a horse."

"You rode all the way home from Tennessee?"

"Fifty miles."

Serafina looked at him in shock, amazed by his story. He was filled with a rebellion she'd never seen in him. Mr. and Mrs. Vanderbilt, and all his aunts and uncles up in New York, were going to be so worried about what happened to him, and angry when they found out what he did. He had disobeyed them! And leave it to Braeden to solve his problems with a horse! He and his new horse must have been riding hard to get back home so quickly.

But as she stood in front of him, she became aware of the beat of her heart in her chest, and it began to drown out everything else. Her thoughts felt as if they were getting washed away in the warm new blood pumping through her body.

Braeden stepped toward her, his eyes looking down at the ground, then slowly rising up to look at her.

As he wrapped his arms around her and pulled her close, it felt as if he was pulling her into a warm blanket. They held each other, and the fretting anxiety and confusion she'd been feeling earlier began to melt away.

"Come on," he said, finally separating from her. "I want to show you something down by the lake."

"Aren't you going to get in trouble for coming back?" she asked as they went down the stone steps that led to the Pergola and into the gardens.

"Oh, yes, most definitely," he said with an odd cheerfulness.

"What are you going to do when they find out?"

"I don't know," he said. "Maybe they won't."

She couldn't help but glance at him in surprise that he didn't have some sort of plan worked out.

"I just wanted to see you one last time," he said.

As they followed the path past Biltmore's famous golden-rain tree, Braeden kept talking. "I know I was born in New York, and that's where my family comes from, but . . . I don't know . . ." He glanced at her and then cast his eyes sheepishly to the ground. "My life is here . . ." he said. "*You're* here."

She felt a pang of happiness when he said these words. It was as if she were becoming physically lighter.

"And you belong here, too," she said, suddenly realizing by the tremble in her voice why he'd struggled to say the words he'd said to her. Why were certain things—even things that were obviously and deeply true—often the most difficult things to say to someone?

"I'm glad you're home, Braeden," she managed to get out as they went down the steps into the Walled Garden, filled with its red and orange spray of autumn mums. "I've been moping around wonderin' what to do, and skittish as a long-tailed cat in a room full of rocking chairs."

"I know what you mean," he grumbled.

"When I'm in the house," she said, "I try to join in, I try to talk to people, I really do, but I feel like I'm just watching everyone else from a distance, like I'm disconnected from them."

"And from me, too?" he asked.

"Not you," she said, "but your aunt and uncle sometimes, and definitely the new guests. Especially the hunters."

"The way some of those hunters strut and brag and make bets on how many animals they're going to kill is disgusting," he said, scowling. "But that's not me and you, and it's not my aunt and uncle, either."

"Then why do they allow the hunters to come?" she asked, genuinely curious, but as soon as she said the words, she knew she shouldn't have. "I'm sorry. My pa would say I'm gettin' above my raising, and he'd be right. I know I don't have any right to tell your aunt and uncle who they should allow into their home. They allowed *me* into their home, and I'm decidedly suspect."

Braeden smiled as they walked. "Come on now, don't exaggerate. You're not *decidedly* suspect," he scolded her. "You're just plain old, regular suspect, a typical shape-changing, rat-catching, basement-dwelling, demon-killing mountain girl. Nothing wrong with that. We seem to need those around here."

She laughed at his description as he continued. "My aunt and uncle have hosted the hunting season every fall for years. It's a tradition in the old families, a way for family and friends to get together, but my aunt and uncle don't actually do any hunting themselves. They enjoy the riding, but not the rest of it."

"Not the killing, you mean," she said quietly.

After crossing through the Rose Garden, they took the brick pathway around the glass-roofed Conservatory. The trail that led down to the lake, which their old friend Mr. Olmsted, Biltmore's landscape architect, had called the Bass Pond, was covered in a carpet of pine needles, soft and quiet beneath their feet.

"I guess I just don't know what to do here anymore," she said.

"You don't need to *do* anything."

"That's just it. I feel useless, like I'm not any good to anybody."

"You're not useless," he said fiercely. And then he added with a smile, "At least not any more useless than I am these days, being a scofflaw fugitive from justice and all."

Serafina smiled with him, feeling better and better as they walked together down the path.

"Come on, I want to show you something," he said, quickening his pace as they approached the lake.

"What is it?" she asked, hurrying to keep up with him.

As they crossed through the last of the trees and approached the shore of the lake, she saw a clump of sticks on the ground, arranged into a small pile and surrounded by a circle of stones.

Braeden knelt down, struck a wooden match, and leaned in to light the dried leaves inside the stack of sticks. As he blew on the glowing embers, the smoke rose up around him.

"Oh yes, we were expecting you. We have your seat reserved for you right here, madam," he said to her with an exaggerated, elevated air and a sweeping gesture of his hand, as if he were inviting her into the most elegant of drawing rooms.

"What is all this?" she asked.

28

"It's a campfire."

"I know, but how did it get here?"

"I built it."

"When?"

"Just a little while ago."

"But how did you . . ."

Seeming pleased with her mystified reaction, he grinned, put his hands behind his head, and lay back on the ground, looking up at the stars.

It was hard for her to take it all in. He had apparently leapt off a moving train, then rode a horse like a mad boy through the mountain wilds to get here. He was in serious trouble. But he seemed so calm and relaxed, as if he finally had everything he wanted.

"Why did you build this campfire, Braeden?" Serafina asked as she sat on the ground beside him.

"I had a feeling you wouldn't like tonight's party too much."

"So you knew I'd be outside, on that particular terrace?"

"I thought you might be," he said, nodding.

"And you built this campfire for me?"

"Well, not exactly," he said. "*You* can see in the dark. So in a way it's more for me than you. But I thought you might like it."

"I love it," she said.

"Look at all those stars up there," he said, gazing up at the sky. "They're really putting on a show for us tonight."

She glanced up in the direction he was looking, but she'd seen plenty of stars in her life. What interested her now was *him*, the quiet, peaceful expression on his face and the way his eyes seemed to be taking in the sky above. She still couldn't believe he was home. It felt almost too good to be true, like it wasn't even real.

"Lean back," he said, "and take a look."

As she lay with her back on the ground beside him, her shoulder pushed up against his and she felt the warmth of it against the coolness of the night.

"Look at Orion the Hunter up there," he said, pointing toward the constellation. "Do you see how the three stars of his belt are pointing toward that one bright orange star over there?"

"I see it," she said, following his pointing finger.

"That's Aldebaran, the Leading Star. Now follow it a little farther in that same direction and there's a small bluish cluster of stars. Do you see it?"

"Yes, I see it," she said.

"My uncle told me that in Greek mythology those are the Seven Sisters of Pleiades," Braeden said. "But the Navajo called them *dilyéhé*, and the Persians called them *Parvin*. Everyone has a different name for the Seven Stars."

As she looked up at the small cluster of stars, she saw the seven he was talking about, but her feline eyes began to pick up the sparkling dots of light with more and more clarity. There were indeed six or seven particularly bright blue stars gathered together, but there were also hundreds of smaller, fainter stars sparkling in between them, all glowing in a hazy, bluish light, as if all the varied, dancing stars of the cluster were of one living spirit.

When she pulled in a long, steady breath, it felt as if a whole new kind of air were filling her lungs.

"A few days ago," Braeden said, "I was arguing with my uncle about why I had to go to New York. He could tell I was frustrated, so he told me a story he knew from the Bible. A guy named Job was mad at God because he couldn't understand why certain things happened the way they did. God said that the world was the world, beyond Job's comprehension and control. 'Can you bind the chains of the Pleiades or loose the belt of Orion?' God said to Job. 'Can you bring forth a constellation in its season and guide the Bear with her cubs?'"

She wasn't sure she agreed with or even fully understood what he was trying to say, but she liked the way Braeden's voice sounded when he recited the words.

"I think the part about the bear is talking about Arcturus," he continued, his shoulder brushing hers as he pointed to one of the other stars. "It's that really bright reddish one over there. Do you see it?"

"I see it," she said.

"But this is what amazes me," Braeden said. "My uncle said that the Book of Job was written two thousand five hundred years ago. That means that way back then those people were looking up at these same seven stars, just as we are now, giving them names, telling stories of their origin and their powers. And the Persians were doing the same thing, and the Vikings, and the Navajo out West, and the Cherokee here in these mountains, and people all over the world, for thousands of years."

"That *is* amazing," she said, taken with his spirit of

wonderment for the world. Where did it come from? Where did he get all the energy? By all rights, he should have been dead tired, and frantically worried, but he seemed to be brimming with the fullness of life.

As they huddled together in the crisp autumn night, the stars of Pleiades and a thousand others reflected on the smooth, mirrorlike surface of the lake, seeming to scatter it with glistening diamonds.

She wasn't sure why or how, but deep down into her living, breathing soul, she didn't feel nearly as anxious as she had earlier that day, or in the days and nights before. She wasn't scared. She wasn't jittery. She felt more content in this moment than she had in a long time.

Letting her mind wander, she imagined herself and Braeden leaping onto moving trains and fast-running horses, soaring up into rising planets and streaking down as falling stars. They swam through tepees of glowing embers and glided over lakes of mirrored glass, curled in clusters of sparkling light.

When the stars above her began to fall from the sky, she sucked in a sudden breath, not sure what she was seeing.

"Look!" Braeden gasped excitedly, clutching her arm as long, thin streaks of blazing light shot across the darkness. "It's a meteor storm!"

She'd spent so much of her life outside at night that she'd seen many falling stars flashing silently through the lonely heavens, but it had never looked or felt like this before, with Braeden beside her, the burst of meteors coming down one after another.

"Isn't it amazing?" Braeden asked breathlessly.

But the abrupt sound of men's voices coming from the top of a nearby hill interrupted her reply.

She quickly turned to look, then pivoted again to a much closer sound rushing toward her.

She saw it immediately: the startling sight of a pure white deer running through the woods.

She gripped Braeden's arm in surprise, so astonished by what she was seeing that she couldn't utter a sound.

In the light of the stars, the creature's white fur seemed to almost glow with incandescence as it ran through the darkness of the trees, leaping effortlessly over fallen branches and narrow gullies, and seeming to glide through the ferns.

Even as she was watching it, she knew it would be—for the rest of her life—one of the rarest and most beautiful things she would ever see.

And then a gunshot rang out.

The white deer stopped.

A single red spot stained her side.

Her head slumped.

Her knees buckled.

And her eyes closed as she crumpled slowly to the ground.

"No!" Braeden screamed, rushing toward her.

The wounded deer did not die immediately. She was trying desperately to get back up onto her shaking, weakened legs. She took three tentative, trembling steps, her head moving one way and then another, as if each step required vast effort, and then finally, she began to run, run in blind terror, away from the danger.

Another gunshot split the night air.

Erupting with powerful anger, Serafina sprang out her claws and snarled her fangs, her long panther body twisting as she whirled toward the sound of the hunters and sprinted toward them.

The frantic, running deer crashed into the water of the lake, shattering the smooth reflections of the stars, and tried to swim. But the deep water and her bone-shattering wound were too much for her. She thrashed in desperation, her head barely above the water as her front legs kicked and flailed around her, her eyes wild with fear, and her pink tongue protruding from her mouth in a bleating scream.

Braeden plowed into the water to reach her as another shot came ripping toward them.

Serafina raced up the hill, snarling and making as much noise as possible to draw the attention of the hunters as she charged straight toward them. There were at least three of them, all with rifles, but she didn't care. The anger boiled up inside her, filling her lungs, driving her muscled legs. She wanted to tear the men apart with her rage.

As one of the hunters spotted her black body and yellow eyes rushing through the darkness toward them, he stuttered in fear, "Wh-what is that?"

"Run!" said another.

The third shot at her, but was shaking so badly that the bullet struck a tree trunk behind her.

She lunged straight at him. The slash of her claws knocked the gun from his hands and scraped the skin of his neck.

Screaming, he tried to turn and run, but tripped and

toppled to the ground. He scrambled back up onto his feet and fled with the others as they ran toward the house.

Serafina wanted to chase them. She wanted to *kill* them. She knew she could easily catch up with them and pull them down one by one with her teeth and claws. But a sudden dread flooded into her mind and she stopped.

She quickly turned and looked down the hill toward the last place she'd seen Braeden.

How many shots had been fired?

Where had all the bullets struck?

She burst into a run toward the lake.

As she reached the shore of the lake, she frantically looked around her, searching for Braeden. But he was nowhere to be seen. She scanned the grass and the shoreline, dreading the sight of a crumpled, bullet-wounded body lying on the ground. Then she gazed out across the surface of the water.

Braeden splashed up out of the lake and walked toward her, panting and dripping wet, the white deer cradled in his arms.

"I've got her," he gasped with a shaking voice. "But I think they've killed her," he said as he lowered the deer gently to the ground and knelt beside her.

Serafina shifted into human form as she came toward him, and then knelt down with him next to the small body of the deer.

It was only then that she realized how young the deer was. She was just a fawn. And her fur wasn't tan, but pure white over her entire body. She had black eyes and a black nose, so she wasn't an albino. Serafina had never seen anything like her. Whatever she was, and wherever she came from, it was clear that she was a rare and precious creature. But the fawn was bleeding from her side, gasping her last labored breaths, her head hanging limp and her long, spindly legs tangled up like broken sticks.

"I'm so sorry, Braeden," Serafina said gently, knowing that there was nothing more difficult for him than seeing an innocent animal suffer.

He placed his hands on the deer's side and neck.

Serafina had seen him restore the cracked bones of a badly wounded dog, mend the broken wing of a falcon, and help many woodland creatures. He had been blessed with the ability to commune with and heal animals, but with it came its own kind of suffering, too close to the life and death of the world.

"I can't let her die," he said.

Serafina watched as he closed his eyes and held the deer in that position, infusing her with his healing power. She'd seen him use his abilities before, but it always amazed her.

She glanced in the direction the hunters had run, wary of their return. She thought there was a chance they were local poachers who had been out hunting the Biltmore grounds at night, but the way they had immediately fled toward the house made her think that they probably weren't.

Her pa had told her that most deer hunters had a sort of

unwritten code that they followed. They didn't hunt at night or use electric light to mesmerize deer. They didn't shoot young deer. And they wouldn't shoot a deer that was trapped, too close to them, or special in some way. She was pretty sure they would never shoot a *white* deer. It was just too unusual, too easy to see. But these hunters had done exactly that. As if the trophy of a rare, all-white deer was just too much to pass up on.

As Braeden continued to work on the wounded deer, she knew there was little she could do to help, but she sat on the ground beside him and scanned the trees and the distant fields for danger, giving him the time and protection he needed.

They had been together long enough to know what they were both good at, and tonight, clawing was her job and healing was his.

Glancing up into the night sky, she saw that a thin veil of silvery clouds had floated in, very high, long, feathery strands obscuring most of the planets and the stars. Although it remained flat and calm, the water of the lake appeared gray in color now, and the reflection of the stars had disappeared.

When Braeden was finally done, he looked up at her. She was shocked to see how sickly and pale his face had become, filled with worry, and he was shivering from the cold.

"We need to get her warm," he said, struggling to get onto his feet with the deer in his arms.

"And you, too," she said, pulling him up until he was able to stand on his own.

As he carried the wounded deer toward the house, she stayed close to him, on guard all the way. They slipped in through the side door, and then crept up the darkened stairs to Braeden's bedroom on the second floor.

Braeden quickly lit a fire in his bedroom fireplace, then sat in the chair near the fire's warmth, gathered the deer in his arms, and wrapped her up in a warm woolen blanket.

"If I can get her through the night, then I think I can save her," he said, his voice weak, but a little hopeful.

"Who do you think that was out there?" Serafina asked.

"I couldn't see them," he said.

But as she looked at Braeden sitting in front of the fire, another worry came into her mind. "What are you going to tell your aunt and uncle in the morning when they discover you here?"

Braeden shook his head, clearly too tired and worried about the fawn to think about that.

"You need to sleep," she said. "You traveled hard to get here, and then you helped the deer. You look exhausted."

"Yeah," he said softly. He seemed almost sad that their evening together was finally coming to an end.

"Are you going to be all right here?" she asked as she wrapped another blanket around his shoulders.

"Yeah, I just need to sleep awhile," he said.

"Whatever happens tomorrow with your aunt and uncle, we'll get through it together, all right?" she said, hesitating near his door.

Braiden nodded, looking up at her. "Stay bold," he said gently.

"I'll see you in the morning. Stay bold," she said in return, and slipped out.

She made her way downstairs to the first floor, then down to the basement, through the vast network of corridors, kitchens, and storerooms, until she reached the workshop.

Over the last few months, her pa had been working on so many new mechanical projects that he had added two more workbenches, three more rows of storage shelves, and, thanks to Mr. Vanderbilt, a rack of brand-new tools: hammers, screwdrivers, pliers, saws, and metal cutters. Her pa was in seventh heaven.

And thanks to *Mrs.* Vanderbilt, the kitchen was now providing most of their meals, so they didn't have to cook them over the burning barrel as often as they used to. Biltmore had various types of kitchens, a prestigious chef from France, and many supporting cooks and staff, including her friend Mr. Cobere, the butcher and meat cook who worked in the Rotisserie Kitchen down the corridor. But even so, her pa was right determined to teach Biltmore's fancy cooks how to smoke up a good old-fashioned Carolina barbecue pulled-pork sandwich.

Her pa was a big man, strong of arm and thick of chest. He lay sleeping in his cot now, snoring away like he did every night. His snoring probably would have bothered most folk who weren't his kin, but she was so used to it that she probably couldn't fall asleep if the timbers weren't shaking at least a little bit.

Her pa's face looked placid, as if he was dreaming of equipment that never failed and machines that always did what they were supposed to. But then she realized that wasn't quite right. If the electrical generator, dumbwaiters, leather-strap-driven clothes washers, and all the other newfangled contraptions in the house always functioned properly, then her pa wouldn't have a job to do and he'd be miserable, just as she had been earlier that day. *Useless.*

She was dead tired and worried about Braeden now, but she felt so much better than she had.

She thought it was interesting. If all the horses in the stable behaved perfectly on their own, was there still a need for the horse trainer? If all the souls in the church were already angels, what would the pastor do? If a mother's baby cared for itself, would she love the baby as much? It seemed as if human beings longed for everything to be easy, she thought, but deep down, we didn't want it. It seemed as if everyone had a job to do, a role to play, to fix the always breaking world.

She crawled into her little cot behind the equipment and curled up beneath the soft sheets and warm blankets that Mrs. Vanderbilt had given her.

Her two young cats, Smoke and Ember, came trotting across the workshop floor and hopped effortlessly into her bed. They curled up with her in their usual spots and started purring, one of her favorite sounds and feelings in the whole world. She couldn't help but purr back to them in return.

Smoke was a large dark gray cat, strong and quiet, with watchful green eyes. Ember was a skinny little orange tabby, talkative and opinionated, fast and lean, and she loved to run and pounce. She was small, but there was a wild, bushy-tailed fierceness to her that Serafina loved.

She had found them as tiny kittens in the ashes of the crumbling chimney of an abandoned building, their eyes still closed, mewing for their momma. But their momma had passed away. Serafina took them home that night, and with her pa's permission, began to take care of them. As they learned the darkened air shafts and shadowed passageways of the basement, and figured out how to sheathe and unsheathe their claws, it seemed only natural that she give them a job as her rat-catching apprentices.

Most of the night was over, but she was grateful to sleep for a few hours before her pa woke for the day, and more than anything, she was grateful to have seen Braeden again. There was something about his voice, his smile, and the way he looked at the world that always made Biltmore feel like home.

Within seconds after resting her head on her pillow, she felt so comfortable and nuzzled-in that it was as if she'd never moved from there, as if she'd been sleeping there all night, just dreaming away.

"Wake up, Sera."

Several seconds went by.

"Serafina," the voice came again.

She swam slowly up through the thick black molasses void of deep sleep, unsure where she was.

And as she came awake she felt the slow shock of entering a world different from the one she'd been in moments before.

"Wake up, Sera," her pa said as he shook her shoulder. "You've got to get up."

As she rubbed her sleep-crusted eyes and looked up, her pa was standing over her, his face filled with a frightful scowl.

"What's wrong, Pa? What time is it?" she asked as she

sat up and hurriedly looked around the workshop. "What's happened?"

"The master is comin' down."

"Mr. Vanderbilt down here? Now?"

"What sort of trouble did you get into last night?" her pa asked.

Her stomach dropped at the question, but there was no place to hide. His voice wasn't angry or accusing, but it was clear he was trying to figure out what was about to happen.

"Serafina," Mr. Vanderbilt said as he strode through the door and into the workshop.

Startled, Serafina jumped out of bed and quickly straightened her wrinkled dress.

"Don't worry about that," Mr. Vanderbilt said. "I'm sorry to come down here, but I need to talk to you."

They caught Braeden, she thought. *They caught him bad, and he's in big trouble for sneaking back to Biltmore. And they know I helped him.*

"What's wrong, sir?" she asked, struggling to keep her voice steady.

Mr. Vanderbilt shook his head, his hand held to his tightly pressed lips, as if he himself was still trying to comprehend what was happening and how to describe it. She had never seen him this upset.

Seeing the master's distress, her pa grabbed him a workbench stool to sit on and steady himself, and her pa did the same. It was a right peculiar situation to have Mr. Vanderbilt—the great gentleman of Biltmore Estate—sitting with her and her pa in the basement workshop, but that was the situation she suddenly found herself in.

Mr. Vanderbilt was normally well rested and relaxed, reading his books and enjoying the company of his guests, but today he had a worn, haggard look to him and was filled with the tight breaths and nervous glances of an anxious man.

"I know that you have—" he began.

"Sir, let me explain," she tried to interrupt, thinking there must be a way to help Braeden through this.

But Mr. Vanderbilt plowed ahead. "I know that you have helped this house in the past," he said. "When the children went missing a year ago, and the other times as well . . ."

"Yes . . ." she said slowly, trying to understand where he was going with all this.

"I think of you as one of Biltmore's friends, Serafina, one of its protectors," he said. "You have been especially adept when it comes to . . ." He paused there, as if he didn't quite know how to say it, and then he finally said, "Certain kinds of forces."

Serafina stared at him in shock.

"I need your help," he said.

"Did something happen, sir?" she asked. "Did you see something?"

"I don't know what I saw," he said, wiping his mouth as he glanced over at her pa, then looked back at her.

Serafina's temples started pulsing. This wasn't about Braeden. And Mr. Vanderbilt wasn't angry. He was *scared*.

"If it's all right with your father," Mr. Vanderbilt said, "I would like you to move up onto the second floor. Today. Before nightfall."

"The second floor?" her pa said in surprise. The second floor was reserved for the Vanderbilt family members.

"The Louis XVI Room," Mr. Vanderbilt said.

"The room next to the Grand Staircase . . ." Serafina said slowly, understanding his thinking.

"Yes," Mr. Vanderbilt said.

"Where I can observe the comings and goings of the house . . ."

"That's right."

"And where I can watch over Mrs. Vanderbilt and Baby Nell . . ."

"Exactly," Mr. Vanderbilt said, lifting his dark eyes and gazing at her. "I think it would be best if you were closer to Cornelia's room than you are now."

Serafina nodded. If there was danger afoot, then it made perfect sense for her to be up there.

Mr. Vanderbilt turned and looked at her pa. "But we will only do this if we have your father's permission."

Her pa looked startled. She suspected that he knew she was different from other people, but he didn't know exactly what powers she had developed in the last year, or exactly how she had used them. And here was the master of the house asking for her help in matters too dark to say out loud. But if there was one thing her pa understood—if there was one thing he'd taught her—it was loyalty to the ones she loved. If Mr. Vanderbilt needed her, then she had to help.

Her pa looked at her, his dark brown eyes serious and unblinking. "It sounds like there's a job that needs doing," he said.

Serafina nodded, understanding, then turned back to Mr. Vanderbilt. "I'll move upstairs today, sir."

"And if you're willing," Mr. Vanderbilt said, "there's one more thing I need you to do."

"Just name it, sir."

"Starting tonight, I want you to come to dinner in the Banquet Hall each evening."

"You mean, with all the guests?" she asked in surprise.

"I want you to get a clear view of the people here and their interaction with one another."

She had no idea how a country cat like her was going to fare in a room chock-full of fancy folk like that, but she said, "I will do it."

"I know that formal dinners aren't something you're used to," Mr. Vanderbilt said. "But I will provide you with the funds to acquire the dresses and shoes and whatever else you need. And I'll ask Mrs. King to assign a lady's maid to help you."

"Begging your pardon, sir, but if it's possible, I would love for Essie Walker to help me. She's a good friend of mine and she's helped me before."

"I'll talk to Mrs. King about it right away," he said as he rose to his feet. "Mr. Doddman, the new security manager, and I have business in town to attend to, but I will see you at dinner tonight."

She wanted to ask Mr. Vanderbilt more questions, to get a

better understanding of what had occurred that would cause him to take these actions, but he rose to his feet, quickly thanked her and her pa, and left the room as swiftly as he'd come.

In the wake of his departure, there was an awkward, unsettled air in the room.

"Well," her pa said finally. "That's a slug of a thing to wake up to on a Monday morn."

"It sure is," Serafina agreed. "The master seemed so scared."

"Something must have spooked him pretty bad."

She turned slowly toward her father. "Are you truly all right with me doin' all this, Pa? I'll just be upstairs, but I won't go if you don't want me to."

"I think you better lend a hand where a hand's needed," he said. "For Mr. Vanderbilt's sake, and for yours, too."

"Pa?"

"Look, Sera," he said gently. "I know you've been frettin' away, feelin' a bit worse for wear, worrying about this and that, jumpin' at the slightest sound. I can't say I won't be down here worrying about ya, but I know ya wanna help up there, and I want ya to."

"I'll come down every morning and we'll eat breakfast together just like we always do."

Her pa nodded, agreeing, but she could see by the misty squint in his eye that he didn't want her talking like that anymore.

"You're a good, girl, Sera," he said softly. "And I suspect that most of the people up there are decent folk, but stay on your guard. Some of them might not take to you right away—for the wrinkle in your dress, or the keen look in your eye, or for whatever reason—for you being a girl of these mountains instead of wherever they come from. And it's clear the master's seen somethin' unsettling, so keep your wits about ya, ya hear?"

"I hear ya, Pa," she said. "I hear ya well and good. I'll be real careful."

After they ate their breakfast, and her pa slung his tool bag over his shoulder and went off to work, Serafina knew that she had to tell Braeden right away what was happening.

She ran down the basement corridor and up the narrow stairs to the first floor. In the Main Hall, a party of men and women dressed in hunting jackets and leather boots was just going out through the front doors. She continued on up the wide, curving expanse of the Grand Staircase, the sunlight pouring in through the spiral of slanted windows. As she reached the second floor, she tried to glance into the Louis XVI Room that Mr. Vanderbilt had asked her to move into, but the door was closed and she didn't have time to linger.

On the way down the second-floor corridor, she passed two uniformed maids coming in the other direction. She had been walking openly in the house for months, but it still felt peculiar to allow herself to be seen. With her long jet-black hair and her unusual amber eyes, they knew who she was, and that she worked for the Vanderbilts, but they did not truly know her, not deep down, and they did not know her purpose. But they knew enough not to bother her.

When she came to the T at the end of the corridor, she

paused. To the left, the door to the nursery was ajar, and she could hear Mrs. Vanderbilt singing to Baby Nell. But Serafina slipped down the corridor on the right, past several doors, and finally reached Braeden's room.

She rapped on the oak door, then turned the knob, saying, "Braeden, you won't believe what's happened," as she entered the room.

But there she stopped cold.

The room was empty.

It was a large corner suite with fine walnut furniture, a carved marble fireplace, maroon damask wallpaper, and windows facing the mountains to the west on one side and the South Terrace on the other. The sunlight pouring into the room made it seem so different than it had been the night before.

Serafina frowned.

The bed was made. None of Braeden's clothes or shoes or other belongings were lying about. There was no sign at all that he'd been there.

She checked through the small door that led to the bathroom and the water closet, and the other door that led to the clothes closet. Nothing.

She walked over to the bed, checked the nightstand and the dresser, and looked out the window to the terrace below.

The blanket that he had wrapped the deer in the night before was folded neatly, resting on a small table near the window, as if it had never moved.

Perplexed, she got down on the floor and felt the Persian rug with her fingers. Braeden had gone into the lake, so he must have tracked water into the room. But the rug wasn't wet. Could it have dried so quickly?

She tried to stay calm, but her lips pursed and she began to breathe through her nose as she gazed around in bewilderment at the empty room.

She looked under the bed and into the brass grate that covered the heating shaft that they had once used to escape the room.

She checked all the places she and Braeden had hidden before.

But there was no sign of him.

There was no Braeden at all.

He wasn't just gone.

It was like he'd never been there.

She rushed headlong out the side door of the house, her mind swirling with confusion as she ran. *Was Braeden hiding from his aunt and uncle or did he already go back to New York?*

She raced through the garden, hurrying past the finely dressed ladies and gentlemen strolling casually along the flowered paths, and dashed toward the lake.

In the muted light of the cloudy day, the rippled surface of the water looked moody and dull of color, much different from the shining black mirror that had reflected the stars the night before.

When she arrived at the edge of the lake, panting from the run, she went straight to the spot where the campfire had been.

But the campfire wasn't there.

She stopped and looked around her.

This can't be. . . .

She studied the ground, but there was no sign that she and Braeden had been there, no ashes or kindling where their campfire had burned, no impressions of their bodies where they had lain on the grass.

Nothing.

She searched up and down the shoreline, but there were no footprints where he had entered the water or come back out after saving the white deer. She looked out across the water and then up toward the hill where the hunters had been.

Could I have imagined it all? Could I have dreamt it?

She growled in frustration. It had felt so real! Had she just *wanted* Braeden to come home to see her? Had she just *wanted* to fight an enemy? Was all this just another trick of her mind?

But if Braeden hadn't actually come home—and if there was truly nothing wrong at Biltmore—then what had Mr. Vanderbilt seen that had frightened him so badly?

Her stomach sank.

What if *that* hadn't happened, either?

She thought about Braeden's ghostlike arrival on the terrace the night before, and the master of Biltmore coming down to the workshop and asking her to move upstairs. . . .

She stared glumly down at the ground.

It all seemed so unlikely now.

At what point did she wake up? Where did the dream end and the reality begin?

As she pulled in a long, ragged breath, a deep and aching loneliness settled into her chest.

She looked out toward the mountains to the north. Was Braeden back on a train to New York? Or had he been up there all along and she had just imagined his return? Or was he here on the property someplace, too frightened to face his aunt and uncle?

And then a darker thought crept into her mind.

What if he had come home last night but then something had happened to him after she left him? Had some sinister new adversary found its way into his bedroom? Should she tell Mr. Vanderbilt everything that had happened during the night and that they should start looking for Braeden?

But was she even certain that he was missing? She'd seen no signs from Mr. and Mrs. Vanderbilt or any of the servants that there was any kind of worrisome telegram from New York. And there was no way for her to reach Braeden directly without raising too many alarms.

It felt as if her thoughts were fraying in a hundred different directions at once.

Still trying to think it through, she started making her way back toward the house.

It had been an easy, downhill run through the gardens to the lake, but the walk back up was steep, dragging at her legs.

She decided that she would find her pa and ask for his help. If Mr. Vanderbilt's visit to the workshop had been a figment of her imagination, then he would dispel that notion soon enough.

You've been makin' up stories in your head again, girl, he'd say. *Better keep your feet on the ground.*

She ascended the stone steps and entered the long promenade of the Pergola, with its profusion of wisteria hanging down from the lattice above and its line of vine-entangled columns that overlooked the flowers and trees of the garden. The other side of the Pergola ran along a stone wall adorned with fanciful statues and exotic plants. Gentle spouts of water poured from the mouths of scaly stone fish and mythical creatures, splashing into small bubbling fountains. A clutch of children was leaning into the basin of the nearest fountain, giggling and squealing in excitement as they grasped frantically at what looked like a large frog in the water. But it was perplexing because she had never seen any frogs there before, and it seemed far too late in the year.

She walked past several couples and small groups quietly enjoying the coolness of the Pergola's leafy shade, but then she noticed someone coming down the path at a hurried tilt. It appeared to be the girl who had arrived with the carriages the day before, walking fast, her long dark brown hair shifting wildly as she glanced behind her. The girl seemed so agitated by whatever was driving her forward, Serafina wasn't sure she would even notice her, but as they passed each other on the path, the girl looked up and gazed at her with the most striking sapphire-blue eyes Serafina had ever seen.

Serafina reflexively tried to nod politely as they passed, as she had seen the gentle ladies do, but the girl immediately lunged toward her.

"You live here, don't you?" the girl said, reaching out her hand.

Serafina was surprised by the speed at which the girl had surmised that she was a resident of Biltmore rather than another guest. "I work for the Vanderbilts," she said. "My name is Serafina."

"I'm Jess," the girl said quickly, her attention flitting from Serafina's eyes to her hair to her clothing, as if rapidly cataloging everything about her. It reminded Serafina of how the girl had studied the details of the house the day before.

Jess wore a well-made slate-blue dress, and it was clear she was educated. As far as Serafina knew, all the new guests were American, mostly Northerners, and Jess certainly seemed American in her appearance and clothing, but it almost sounded as if she spoke with the trace of a foreign accent.

Where are you from? Serafina was about to ask her, but as quickly as the girl had arrived at the Pergola, she was gone again, moving swiftly down the path.

"Be careful, Serafina," she whispered as she turned the corner around the hedge and disappeared. "And warn the others!"

"Warn the others?" Serafina said to herself as she continued up the stone steps toward the house. What did the girl mean? Warn *who* about *what*?

Jess had only arrived the day before. What could she possibly have involved herself in so quickly that she was giving warnings?

Crossing the terrace in front of the house, Serafina passed behind the row of stone columns, each one carved with a different elaborate pattern and topped with griffins, gargoyles, and other fantastical creatures. She entered the house through the small side door that led beneath the sweeping arc of the Grand Staircase, and then went down the narrow servants' stairs that led to the basement. For every awe-inspiring room in the mansion, there was a smaller, hidden path behind it—like the darkened passageways behind a magnificent theater stage—and she knew them all.

When she arrived in the workshop and saw that her pa wasn't there, she hurried down the corridor, past the clattering din of the busy kitchens and workrooms, all bustling with servants, and went down the brick stairs into the subbasement.

She found her pa on his knees at the base of one of the huge coal-fired, steam heating boilers, his metal-and-wood tools scattered around him.

"This one's giving me fits again," he grumbled as he wrenched on one of the valves.

She had once heard Mr. Vanderbilt say with pride that Biltmore was one of the first homes in America with a central boiler to provide heat to all its rooms. She had no idea how her pa could make heads or tails of the contraption, with all its twisted tubes and steaming pipes, but that's what he liked to do, and Mr. V depended on him for it.

"Pa, I hate to bother you, but I need to ask you somethin' about this morning," she said.

Her pa set down his wrench and looked at her. "What's on your mind, Sera?"

She narrowed her eyes, not quite able to read his initial reaction.

"Did the master . . ." she began. She wasn't sure if it was embarrassment or just plain cowardliness, but her words faltered.

"I can't hardly believe it none, either," he said. "It doesn't seem real, the idea of you actually moving out of the work-shop, goin' on upstairs with the Vanderbilts—doesn't seem like it could be happening. Is that what you're battlin'?"

A wave of relief passed through her.

"But that's what Mr. V asked me to do, right?" she asked, just to be sure.

"White as a haint he was, and wants you up there lickety-split," her pa said.

She nodded, satisfied. At least she hadn't conjured up *that* part of all this.

"But we'll be all right, Sera," her pa said, his voice getting a smidge grave. "It's just a flight or two of stairs. . . ." But even as he said the words, his normally strong, gruff voice cracked a little.

"Aw, Pa," she said as she moved into his chest and wrapped her arms around his bearlike body.

"Just a flight of stairs," he mumbled again, sounding like he was trying to reassure himself as much as her. "You know that I'm real proud of you, Sera, real proud, and I love ya somethin' fierce."

"I love you, too, Pa," she said, holding him tight.

After she had reluctantly said good-bye to her pa and walked glumly away, tears wetted her cheeks, but she didn't let herself sniffle until she was out of his earshot.

When she stepped into the workshop to gather her belong-ings and begin her move upstairs, she felt a heaviness in her arms and her legs. She had grown up in this place, slept here, played here, eaten her meals with her pa here. This was where she had started her hunts each night and returned each morning. This workshop was her home.

As if to make the point, her cat Smoke sat on one of the timber frame beams, staring at her. Ember walked with jaunty steps along the stone ledge above the benches, chirping complaints and looking down at her with her round, feline eyes.

"What are y'all looking at me like that for?" she asked. "It's just a flight of stairs!"

But she could tell by the looks on their faces that they weren't impressed with her argument.

"I'm sorry," she said, "but I've got to. Mr. V needs my help."

But even saying these words out loud made her feel like a naive little child. How ridiculous it was to think that Mr. Vanderbilt actually needed her. He was the richest, most powerful person she had ever met. Why would a man such as that need her help? With all her eye-flitting, scaredy-cat flinchiness and her strange dreams in the night, could she even be trusted to identify the dangerous visitors among the harmless ones? Was Mr. Vanderbilt asking for her to do this because he genuinely thought she could help protect his family? Or was there something else going on with him that she didn't understand?

She walked over to her little bed and picked up the piece of shredded red cloth she'd saved from the gown Braeden had given her more than a year before. It had been torn to pieces during her battle with the Man in the Black Cloak that fateful night in the Angel's Glade, but she'd always loved that gown.

And thinking about the gown made her think of Braeden. "*You're* here," he had said to her by the lake, so quietly, but so fiercely, as if that simple fact explained everything. Remembering the sensation of his breath touching her ear when they embraced, a chill ran up her spine.

Flustered, and seeing Smoke and Ember still looking at her, she said, "Don't y'all have mice to catch or something? Go make yourselves useful!"

Pretending to be annoyed by her tone, they dropped down from their perches with soft thumps of their furred feet on the floor, trotted out of the workshop with mildly perturbed meows, and went out to start their day.

They'll probably go to sleep on a windowsill someplace, not a care in the world, Serafina thought.

Dragging her mind back to the reason she was here, she gathered up the blanket, sheets, and pillow that Mrs. Vanderbilt had given her and prepared to go. She didn't have much in the way of belongings. She meant to just walk out of the room in a quick-like fashion, and not look back. But the moment caught her. She stood in the middle of the workshop and looked around. It was the place of almost every happy memory she had shared with her pa.

Finally, she took one last look, pulled in a long, deep breath, and left the room.

As she made her way up the servants' stairway carrying the bundle of her bedding and belongings in her arms, she noticed a streak of motion out of the corner of her eye. Startled, she turned quickly to see what it was, but the animal dashed away and was gone before she could get a good look at it.

Was that a rat? she wondered, but it had moved more like a small cat or woodland critter. It couldn't have been Smoke or Ember, so maybe it was a little mink or something that had gotten into the house.

A black-and-white-uniformed maid passed her on the stairway, her arms too full with laundry to say hello. But it jostled Serafina back to attention, and she continued up the stairs.

In the Main Hall, she noticed Cedric, Mr. Vanderbilt's Saint Bernard, along with Gidean, Braeden's Doberman, lying on the floor.

"At least I'll have some good company up here with the fancy folk," she said to the dogs. Creatures of her ilk didn't usually take too kindly to the canine type, but she had come to know and trust these dogs as good old friends, true of heart and fierce in a fight.

Her nose itched nervously as she walked through the Main Hall of the house in plain view—right past the butler and maids and all kinds of guests—holding her bundle of belongings in her arms.

Although she kept her chin low and her gaze lower, so that no one could accuse her of putting on airs, it still felt like she was striding up the wide, sweeping curve of the Grand Staircase to the second floor like she suddenly owned the place.

The ivory-colored limestone steps of the Grand Staircase blazed in the morning light, with the elegant, deeply filigreed wrought-iron railing on one side and the curving cascade of windows on the other. The staircase spiraled up through all the floors of the house, with a great, multistory wrought-iron chandelier hanging down through the center of the spiral.

When she reached the second floor, the stairway opened up to a living hall with plush Persian rugs, comfortable places to read and talk near the fireplaces, and fine English tables adorned with many of the small bronze animal sculptures that Mr. Vanderbilt had collected on his trips to Europe. A small alcove led to Mr. Vanderbilt's bedroom, and then down a short corridor to Mrs. Vanderbilt's rooms, while the hallway on the left led to baby Cornelia's nursery, Braeden's room, and several others.

It made her feel a bit queasy in the stomach to think she was going to live *here*, this close to the family, but she had drawn her lot in life, and this was it. She was now an official inhabitant of the second floor.

She turned and faced the closed white door of the Louis XVI Room.

Stoking her courage, she drew in a breath, pushed opened the door, and stepped into what was now her new bedroom.

The first thing she heard was a purr.

And the first thing she saw was the cats. *Her* cats! The soft, gray-furred Smoke, who was keeping watch from the window-sill, gave her a quiet, thoughtful meow, as if he wasn't quite ready to accept that this was their new home. He had seemed even more guarded and wary of his surroundings than usual for the last couple of days, and she knew the room change wasn't going to make it any easier for him.

The not so reserved Ember was stretched out on the large, queen-size bed, happily luxuriating, purring and meowing loudly, as if she were saying, *This bed is so much nicer than the old one!*

"How did you two get in here?" Serafina asked in surprise. She had assumed she'd go down to visit them in the basement every once in a while, but here they already were, all moved in. "Well, just because we're up here now, don't think you can shirk your duties in the basement," she told them firmly. "I saw a big old rat or something down there, so keep your eyes peeled for varmints. If you see something, it's your job to get it."

Smoke just stared at her, almost apprehensively. But Serafina knew he was well capable of catching even the largest rat.

Ember, on the other paw, closed her eyes and flexed her claws in and out, piercing the fine silk fabric of the bedspread, as if she was more than happy to pounce on some scurrying little thing.

"And there'll be none of that on the silk, Miss Ember," Serafina scolded. "Keep your claws in your paws or Mrs. V will kick us out for sure."

When Ember complained with raspy, chirping meows, Serafina said, "Hush up now. I don't wanna hear no sass."

But regardless of her firm tone with little Ember, she was secretly relieved that they had found their way up here and that she wasn't going to be alone.

Finally, she turned away from her feline companions and took a good long look at her new room.

She'd been in this room several times before, but the morning sunlight pouring in through the open windows basked the Louis XVI with a grace that made her sigh. It was a lavishly appointed, oval-shaped bedchamber with a gently domed cream ceiling and elegantly curved walls—the wallpaper, draperies, pillows, and even the upholstery on the gold-leafed, French-style furniture, all done in a fine silk fabric of red peony flowers.

There was a cushioned chaise lounge for relaxing and a sitting area with a low table for morning breakfast and afternoon tea. *If Braeden was here, that's where we'd sit and have our meals,* she thought wistfully, but then the bad thoughts started creeping into her head again. She still didn't know if he'd returned to New York, or was in trouble and needed her help, or had never come back to begin with.

She felt so helpless. She wanted to spring out her claws and tear something. She wanted to find an enemy and fight it. But she had looked all over for Braeden and he had just disappeared. When the heating register in her new room ticked, she flinched wildly and spun toward it before she could stop herself.

Just get hold of yourself, she thought. *One way or another, you'll figure this out.*

Trying to calm down, she turned and looked at the other side of the room.

There was a canopied bed with a red silk bedspread and a makeup table with delicately curved legs and a gold-leafed mirror. She could smell the scent of silk and freshly laundered linens, but it was the red roses in the vase on the mantel of the white marble fireplace that filled the room.

It seemed to her that Mr. Vanderbilt couldn't possibly have picked a room more different than her dark little corner down in the workshop with its rough-hewn stone walls, its greasy tools, and its smell of oil. Up here on the second floor, she would have probably felt more at home curled up in the back of a dark closet or maybe inside a cabinet rather than this luxurious bedchamber. But here she was, a denizen of the basement and a devout creature of the night, swimming in a world of silk and gold and blazing light.

But just as she began to doubt Mr. Vanderbilt's judgment, she stepped over to the window and saw the view it provided her of the front courtyard. Even now, at this very moment, she spotted Mr. Kettering, one of the gentlemen guests, walking up the Esplanade toward the stables. Dressed in his tan-colored hunting coat and carrying a rifle over his shoulder, he looked tired, but satisfied. Another hunter walked with him, and their servants followed with the carcasses of two antlered bucks. Their early morning hunt had been successful.

The room Mr. V had picked for her didn't just provide the perfect position to guard the stair's entry point onto the second floor; it was also an ideal spot from which to observe the front courtyard, and all the comings and goings of the house. It was a stark and welcome reminder that she wasn't on the second floor because she was a cherished member of the family or an honored guest. She was a *guardian*. And that suited her just fine. It was a job she understood, a job she wanted. She just hoped she could do it. What use would she be if she couldn't tell the difference between what was real and what wasn't? What use would she be if she flinched at every sound?

As she looked around at the opulence of the room, it was still hard to believe she was here. Even this felt like a dream. How was it possible that a little rat-catching girl from the basement was suddenly living in a beautiful bedroom on the second floor?

"But this is real," she told herself firmly. "And you have a job to do."

A rap on the open door behind her startled her out of her thoughts.

"Y'all look like three kittens in a basket up here," Essie said as she entered the room, looking at Serafina, Smoke, and Ember with a warm and happy smile. Essie was wearing her usual black-and-white maid's uniform, her cheeks beaming, her dark hair stuffed under her white cap. By training, a maid was supposed to remain formal, quiet, and restrained, but Essie was just a couple of years older than Serafina, and they knew each other far too well for all that nonsense.

"Tickled fine to see you, Miss Serafina!" Essie said, her Southern mountain accent sounding warm and familiar.

"Good to see you, too, Essie!" Serafina said, walking straight toward her and abruptly hugging her.

"Oh my," Essie said in surprise, flustered at her show of emotion. "Thank you, miss, thank you."

And this is real, Serafina thought as she tightened her arms around Essie.

"You reckon you're all right, miss? Has somethin' hard-gone happened?" Essie asked.

"I'm fine, Essie," Serafina said quietly, "just happy to see you is all."

"Well, I danced my own little jig when I heard the kitchen all a-gossiping about y'all movin' upstairs," Essie said.

"It came as quite a jolt to me as well," Serafina admitted.

"And now we gotta get workin' like it's harvest day, right?"

Serafina nodded. "Mr. V wants me ready by dinner tonight."

"Oh Lordy, these men with all their ideas! They have no conception of what goes on to put a lady in a dress and a proper pair of shoes!"

Over the next few hours, Serafina got out of her old clothes, took a bath, and worked through the process of getting ready. Essie helped her wash her long black hair and brush it smooth, and then sat her down at the little table and applied various kinds of makeup to her face in what she called "the style of the day," which Serafina didn't quite understand, since dinner began at eight o'clock.

Just as they were finishing up with all their preparations, there was a knock at the door. Mr. Pratt, a tall, handsome footman in formal black-and-white livery, entered the room with a dark green dinner gown held gently in his white-gloved hands.

"Thank you, Mr. Pratt," Serafina said, happy to see her old colleague. He was a lean but not quite gangly bachelor in his mid-twenties, with a sharp-looking face and slicked-back dark hair. It amused her how he was the quintessence of formal reserve and stately decorum when he was upstairs in view of the Vanderbilts and their guests, but quite the boisterous rogue when he was downstairs in the kitchens.

"You're most welcome, Miss Serafina," he said, gave her a hidden smile, and bowed out of the room.

Once he had gone, Essie helped her climb her way into the new dress and buttoned up the back for her. After applying a few more flourishes to her shoes, her ears, her neck, and her hair, Essie stepped back and looked at her. For several long seconds, she just stared at her and did not say a word, but then she finally spoke.

"I sure do wish the young master could come a-jumpin' back home and see how beautiful you look."

"You're being very kind," Serafina said.

"No, I am not. If I could wish upon a star, I'd bring him right back from that school up there. He doesn't need all that Northern bunk. I reckon he's a proper Southern gent now, don't you?"

"You got that right," Serafina said, smiling, but then turned more serious. "You haven't heard any news about Master Braeden, have you?"

"Aw, you really miss him somethin' awful, don't you?" Essie said. "I'm sure he's fine up there, otherwise we would've heard about it."

Serafina nodded, hoping Essie was right. "I'm afraid my company tonight is going to be far less agreeable than Master Braeden."

"Oh, yessin," Essie agreed. "And have ya heard about the thief in the house?"

"The thief? What are you talking about?"

"Things goin' missin'," Essie said, "Everybody's on about it."

"What kind of things?"

"I don't know what all, but I heard that some of Mr. V's expensive bronze animal sculptures have disappeared, for one."

"That *is* peculiar," Serafina said, wondering. But over the last few months of peace and quiet, the convolutions of her mind had snagged on so many wicked snares, and she had startled at so many empty shadows, that she didn't know what to trust anymore, whether it was backstairs gossip or the odd comment of a newly arrived guest. All she knew for sure was that the master of the house wanted his rat catcher at dinner tonight.

When she finished fastening up the gown and straightening out the fall of its skirt, Essie touched Serafina's shoulders and gently rotated her toward the full-length mirror.

"Whoo-eee! Take a look at that, why don't ya," Essie said, seeming at least as proud of her own handiwork as she was of Serafina.

Serafina stood in front of the mirror and gazed at herself in amazement. She had worn a fancy dress a few months before, but she had never looked quite like this. She had certainly filled out here and there. And her face . . . What did she see? Was that confidence? Fear? Determination?

But she couldn't help but take a hard swallow. She'd never stepped into a room full of high-society ladies and gentlemen without Braeden by her side. But this time she was going to walk right into a snake nest full of them all on her own.

With her long, shiny black hair falling down onto her shoulders instead of bound up in a traditional bun, her large amber eyes, and her sharp, feline cheekbones, she knew she wasn't going to blend in with the other high-society girls. Essie had colored her cheeks, shadowed her eyes, and done her best to mask the traces of long, jagged scars on her neck and face, but the wounds were still visible. She was pretty sure the gentle folk at dinner were going to take one look at her and grimace a nasty scowl. But even so, standing before the mirror at that moment, it was the first time in a long time that she looked at herself with a strong and steady gaze and thought: *This is me. The Guardian of Biltmore Estate.*

"Thank you so much, Essie," she said softly.

"Don't let none of them fancy folk give you any guff, Miss Serafina."

"I sure won't," she said, nodding with a smile.

$\mathcal{S}$he had come down the Grand Staircase hundreds of times, under all sorts of circumstances, but never like this, all washed and polished, her hair brushed and shaped, wearing her beautiful new forest-green gown for all to see. But more than all that, there was something else that had changed. This time she had come with a mission. Mr. Vanderbilt hadn't said the words out loud, but she knew her purpose: *Find the rat.*

She wasn't sure what the fancy folk were going to make of her when she entered the room, but as she crossed through the candlelit Main Hall on her way to dinner, Mr. Pratt and another footman, standing at attention near the house's front doors, smiled.

"You look good, Miss Serafina," Mr. Pratt said encouragingly, and her chest filled with a little hope.

The servants of the house didn't know exactly what her purpose was—rumors had run rampant over the past few months—but more and more, they were getting to know her and see her as one of them.

But as she walked along the wide, formal corridor, past the tropical plants of the Winter Garden, and approached the Banquet Hall, her heart began to thump in her chest, and she could feel the perspiration rising beneath her dress. The footmen, the laundresses, and maids—whether they were brought over from England, or Northerners, or Southern mountain folk—these were her people. But the well-heeled ladies and gentlemen at dinner were some of the richest high hats in all of America—ambassadors to foreign countries, famous writers and painters, lords and ladies from Europe, owners of railroads and steamship companies, wealth and privilege of every ilk and strain. And she knew from experience that she couldn't trust a single one of them until she caught the devious rat she suspected to be hiding among them.

As she passed the bronze sculpture of Mr. Vanderbilt in the corridor, she whispered, "Wish me luck in there, Mr. V."

And then she pulled in a deep breath and stepped into the radiant light of the Banquet Hall.

The grand room's barrel-vaulted ceiling was so high that a flock of Braeden's crows could have an aerial battle in its heights, and its massive carved stone fireplaces were blazing with great fires, but it was the silk-wearing denizens of this magnificent cave who held her attention.

She seemed to have arrived just at the moment when dinner was about to begin. More than fifty ladies and gentlemen in formal dinner attire were already sitting at the enormously long table. The grand event was set in lavish Vanderbilt style, with silver serving trays, crystal goblets, and fine Biltmore china among vast sprays of flowers, and a silver candelabra rising above, casting it all in a glowing light.

She carefully scanned the dinner guests, one after the other, looking for any signs of danger. And she listened intently as they talked quietly among themselves, many of them whispering in anticipation that their host would soon announce the beginning of the evening's festivities.

Mr. Kettering, the hunter she'd seen from her window earlier that day, came into the room behind her, looking flustered that he was late. He smiled at her in a friendly, almost nervous manner, and she nodded to him in return.

"Oh, Serafina," Mrs. Vanderbilt said as she bustled toward her and guided her gently forward into the room. "Come in, come in. Mr. Vanderbilt told me that you would be joining us. Your seat is just here, my dear." The mistress of the house gestured toward an empty chair at the table, and then hurried back to help Mr. Kettering find his place.

The embodiment of the perfect hostess, Mrs. Vanderbilt seemed to know all the guests personally, why they were there, and where they should sit.

As Serafina took her seat, she was careful not to pull the

tablecloth with her legs or disturb the beautiful place setting in any way. She noticed that a few of the ladies and gentlemen sitting near her were staring at her. They did not appear alarmed or indignant to see her among them, but they seemed keenly interested in her, as if wondering just what sort of exotic creature she was.

Once she took her place at the table, she realized she was sitting in the exact seat in which Braeden normally sat. It felt so wrong, like Braeden had died and now everyone—including *her*—was just fine with it and going on with their lives. *He should be here,* she thought fiercely as a pang of lonesomeness swept through her. Somehow, she'd managed to lose track of her best friend, and now she had taken his chair!

"Hello, young lady," a woman said in a kindly, aristocratic voice tinged with a New York accent.

"Hello," Serafina said, a little surprised that the woman next to her had turned to speak with her.

She was an elderly, stately woman, in an expensive gown and wearing an elaborate diamond necklace. "My name is Mrs. Ascott. What's yours?"

"I'm Serafina," she said, sitting up.

"That's a very nice name. And from where do you hail?"

Serafina thought it might be a bit melodramatic to say "The basement," so she said, "Around these parts."

"Ah!" the woman said, seemingly delighted. "So you're a local girl."

"Yes, very local," Serafina agreed.

In between her comments about the loveliness of the

table settings and the particularly breathtaking hue of the Vanderbilts' candlelight, Mrs. Ascott took a sip from her water glass. Serafina tried to drink from her own glass, but ended up taking too big a gulp, and the water dribbled unceremoniously down her chin as she quickly growled and wiped it away. She despised drinking water that had been sitting still in a glass. She was far more used to drinking straight from the faucet in the utility sink in the basement.

As Serafina tried to focus on the job she'd come for, Mrs. Ascott spoke with her in a polite and pleasant fashion. But Serafina couldn't help glancing down the length of the long table full of glittering guests. Her ears were keen enough that she could hear almost all of their conversations. The flurry of words came to her in a crisscrossing jumble of traveling stories, hunting tales, and comparisons of the latest clothing styles. But none of them seemed like evil conspiracies or treacherous plots. Despite what she had been imagining in her twitchy mind, everyone here seemed harmless.

Was this where she belonged now? Were these her new people? If she was wearing an extravagant gown, and hobnobbing with the most fashionable members of society, did that make her a civilized person?

At the very end of the table, several gentlemen were talking to Mr. Vanderbilt. Dressed for dinner in an immaculate black tailcoat and white tie, and freshly shaven and prepared for the evening, he looked so different than the bristled, haggard man she'd seen earlier that morning. And she knew she must look so very different to him as well. When he noticed her looking at him, she saw the recognition in his dark eyes, but he did not nod or draw attention to her in any way. *This was business. Find the rat.*

But then an irksome doubt flitted into her mind like an annoying little bird. What if he hadn't actually needed her help, but had given her a job and invited her upstairs because he felt sorry for her? Maybe Braeden had asked him to do it, or her pa. Maybe she was just imagining all these dangers and dramas and adventures-in-the-night, just remnants of a past that her troubled mind was having difficulty letting go of. *The nerve-racking peace and quiet,* she had called it. What if the people who cared for her were even more aware of her problems than she was herself, and they had conspired to help her?

But before she could dwell on it too long, she spotted the furry, dark gray shape of Smoke slinking slowly under the table, right between the feet of an unknowing Mrs. Ascott. And there was Ember madly clawing her way up the rare sixteenth-century Flemish tapestry on the wall. Serafina hissed in exasperation, just loud enough for Ember to hear, letting the little scoundrel know that she better make herself scarce and quick.

"Oh, are you all right?" Mrs. Ascott asked her, seeming to think that she had choked on her drink again.

"I'm all right, thank you," Serafina muttered, trying to avoid sounding and looking like a wild, snarling, yellow-eyed beast.

But glancing quickly at the people around her, she was

relieved to see that most of them were far too occupied with chatting with their neighbors and drinking their wine to notice anything else.

All except one.

The dark-haired girl named Jess was sitting right across from her, and the girl's sapphire-blue eyes were staring straight at her.

Serafina wanted to confront Jess right then and there, to ask her what she'd been talking about earlier, and why she was always watching her so intently. But just as Serafina opened her mouth to speak, Mrs. Vanderbilt rose to her feet.

Gathering everyone's attention, the lady of the house stood beside her husband and began to address all of her guests.

"If everyone would please stand," Mrs. Vanderbilt said. "George will be saying grace for us."

Murmurs of quiet approval and respect ran through the crowd as Mr. Vanderbilt nodded. "Thank you, Edith," he said, "And thank you for arranging this wonderful gathering here for all of us tonight."

Enthusiastic cheers of agreement exploded from the crowd,

everyone thanking Mrs. Vanderbilt, who beamed in modest gratitude.

Serafina could see from his soft smile that it pleased Mr. Vanderbilt that everyone loved his wife. But then he turned more serious, and a contemplative expression came over his face as he folded his hands in front of him and bowed his head in prayer.

When all the guests around the table bowed their heads, Serafina lowered her head with them as Mr. Vanderbilt said grace.

"Amen," everyone said in unison when he finished.

A handsome young man wearing the dark blue-and-gold dress uniform of a United States cavalry officer rose to his feet and held up his glass.

"If I may have everyone's attention," he said, his voice as soothing as a cup of warm autumn cider. "There's one more thing to do before we begin our dinner."

"Oh, it's Lieutenant Kinsley," Mrs. Ascott said excitedly as she leaned toward Serafina. "Such a lovely boy."

He looked surprisingly young to be an officer, fresh-faced and neatly kept, with wavy blond hair swept to the side, soft gray eyes, a cleft chin, and a well-trimmed blond mustache. He stood with the erect posture of a fencer, and wore a cavalry saber belted at his side. And it was clear from his sly but good-natured smile that he knew he was standing among welcoming company.

"If you would please raise your glasses," he said as he lifted his crystal wine goblet, and everyone around the table followed his request. His smile and his eyes were almost sparkling when he turned toward Mr. and Mrs. Vanderbilt with obvious affection. "I would like to propose a toast to our grand and admirable hosts, George and Edith. May Biltmore always reign!"

"Hear, hear!" everyone cheered. "Hear, hear!"

They all raised their glasses, smiling and nodding, as they looked upon Mr. and Mrs. Vanderbilt, who smiled back in return. And then, together, everyone drank from their glasses.

"You are too kind," Mrs. Vanderbilt said graciously.

"And one last toast," Lieutenant Kinsley said, raising his glass once again as he looked at the people gathered around the table. "We have come down to these Southern mountains to be with our good friends, both new and old, in this year of 1900, the start of a bold new century. As you all know, it is tradition in our families to come together at this time of year to spend the hunting season with one another. And I, too, look forward to our 'time in the woods,' for the challenge and the camaraderie it brings. I would ask that we hunt with honor and respect, not just for the beautiful hunting grounds that our generous hosts have provided us, but for the natural world we are about to enter. For it is in the mystery of these forests that we begin to find our true selves. So, finally, I would like to propose a toast to everyone here tonight. May all of our hunts be bountiful, all of our card games be exciting, and all of our teatimes be . . ." Here he seemed to be unable to find a suitable elegant phrase. "Full of tea!" he said finally, laughing, and everyone laughed with him. "And most importantly," he said, turning more heartfelt now, "may our time with our beloved friends and family be fulfilling to our souls."

"Bravo!" many of the guests shouted, nodding warmly.

"Hear! Hear!" others called as they raised their glasses and drank.

She wasn't sure if she belonged among these ladies and gentlemen or not, but watching what Mrs. Ascott, Mr. Kettering, and the others did with their glasses, Serafina raised her water glass and participated in the toasts with everyone else. There was something that she liked about this simple gesture of honoring the people around her, sharing in that moment with them. It made her feel as if she was one of them, part of their family. And she marveled at the bold young lieutenant, the way he was so relaxed and charming in front of everyone. She had been so nervous to even attend the dinner. She couldn't even imagine standing up in front of all these people and speaking to them. And she had to admit that, despite what else was going on, the lieutenant's toast had made her feel at home, as if things were going to be all right after all.

And as Lieutenant Kinsley sat down, his gray eyes looked across the table at her and he smiled kindly.

Serafina thought for a moment that he might try to speak with her, but as the footmen around the table began to serve the first course, a loud, overbearing voice at the other end of the table broke in.

"Well, I will tell you this," the man bellowed to those

around him. "It's not the gun, but the hunter pulling the trigger that makes the difference in the kill."

The man reminded her of an old, musclebound bull, with a swollen chest and bulging shoulders. He had a square jaw, a blockish head, and deeply tanned, weathered skin, like he'd spent years of his life outdoors.

"But since you're asking the question," the man continued, his booming voice filled with self-importance, "I do my hunting with the most effective weapon that has ever existed, the venerable 1873 Winchester Henry Repeating Rifle." As he talked, he sat with his chest stuck out like a rooster showing off for hens, which in this case were the men and women gathered around him at the table, listening excitedly to his stories. "You see, the Henry Repeating Rifle is known as the Gun that Won the West. I fought with it in the Indian Wars and I've hunted with it all through North America, South America, and Africa."

Many of the people around the loudmouthed hunter seemed enthralled with him, but Serafina noticed that Lieutenant Kinsley, who was trying to eat his soup, glanced at the man with a flicker of distaste. The lieutenant didn't seem to like the man any more than she did.

"And what do you make of Africa, Colonel Braddick?" one of the ladies asked, filled with starry-eyed admiration for a man who had traveled to such distant places.

"Oh, the hunting there is marvelous," the colonel said. "I'm proud to say that I bagged all of the Big Five: Cape buffalo, black rhinoceros, African lion, elephant, and leopard—the five game animals renowned for being the most difficult and dangerous to hunt on foot. But I wasn't done there. I went on to kill every species the safari continent has to offer: Thomson's gazelle, hippopotamus, warthog, greater kudu, springbok, impala, eland, zebra, serval cat, caracal cat, cheetah— You name it, I shot it."

Serafina felt her gut tightening as she listened to this man bragging about his trophies. She had taken pride in doing her job as Chief Rat Catcher, so she understood the thrill of the chase, but it seemed so wrong to go around hunting all those beautiful animals. They weren't harming anyone, and he didn't need them for food. He just wanted to kill them for killing's sake.

She couldn't understand why Mr. Vanderbilt had invited people like this into his home to go out into the forest and kill its animals. It seemed so wrong. Why was he allowing this?

"With all your honors and success, Colonel, what keeps you going at it?" a wealthy gentleman named Mr. Suttleston asked. "I mean, it can't be easy trekking through the wilds of Africa."

"It's the challenge of it all, really," the colonel replied philosophically. "I love the idea of using my abilities to track down an animal. Perhaps it's the most powerful, or it has the largest rack of antlers, or it's the rarest and most beautiful of animals— doesn't really matter—it's the challenge I love. The trophy head on the wall isn't just a record of a killing; it's a badge of honor, a remembrance of personal skill and experience coming together into a single striking moment."

"With all you have done, you must find the hunting in

North Carolina to be rather tame by comparison," said a rotund, bearded Southern gentleman as he thirstily drank his wine.

"Oh, you're right," Colonel Braddick said. "The hunting here is only a mild diversion for me, and it won't be anything I'll be boasting to my friends about, but I do have certain interests here."

"What are you after, Colonel?" Mr. Kettering, the deer hunter, asked.

"In these grand United States of ours," the colonel began to answer, "I've killed mule deer, white-tailed deer, mountain elk, moose, gray wolf, buffalo, pronghorn antelope, grizzly bear, black bear, bobcat, coyote, boar, and all the rest."

"Speaking of bores, maybe you could just shut up for a little while so we can enjoy our meal," Lieutenant Kinsley said beneath his breath as he sipped his soup.

Serafina gasped in surprise that he would say such a thing, but then realized that he had said the words so softly that only she and Jess had heard them. Jess didn't seem to react to the comment. She remained strangely motionless. But Serafina couldn't help cracking a little smile of appreciation.

"There is only one American beast that has managed to elude me," Colonel Braddick continued loudly. "Let's just say I've got a score to settle with this particular breed of varmint."

The colonel pulled up his sleeve for all to see the thick white lines of old scars on his arm. "This was done by none other than America's largest and fiercest feline predator, the cunning and dangerous creature known as the North American mountain lion. Some folks call it a cougar, a puma, or around these parts, a panther or catamount."

Most everyone was listening to the colonel with rapt attention, but Serafina noticed that Mr. Vanderbilt seemed far more alarmed by this loudmouthed guest than impressed by him. The master of the house looked over at Lieutenant Kinsley, who looked back at him with serious, knowing eyes, as if they were both in agreement that something needed to be done about this man. It was at that moment that she realized just how close a personal friend the young Lieutenant Kinsley was to Mr. Vanderbilt.

"What about the other wound you have there, Colonel Braddick?" one of the younger gentlemen asked, pointing to what looked like a fresh cut on his neck.

"Oh, that's just a little scratch I got last night," the colonel said, pulling back the collar of his shirt and showing off four jagged lacerations.

Many of the guests around him recoiled from the gruesome sight of it, while others stared in wide-eyed fascination.

But Serafina's pulse quickened as she looked down at her own fingernails. *Could it have been?*

"What in the world did that?" one of the women asked, clearly impressed.

"Well, the boys and I were out scouting for signs of game last night, just minding our own business, and one of the local varmints attacked our group totally unprovoked, just pounced on us out of nowhere for no reason. That's the mettle of these wild creatures. They'd sooner kill ya than look at ya."

"Tell us what happened, Colonel," one of the admiring young men said breathlessly.

"Well, I was fearful for the safety of the other men, so when the beast attacked, I charged straight at it. I fought the big cat, my bare fists against its razor-sharp claws. We tumbled head over heels down the side of a mountain. First I was winning, then he was winning. There was no telling which way it was going to go. But finally, I got my Bowie knife out and stabbed him just as he sunk his teeth into me. And at that point, the cowardly beast ran away."

It was startling to hear the colonel tell so many lies in so few sentences.

"That's amazing!" one of the guests gasped, and even the footmen had stopped to hear the hair-raising tale.

"You say it sank its teeth into you . . ." Lieutenant Kinsley said quietly. "And yet—mysteriously—there are no puncture wounds in your chest. . . ."

"So, you see," Colonel Braddick continued, nearly shouting, "ever since that first run-in that mangled my arm years ago, and now this encounter last night, the mountain lion is the only game animal—on any continent, mind you—that's gotten away from me. And I take that as a personal affront. When my friend Turner here said he was coming to visit George Vanderbilt's little cottage in the mountains, I was obliged to invite myself along for another try. And after last night's battle, I think I've come to the right spot to bag the trophy I'm looking for."

When Serafina glanced over at the colonel's friend, Mr.

Turner, the poor man looked positively sick to his stomach that he'd made the mistake of bringing this rude and vulgar man into the private dining room of George and Edith Vanderbilt.

Mr. Turner looked at Mr. Vanderbilt with a profoundly apologetic expression on his face, but the master of the house wasn't looking at him. Mr. Vanderbilt's dark and penetrating eyes were locked steady onto Colonel Braddick now, as if he were studying every minute detail of a monster that he was going to slay.

As the colonel carried on with harrowing tales of his "astounding skill" with a rifle, and people encouraged him with questions, Serafina's blood boiled. She was sitting here at the dinner table, with her pretty hair and her pretty dress, pretending to be one of these people. But she wasn't one of them. These humans wanted to hunt and kill the animals of the forest. They wanted to hunt and kill her own kind, her own brother and sister. Why would she want to be one of them? Why would she want to *protect* them? Why would she want to be a protector of Biltmore if *this* was Biltmore?

She imagined seeing this great white hunter, this famous Colonel Braddick, alone out in the forest, up on his horse with his rifle in his hands. She would stalk him from behind, moving slowly at first, her long slinking black body crouched low to the ground, then charging so swiftly and so silently that he would never even see her coming. She would launch herself at him, rip him from his screaming horse, slam him to the ground, and tear him to pieces with her teeth and claws. Then he would truly know what a "Southern varmint" could do.

As she sat there at the table with a pretty bow in her hair, she could feel her nostrils flaring, the sweat oozing from her pores. She wanted to do it so bad that she could taste it like blood between her fangs.

Regardless of how she had been feeling a few moments before, she knew now that she didn't belong here in this so-called civilized place. She didn't fit in among these people laughing and smiling at the colonel's stories. She was a creature of the night. A slinking, clawing animal with the soul of a panther.

She squeezed her eyes shut, trying to block out the violence of her thoughts.

The house, the forest, the wind, the trees, the people, the beauty, the peace, she didn't trust any of it. But most of all, at this moment, she didn't trust *herself.*

"I once shot and killed a running cheetah at a distance of five hundred yards," Colonel Braddick was saying cheerfully to his admirers. "So the next time I see a mountain lion in these hills, you can believe me when I say that it's going to come to a quick end."

In one last bid to maintain her quiet and civilized composure, Serafina glanced over at Lieutenant Kinsley. It was clear that, like her, he had been struggling to sit passively through this braggart's boasting. And now, finally, the lieutenant raised his eyes, looked at the colonel, and spoke loud enough for all to hear.

"But if mountain lions are as cunning and elusive as you say, Colonel," he asked, "how do you plan to find one to shoot?"

Lieutenant Kinsley had phrased his question such that it seemed as if he was genuinely interested, but it was evident to Serafina that the young officer was baiting him. The fight was afoot now, sides were being taken, and she knew hers.

"Well, it's true that mountain lions are the most cowardly and treacherous of wild beasts," the colonel said. "But I am a man of great experience and tracking ability. If I work long and hard enough, I'll find my quarry and kill it. You can be sure of that, Lieutenant."

As the evening proceeded through the seven courses of the meal, Colonel Braddick continued with what were meant to be enthralling stories of his bravery and grit.

All the while, Serafina watched as the dark-haired girl named Jess sat quietly across from her. The girl ate her food. She drank her water. She never looked at Colonel Braddick, and she didn't seemed to be listening to him. But she glanced at the other guests and the details of the room, one after another in rapid succession, her eyes glistening in the candlelight as she took in her surroundings.

When Jess's eyes finally fell upon Serafina, the girl studied her for just a moment before her eyes flicked away again. But

Serafina had the impression that Jess took in more information in that split second than another person might do in an hour.

After dinner, as everyone was getting up from the table, Mrs. Ascott said, "Well, it was very nice to meet you, young lady."

It took Serafina a beat to realize that the woman was speaking to her. Flustered, she said, "And it was very nice to meet you as well, Mrs. Ascott." She bowed slightly, as she had seen the other girls do. "I hope you enjoy your stay at Biltmore."

"Oh, yes, of course. How could I not enjoy myself in such a peaceful and lovely place as this?" Mrs. Ascott said warmly, gesturing to the grand scale of the room.

Serafina turned and looked across the table to say good-bye to Jess, but was disappointed to see that she had already left.

When someone close beside her touched Serafina's arm, she jumped, startled, and turned quickly.

"I didn't mean to—" Jess began to say apologetically.

"No, it's fine, it's just me," Serafina said, trying to explain. "I'm just—"

"I liked seeing your friends earlier," Jess interrupted. "I wished they had stayed a little longer."

"My friends?" Serafina said in surprise, then realized who she must be talking about. She didn't think anyone had noticed her little rat catchers slinking around in the shadows of the huge room. "How did you know they were mine?" Serafina asked, not trying to deny it, but mighty curious.

"I saw them listening to you," Jess said.

"They're usually decidedly bad at that," Serafina said with a smile.

Jess smiled in return. "What are their names?"

"The dark, quiet one is Smoke and the little orange ball of clawed fur is Ember," Serafina said.

Jess was about to say something in reply, but visibly winced when Colonel Braddick's voice clanged like a broken bell across the Banquet Hall.

"Come on, gents, it's finally time to get this party started," he bellowed, putting his arm roughly around the squeamish Mr. Turner and dragging him from the room. "I didn't think that meal would ever end! Seven courses? My God, who on this planet ever needs more than five?"

As Colonel Braddick, Mr. Turner, Mr. Suttleston, and some of the other hunters left the room, Jess said calmly, "They're going to go play poker now."

Three seconds later, Colonel Braddick's voice rose above the others. "Let's play some poker in Vanderbilt's Billiard Room!"

Colonel Braddick and his group pulled their cigars out of their breast pockets as they headed to their card games. Many of the other guests wandered over to the Salon to enjoy an after-dinner coffee or stepped outside onto the Loggia to partake of the late night air. Another group availed themselves of a tour of the Winter Garden with Mrs. Vanderbilt. But Serafina noticed that Mr. Vanderbilt and Lieutenant Kinsley remained in the Banquet Hall, standing near the fireplace at the far end of the room, talking privately in hushed voices, sometimes looking toward the Billiard Room, as if they were hatching some sort of plan.

The bellowing voice of Colonel Braddick could still be heard ringing through the corridors of the great house.

"Listen," Jess said, leaning toward Serafina with a conspiratorial whisper. "Don't let him fool you. He'll drink and gamble most of the night, but that won't stop him from getting up early in the morning to go hunting. You need to leave here and warn whoever you need to warn."

Serafina looked at her in surprise. This girl was getting downright spooky now. "What do you mean?" she asked. "Warn who?"

"I saw your reaction earlier," she said. "You weren't just put off by his story about mountain lions, you were angry and you were *scared*, and not for yourself. I could see it."

Serafina just gazed at her, unsure of what to make of this peculiar girl with the eyes of a hawk. Should she pretend she didn't know what she was talking about? Should she deny it? Was there even any point in denying it? The girl seemed to already know.

"You have to understand," Jess said. "He's not just an aggravating braggart. He's a liar and a cheater as well. He said that in the days ahead he's going to use his skills and experience to track a mountain lion, but the truth is he's already hired a local man with a pack of hunting dogs to do the work for him. As soon as the tracker finds a mountain lion, the colonel will go to its den and shoot it. Then he'll tell everyone grand and exciting stories about what a great hunter he is."

Serafina tried to stay calm, but a jolt of new fear ran through her. Her brother and sister were out there. And Colonel Braddick was going to hunt them down.

"How do you know all this?" Serafina asked in amazement.

But before she could answer, Colonel Braddick's voice rose up above the voices of the other men in the Billiard Room. "Oh yes, I'm sure she'll be tagging along," he replied to a question that someone had asked him. "She's a good, obedient girl, tougher than you might think out on the trail, but I gotta tell ya, gents, she's a god-awful terrible shot with a rifle. She couldn't hit the side of a barn if her life depended on it. And sometimes she's unbelievably loud with her feet when we're trying to stalk up on a good kill. She sounds like a herd of tramping elephants in those girly boots of hers!"

As the entire room of men erupted into laughter, Serafina looked at Jess. Her face was quiet of expression, almost emotionless, as if she had heard that same joke so many times it didn't affect her anymore.

"You're Colonel Braddick's daughter," Serafina said softly.

"He makes me go out on his hunts with him," Jess said. "But I'm a liar, too."

"What do you mean?"

"My bullet always hits a tree," Jess said.

Serafina smiled, liking that answer and the girl who had said it.

"She's like any girl, I guess," Colonel Braddick was telling his friends, "totally worthless at the practical things in life. But I gotta bring her along or she'd have no place else to go, poor little soul. Her mother's been gone all these years now, left us to fend for ourselves nearly from day one. Tuberculosis, God rest her soul."

As Colonel Braddick droned on in the distance, Jess stepped closer to her.

"We lived and traveled in Africa for years," Jess said. "When I was very young, I remember my father asking me all kinds of questions when we were out hunting, day after day, year after year."

"What kind of questions?" Serafina asked.

"He'd ask things like 'Which of these game paths do you think looks more trodden than the other?' and 'What kind of animal makes this kind of track in the dirt?' For a long time, I thought he was asking me because he was trying to teach me, and maybe he was, I don't know. . . ."

"But what happened?" Serafina urged her, fascinated by her story.

"I had heard that the African leopard was one of the most elusive and beautiful animals in all the world. I had always wanted to see one. I learned where they lived, what kind of tracks they made, and how they behaved. Finally, I spotted a gorgeous leopardess sleeping high up in an acacia tree, nearly impossible to see."

"Was she amazing?" Serafina whispered, envious of seeing such an animal.

"My father shot her," Jess said bitterly. "It was at that moment that I realized the true purpose of my father's questions. For the last few years, he wasn't teaching me. He had no idea that leopards frequented this particular part of the savannah or that they preferred acacia trees. And he had no idea of the particular way in which they draped their sleeping bodies over a branch so that their spots camouflaged them just right. And his eyes weren't that good."

As Serafina listened to Jess's story, she began to understand the level of trust that Jess was putting in her. She must have seen something in her, not just that she *could* share this story, but that she *should* share it.

"My father had used my skills to track the leopardess and kill her," Jess said. "And I realized that he had been doing that for years. I swore in that moment that I would never show my true self to my father again."

"I'm so sorry, Jess," Serafina said, touching her shoulder.

"But truth is, I thank my father every day," Jess said.

"What do you mean?"

"A daughter grows up watching her father, seeing everything he does. Whether he realizes it or not, he is teaching her. From *my* father, I learned what I most don't want to be."

Serafina looked at Jess, and Jess looked back at her. This time Jess's sapphire eyes did not flit away. She held Serafina's gaze. It felt as if it was in this moment that the two of them were truly meeting each other.

"I understand," Serafina said, touching her arm in the way Jess had tried to touch hers earlier. "Thank you for warning me about your father. I mean it. I truly appreciate it."

"You'd do the same for me, right?" Jess said, a tinge of hope in her voice as she looked up at her.

Serafina nodded. "Yes, I would," she said, but she couldn't help but wonder exactly how Jess had determined that about her so quickly. "Do you *know* me somehow?"

"No," Jess said, a little surprised by the question. "I just got here yesterday. You saw me arrive."

"Wait," Serafina said, startled. "Did *you* see *me* when you arrived?"

"You were on the terrace, behind the stone railing," Jess said.

This girl truly does see everything, Serafina thought. And as they were talking, Jess's eyes flicked over to the main corridor.

A messenger had come in and was now walking toward Colonel Braddick.

A moment later, Colonel Braddick and several of his men hurried out of the Billiard Room.

"He never leaves a card game that quickly," Jess said, her voice tight with worry.

"What's it mean?" Serafina asked, feeling herself already relying on this girl's startling powers of observation.

"The local tracker he hired must have found something—"

"Jess!" the colonel barked. Jess jumped at the shout. "Get out of that gown and into your hunting clothes! We're going out right now!"

"You'd better get going," Jess whispered to Serafina.

"I will, right away, but please tell me: Why are you helping me like this?"

Jess looked her in the eye. "Because I've seen too many dead cats."

Serafina ran through the forest, her four furred feet tearing rapidly across the ground, propelling her forward, her body nothing but a black streak through the murky darkness of the trees. The colonel's pack of hunting dogs chased close behind her, running, barking, howling after their prey. She knew from experience that hounds only bayed like that when they were close on the scent. But they weren't on *her* scent. She had come up behind them and gone far around them. She scanned the forest ahead of her, looking frantically for a flash of tan. Her sister and brother were out here someplace, running for their lives. They must know the baying hounds were coming for them. And there was no escape. A mountain lion could easily kill a single dog, but a pack of twenty mindless, biting hounds—all willing to die to get in a single bleeding bite—was more than most mountain lions could handle.

Finally, she heard the whisking sound of two mountain lions sprinting through the thicket in the distance. Looking across a rocky, mist-filled valley, she saw them scurrying up the slope across from her, instinctively heading for high ground.

Not up there, Serafina thought, recognizing the ridge they were headed for. *Not up there.*

The pack of dogs came out of the forest close behind them, loud now, howling with new fervor. The hounds had been chasing the two mountain lions for miles, all through the night, relentless in their pursuit, and they knew they had finally gotten close to their prey.

With nowhere else to go, the two young mountain lions bounded from rock to rock up the ridge, then scrambled their way up an old, dead tree snagged at the top of it. Their shoulder muscles bulged and their claws ripped into the loose bark as they scaled the trunk and reached the upper branches.

The two wildcats were now stuck at the top. They turned, panting, and looked down at the barking, snarling, howling dogs surrounding the base of the tree.

The cats pulled back their ears and wrinkled their whiskered faces in nasty snarls as they hissed at the dogs.

Serafina ran across the valley to help, but then she heard the sound of the hunters crashing through the underbrush on their horses.

"The dogs've got 'em trapped!" the dog handler shouted in

his mountain twang as the hunters came into view through the swirling fog rolling across the slope of the mountain.

The hunters quickly dismounted and forced their way through the thicket on foot, pushing their rifles out in front of them.

"They've treed two of the varmints!" one of the hunters shouted as he climbed up the rocks to get a better look.

The helpless cats stared down at the barking dogs and shouting humans. The dogs were out of their mind with bloodthirsty excitement, their mouths dripping with spit, their tails wagging feverishly as they paced and circled. Many of the hounds were trying repeatedly to run up the trunk of the tree, one after another, some of them getting up to the lower branches before falling down to the ground, picking themselves up, and trying again, howling all the while.

Even lion-hunting dogs couldn't climb trees, but the dogs didn't seem to care about the illogic of it or their own well-being. They just kept trying over and over again, desperate to sink their snapping jaws into the hides of the big cats.

Colonel Braddick came crashing through the thicket on his horse, the last to arrive. "Get back!" he shouted to his men as he dismounted, handing his reins off to Jess, who was there on her dark bay horse, her rifle in her hands. "Nobody shoot!" the colonel shouted. "This is my shot! My shot!"

Still gasping for breath from the exertion of the chase, the colonel lifted his rifle and aimed at the closest mountain lion.

The crack of the colonel's rifle rang through the night air, echoing off the surrounding mountains. A piece of bark flew up next to the lion as the cat leapt to a different branch of the tree.

Swearing in anger that he had missed the shot, the colonel took several steps closer, levered his rifle, and fired again. Once more, the lion leaped away just in time, slinking from branch to branch as her brother hissed and snarled to keep the frenzied, stupid tree-climbing dogs at bay.

Serafina ran toward her brother and sister as fast as she could, her claws out and ready to fight.

The colonel fired again, and then again, twigs breaking, bark exploding, the lions hissing and snarling, the sound of the repeated shots echoing across the mist-filled valley.

Discouraged by the colonel's poor accuracy, the other hunters began to position themselves to shoot the mountain lions themselves and get it over with.

"My shot!" he screamed again as he moved closer.

Serafina ran straight toward them, her powerful chest expanding with raging power. She was almost there.

But on the colonel's next shot, she heard the bullet thwack into her sister's body.

Serafina watched helplessly as her sister fell from the branch of the tree and tumbled through midair, her limbs flailing as she plummeted toward the rocks below.

15

Her sister's body hit a branch as she fell, then hit another and another, until the cat finally flipped upright and landed on her feet, claws out, right on top of the pack of dogs. Two of the dogs yelped in pain and surprise as the wildcat came down on top of them. But the other hounds turned on the lion, lunging at her with their biting, snapping attacks.

Serafina leapt into the battle, knocking the largest of the dogs away with a powerful swipe of her claws, then clamped her jaws onto another and pulled it to the ground. She swiped another dog as the two behind her latched onto her back with their teeth. Spinning with a ferocious, angry snarl, she grabbed one of the dogs in her fangs and hurled it down the slope of the mountain.

As Serafina fought, her brother came down the tree head-first and then leapt onto the backs of the dogs that were biting his wounded sister, sending them into wild, screeching yelps. His sister managed to get to her feet, and the two of them dashed away, disappearing into the mist-cloaked underbrush.

Serafina felt a quick burst of relief that her sister and brother had escaped, but then one of the attacking dogs lunged teeth-first at her throat. Reacting on pure reflex, she cocked her head and snapped the dog's neck in her jaws. As a second and third dog lunged in at her, she swiped at them with her claws.

A dense fog had rolled across the ridge like the breath of ghouls, making it difficult to see more than a few feet around her, but through a narrow opening in the white swirling mist she caught a glimpse of the colonel and the other men scrambling hurriedly through the brush and back up onto their horses in panic.

She charged toward them. She could see Colonel Braddick up on his horse with his rifle in his hands. She moved so rapidly through the underbrush that she was invisible, her long slinking black body crouched for the kill. Her chest filled with a growling anger. Her fangs were dripping with blood. Her claws sprang out. She launched herself straight at the colonel in a ferocious, snarling attack, determined to make sure the vile human never shot another animal again.

16

As she leapt toward Colonel Braddick and the other hunters she found herself plunging into a wall of fog so thick that she couldn't see anything in front of her. Something large brushed past her. She heard the blowing snort of a startled horse, the crack of steel-shod hooves on the rocky ground. Men shouted warnings to each other as they tried to control their frightened beasts. The horses lunged and turned and lunged again, one rider crashing into another, shouting as their mounts scraped so close that the riders' knees struck and nearly ripped each other out of the saddle. A frightened hunting dog darted past her. She caught a glimpse of a horse's haunch, its dark brown hide glistening with sweat and slashed with bloody gashes.

"There it is!" one of the hunters shouted, sounding as frightened and confused as she was.

"Watch out!" shouted another.

Three dogs tore past her, yelping and crying, glancing over their shoulders as they ran. Her heart hammered in her chest as she tried to understand what was happening. She looked up to see a rider frantically yanking his reins as his horse jostled him one way and then the other.

A burst of light lit up the fog like a flash of lightning and a gunshot cracked the night. And then another gunshot, and another.

"Jess!" Colonel Braddick shouted, his voice ripped with fear.

Serafina hissed as something shoved past her. But then it pivoted and charged straight at her. She dodged the attack and swiped at it with her paw. Her claws raked across something so hard that it didn't feel like skin or muscle, but a mesh of steel, and then it was gone. She heard the collision of something striking a horse's side, the great grunt of the beast, a man shouting, gunfire. One of the bullets grazed Serafina's shoulder, slicing her with a blaze of pain. She struck out with her paw against whatever it was, blind in the fog.

A quick movement dashed behind her. She spun to defend herself, opening her fanged mouth in a hissing snarl. A whimpering dog went limping by, its bloody leg hanging loose from its body.

A sound came rushing in. She sprang to the side. A girl's shouting scream rose up ahead of her, and then the high-pitched neighing of a frightened horse. Serafina leapt forward.

She saw Jess up on her horse as it treaded backward in terror, Jess lifting her rifle and firing at something in front of her, the muzzle flashing, the cracks of the shots splitting the air one after another.

Serafina lunged forward to help Jess, but Jess's horse spooked at the sight of her coming in from the side, its eyes white with fear as it rose up onto its hind legs, rearing and striking. Jess fought valiantly to stay in the saddle, but the horse was out of its mind with panic. It neighed and kicked, rising higher and higher, until it finally toppled, throwing Jess to the ground.

A massive, charging weight slammed into Serafina. It knocked her tumbling across the rocky ground and right over the edge of a drop-off. Her body fell, then struck rock, then rolled and fell again as she plunged down the steep slope of the mountain. She flung out her paws, clawing at trees and rocks, anything to hold on to, trying desperately to stop her fall.

17

Serafina slowly opened her eyes and stared into the darkness.

She did not know how long she'd been unconscious. Her body lay splayed across the ground, racked with pain. It hurt to breathe. It hurt to move. But she knew she had to. Gritting her long panther teeth, she slowly pushed herself up onto her four feet.

There were no more gunshots. No more people screaming. No more horses neighing. All she could hear was the dripping of the moisture from the surrounding branches. Nothing was moving except for the swirls of gray fog drifting between the trunks of the trees like writhing ghosts.

Shaking off the wet dirt and debris that had stuck to her fur, she scrambled back up the slope. She didn't understand what had happened, but she knew she had to get up there to help Jess.

When she reached the top of the ridge, the fog was so thick that she couldn't see anything. Crouching down, she waited and listened for the movement of enemies. She sniffed the air, smelling humans, horses, dogs, trees, wet earth, gunpowder, and ferns.

She let several more seconds pass, just waiting. The chaos of the battle had ended.

Staying low to the ground, she crept blindly forward several feet into the fog.

She found a dead dog lying on the ground, an open wound at its neck.

A few yards beyond the dog she found one of the hunters. She could tell by his simple mountain clothing and the raggedness of his beard that it wasn't one of the gentlemen guests. It was the local man named Isariah Mayfield, whom the colonel had paid to track down the mountain lions with his hounds. Isariah lay crumpled in the leaves, bleeding from a kind of wound she'd never seen before, a single straight slash to the chest.

She shifted into human form. Still staying low to the ground, she crawled forward to help the man, but when she saw Isariah's face, and his open eyes, she knew immediately that he was already dead.

Pulling in rapid, frightened breaths, she scurried along the ground through the fog more quickly now.

She came to Mr. Turner, his eyes wide and his dead hands

still clenching his rifle in terror, and then to Mr. Suttleston, his body facedown.

And then she came to the colonel.

His broken leg bone was sticking out of his thigh where his toppling horse had smashed him against a rock, and there was a large, deep wound to his chest and belly, the blood oozing from it every time he tried to take in a breath.

"Colonel," she said as she rushed toward him. "What attacked you?"

"It's you . . ." he said. "What are you doing here, girl? Where's Jess? Forget about me. You've got to help my Jess, please . . ." he said, his voice ragged and weak.

"I'll find her, Colonel, but tell me what attacked you."

"It was a black panther and—" He gasped violently for a gulp of air, his chest heaving and blood coming out of his mouth.

"Colonel," she said, watching helplessly as his eyes fell closed, his head slowly dropped down, and the last, long, rattling breath of his life came out of him.

She had despised this man. She had hated him with all her heart. But she still couldn't help but feel a pang of remorse to see him die like this.

She looked around her, trying to gaze out into the fog-filled forest. Who or what had done this? Was it still out there?

She slowly leaned toward the colonel and studied the wound to his body. It wasn't a straight cut like the other. And it wasn't the punctures of an animal's fangs. And it wasn't bullet wounds. His chest and belly had been sliced open with four long slashes, like a large cat's claws. Like *her* claws.

A sickening feeling sank into her. She had seen her brother and sister run off, so she knew it hadn't been them. And she knew her mother wasn't in the area.

She looked at the dead body of the colonel, and all around at the bodies of the other hunters and the dogs lying on the forest floor.

She tried to remember the exact sequence of events, everything she had seen and heard. In all the fighting and confusion, was it possible that *she* had done this? Had she, in her panther form, been the one who had frightened the horses? Had she lost her mind in some kind of revenge-fueled rage? She had hated these hunters for what they were doing. But had she actually *killed* them? Had her dark, black panther soul taken her over?

Gasping for breath, she got to her feet and backed away from the colonel's dead body.

Her ankle hit a lump on the ground behind her. Another body. Another victim. She turned to see a girl with long, dark hair crumpled among the roots of an old tree.

"Jess . . ." she cried, filling with anguish as she dropped to her knees beside her friend.

Serafina grabbed Jess's shoulder and turned her over.

She was expecting Jess to be cold and stiff like the others. But she wasn't. She was warm and breathing. Her eyes were closed, but she was very much alive.

"Jess," Serafina said excitedly, her heart leaping with hope.

Serafina looked for a wound, thinking that Jess must have been struck down the same way her father and the other men had been, but she couldn't find any such injuries. Jess's torso, arms, and legs appeared unhurt. But then Serafina found blood in Jess's hair. Serafina remembered seeing Jess shooting her rifle at something in the fog. And then . . . What had caused her horse to rear up in panic?

It was me, Serafina thought. *I sprang to help her, but all Jess's horse saw was a panther charging at it out of the fog.*

She tried to piece everything together in her mind, what she saw, what she heard, but it had happened so fast.

All she knew now was that she had to get Jess back to Biltmore, to a doctor.

But then a small stick broke on the forest floor in the distance behind her.

For days she had been second-guessing herself. For months.

But this time she was sure.

There was something out there moving through the underbrush.

She rose to her feet and scanned the trees.

Then she heard a much closer noise: the dragging of heavy footsteps coming toward her through the woods, the movement of metal mesh, and the clanking of one piece of metal against the other.

The muscles in her legs tightened, telling her to run, to flee for her life. Her heart felt like it was somersaulting in her chest. Her breaths were getting shorter, more frantic.

She knew she shouldn't leave Jess lying here alone and wounded on the ground, but she felt a powerful, overwhelming need to follow that sound.

One way or another she had to know! Had she lost her mind and killed these men? Or was there something out there?

She shifted into panther form and charged into the darkness, straight toward the sound.

She dove headlong through the forest, plowing through the swirling fog, the underbrush catching on her whiskered face.

When the fog became so thick she couldn't even see a few feet in front of her she had to slow down, but she kept moving, listening ahead.

She heard another dull, clanking thud and the heavy, dragging footsteps.

She rushed forward in a fast, slinking prowl, claws at the ready.

But the farther she went, the fainter the sound became.

She stopped and listened into the murkiness of the midnight fog, but the noise had faded.

She waited and listened.

Growling, she doubled back and tried to pick up the sound where she'd heard it last.

Come on, she thought in frustration. *It's got to be here. I'm so close.*

She turned, and then turned again.

As she crept through a thick stand of trees and bushes with low, twisting branches, she used her whiskers to find her way.

The pulsing, rhythmic buzz of the forest's night insects surrounded her now. She could hear dew dripping from the trees, and the whistle of a whip-poor-will in the distance. And then she heard something much softer just ahead, the touch of small feet moving *tap-tap-tap* across the autumn leaves.

She crept forward, ready to pounce.

The fog began to clear in front of her. The clouds overhead were thinning. And the silver light of the crescent moon shone down into a small meadow.

The fur on the back of her neck tingled.

And then she finally saw it.

The creature was standing there, perfectly still, in the center of the moonlit meadow, its head turned toward her. It was staring at her with its black, otherworldly eyes.

It was a small white deer.

She gazed at the deer in awe.

At first she was too startled, too shocked by the sight of it, to understand what it meant. But then it slowly began to sink in.

That night with Braeden had been real.

She hadn't dreamed it.

She hadn't imagined it.

An immense sense of relief, almost euphoria, poured through her body.

It had all been real.

The white deer stood in the middle of the meadow and stared at her. Serafina was surprised that it wasn't frightened of a panther watching it from the edge of the forest. Did it somehow recognize her? Did it know she and Braeden had helped it?

For a long time it did not move. But finally, it walked into the cover of the trees on the other side of the meadow and disappeared.

Serafina felt her heart sink.

Why was it here, on this ridge, in this part of the forest, at this moment?

She knew now that Braeden had definitely come home, but where did he go?

I just wanted to see you one last time, he had said that night. She remembered the tremor in his voice when he said it, the loyalty, the fierceness, but there had been a twinge of sadness and resignation as well.

Did he know all along that he was going to leave again the next morning? Is that what he had been trying to tell her?

But what did the white deer have to do with it all?

With all the peculiar things that were going on, why would Braeden leave without saying good-bye? She couldn't help feeling a hole in her heart, like something that should have happened didn't happen. *Stay bold,* he had said the night before. Had that been his good-bye?

She realized that he hadn't seen many of the peculiar things that she had. It was possible that he had returned to New York without realizing what was happening here. Life at Biltmore had been safe and peaceful for months, so maybe he thought everything was still all right.

But it isn't all right, she thought, feeling an ache in her chest, *it isn't right at all.*

As she turned to go back to Jess, she looked around at the trees and vegetation and realized that she didn't know which way it was.

Her sense of direction was normally very strong in the forest. But now she was confused, uncertain of the path back.

She took a few steps to see if she recognized one of the trees or a jagged rock, or if she could get her bearings in some other way. But nothing looked familiar.

A bout of panic and irritation rippled through her. *What's going on? This never happens to me. What if I can't find Jess?*

As she went deeper into the forest, she looked for any sort of sign or detail that might help her find her way back to her friend.

She felt a slight itching on the back of her neck. The cringing sensation of being followed crept into her shoulders.

She stopped and listened behind her.

For a moment she thought she heard the faint sound of rustling leaves, but whatever was following her stopped the instant she did. When she resumed, it resumed as well, the leaves rustling in the distance.

She couldn't shake the feeling that something wasn't just following her but *hunting* her.

She moved more quickly now, slinking quietly and rapidly through the underbrush.

Whatever was behind her moved just as fast she did, staying right with her, closing the distance between them.

The air rushing in and out of her panther lungs got louder as her breathing became heavier.

She went one way through the forest, and then the other, desperately trying to throw off her pursuer. But at the same time she had to find her way back to Jess.

Finally, she spotted a rock she recognized. She ran in that direction, and then saw a familiar tree.

But as she returned to the area in the forest where the hunters had been killed, her gut tightened with the memory of what happened there, the white-eyed fear of the horses and the bullets flying past her. She remembered the screams of the men and the barking of the dogs all around her.

In the cloud of anger that had boiled up inside her during the battle, and all the confusion of what was happening, had her darkest and most vicious instincts driven her to claw and bite and kill?

Was she transforming more and more into the panther part of herself, just like her mother had, more wildcat than human?

She didn't want to see their faces and the blood, so she skirted carefully around the dead bodies of Colonel Braddick, Mr. Turner, Mr. Suttleston, and Isariah Mayfield.

When she finally reached the spot where she had left Jess, Serafina stared at the empty patch of ground.

Serafina's chest tightened. She looked all around. She circled the area looking for her, but found no sign of her, not even footprints.

She sniffed the ground, searching for Jess's scent, but couldn't find it among the dead humans and trampled earth.

She went farther out into the forest. She searched for hours. But Jess was gone.

Serafina felt an almost overwhelming sense of hopelessness, like the more she tried to help, the worse things got. The more she tried to understand, the more incomprehensible things became.

Growling with frustration, she flexed her claws and began to run, just to get away from the place where the men had died. She ran and she kept running.

Driven on by the anguish roiling in her heart, she made her way toward the abandoned cemetery where so many events of her and Braeden's lives had occurred. She didn't even know why she was going there, except to find some sort of refuge, some sort of protection and understanding.

She crossed through the swampy marsh, then entered the old graveyard, which had been overgrown by the creeping, dripping-wet forest decades before. Black strands of vines strangled the crooked trunks of the gnarled trees. And thick carpets of choking leaves toppled the gray, weathered gravestones to the ground. Over the course of withering years, the roots of the trees had taken grip on the coffins beneath the earth, twisting them and breaking them and wrenching them to the surface, while long beards of grayish-green moss hung down from the branches above.

She shifted into human form as she walked into what she and Braeden had named the Angel's Glade.

Deep in the forest of the graveyard, the glade consisted of a small, open area of perfect, bright green grass encircled by a ring of graceful living trees with leaves that never fell. Surrounded by the death and decay of a long-abandoned world, this was a place of everlasting life.

In the center of the glade stood a magnificent statue of a winged angel holding a sword. She was dark green with age, and spots of lichen and moss covered many of her surfaces. She had long, flowing hair and a beautiful face, but the stain of weeping tears dripped down her cheeks like rain.

Standing in the glade, in front of the stone angel, Serafina lifted her eyes and looked up at her.

"I don't know what to do," she said, her voice pleading, but the angel did not reply.

As Serafina gazed around at the Angel's Glade, it didn't seem as if its grass was as bright green as it normally was. And the trees around the glade weren't as alive. This had once been a place of such awe-inspiring power and glittering magic, but not now. It felt cold and lifeless and alone, as if it too was gone from her world.

There were just so many questions swirling in her mind.

She crumpled to the ground.

In the center of the glade, she lay on her back, with her shoulder pressed up against the stone pedestal of the angel, and looked up into the night. The mist had gone and the air was clear, but very high up in the sky, a thin layer of silver-gray clouds shrouded the stars. She couldn't see the belt of Orion, the blue glow of Pleiades, or any of the stars that she had seen with Braeden. She missed them, her brothers and sisters of the night.

But as she kept looking, she saw a single persistent dot of light directly above her. Not a star, but a planet—the small, glowing orb of Jupiter, shining through the thin layer of clouds, like a valiant friend.

That's my Braeden, she thought, and suddenly her heart felt as if it was drowning.

"I'm in trouble here, Braeden," she cried out, her voice trembling. "I need your help. I don't know what's going on. I don't know what to do. I might have done something real bad. Come home now, just come home, as soon as you can. Please, I need you here. Just come home."

She knew it was impossible, but as she said the words, it almost felt as if he could hear them, as if at that moment, he woke from his bed, looked out into the nighttime sky, and imagined the sound of her voice.

She had to believe that he was safe, that he was up in New York like he was supposed to be, that their bond had not been broken, and that somehow, someday, he would return to her.

As she lay there alone with no idea where she could go or what she could do, it was only the glowing light of Jupiter that kept her from despair.

More tired than she had been in a long time, she wanted to sleep here in the faint but steady light of distant Jupiter, lying on the ground at the base of the stone angel, just as he had done for her in this very spot so long ago, calling her name into the darkness.

But she knew she had to go. She hadn't known the four men well, and she despised what they were doing out here, but the truth was that four human beings had been killed. And Jess was still missing. She had failed Jess! She had lost her! For all she knew, she had actually *killed* her with her own claws, or at least spooked her horse and caused it to throw her. One way or another, her friend was gone!

She didn't know the how or the why or the who. But the rock-hard truth was that she had failed to protect Jess and the hunters from evil—whether it came from her or from somewhere else. She didn't understand this evil. Or how to fight it. Was it inside her? But one way or another, with or without Braeden, she had to do it. She had to go back to Biltmore. And she had to face whatever was to come.

She pulled herself up onto her feet, wiped her eyes, and began the journey home.

21

As she walked across the courtyard toward Biltmore's front doors, her mind was consumed with what was going to happen when she stepped inside. But she spotted her little orange cat, Ember, running between two of the large terra-cotta planters and then darting out of sight. It was unusual to see Ember outside. And even more unusual that Ember didn't come running to greet her. It was as if she was chasing something. *Or being chased.*

Serafina went over to the planter, uncertain.

"Ember?" she said, but the cat did not come.

When Serafina took a few more steps forward and looked behind the planters, she found a small hole that Ember must have slipped down into.

"It appears that you've found a rat," Serafina said, thinking that maybe Ember had finally begun to take her job seriously.

But as she went inside and crossed through the Vestibule, she looked over and noticed scratches on the wall.

She stopped. She didn't remember seeing scratches there before. Had they been there all along and she'd never noticed them?

She took a step closer to them.

The striations almost looked like something Smoke and Ember would do, but they were far too thick, and the limestone walls of the Vestibule were far too hard for their little claws.

Serafina wondered, but she knew she couldn't linger here or follow this path. She had to go inside.

As she opened the doors and entered the Main Hall, the house was in turmoil, servants running, guests crying, dozens of men on the move, many with knives at their sides and hunting rifles in their hands.

"Serafina," a stern voice called.

She turned to see Mr. Vanderbilt stepping away from the group of men he had been talking to and striding toward her.

"I need to talk to you right away," he said. "Some sort of wild animal attacked the hunting party last night."

Serafina stood before him, and tried to keep breathing, but she could barely look at him. She hated the grim tone of his voice, and the desperate look in his eyes, like the world was coming apart at the seams and he had no idea how to stop it.

"From what we've pieced together," Mr. Vanderbilt said,

"Colonel Braddick and several others were tracking a mountain lion, and there was some kind of . . . apparently it . . . the mountain lion turned on them and attacked. Some of the men are saying there were actually two mountain lions."

As he spoke, Serafina felt her lips tightening and her eyes watering. She could hear in his voice all the sadness and confusion churning inside him.

But underneath all of it, she could hear something far worse: the creeping edge of doubt.

Doubt in *her*. And why not? She doubted herself.

Finally, she took a hard swallow and began to speak. "You're right that the hunters and their dogs chased two mountain lions," she said. "They treed them out on the North Ridge."

Mr. Vanderbilt looked at her with his eyes wide, clearly startled that she'd been so close to what had happened that she could actually confirm it.

"Did . . ." he began to ask her. "Did you have something to do with this, Serafina?"

She didn't even know where to begin to answer his question. She had *everything* to do with it!

She wanted to run away, to hide, to get away from it, but she knew she couldn't. Mr. Vanderbilt needed her help. That was the only thing she could cling to. Even as she was, he needed her.

"I helped the mountain lions to escape," she admitted.

"And the mountain lions came back and killed all those men?" he said in amazement and dismay.

"No, sir, that's not what happened," she said emphatically. "The mountain lions did not come back. I know that much for certain."

"Then what was it? What killed those men?"

"There was a dense fog," she said, shaking her head, "so much confusion, fighting and gunshots, all the horses panicking, the dogs running around. I was there. But I do not know what happened. I truly don't."

"Did something attack the hunters?"

"Yes, but I do not know what it was."

"And did you see Colonel Braddick's daughter?"

The question hit Serafina hard. "I . . ." she began, but then faltered.

"Tell me what happened," Mr. Vanderbilt urged her. "We must work together if we're going to deal with this."

She nodded, knowing he was right, and appreciating the way he said *we*, as if at least a little part of him still believed in a little part of her.

"I saw the bodies of the dead hunters in the forest," she said. "When I found Jess, she was injured, thrown from her horse, but she was still alive."

"Then what happened? Did you try to help her?"

When Mr. Vanderbilt asked her this simple question it was as if he were stabbing her in the heart. She knew that it was what she *should* have done. She should have helped her friend. But the anger had been boiling inside her, and then she got so lost and confused when she tried to return to her.

"I heard a noise that I thought was the attacker," she said. "I tried to follow it, but I lost track of whatever or whoever it was. And then, by the time I got back to Jess, she was gone."

"What do you mean she was gone?" Mr. Vanderbilt said.

"I thought she must have woken up and stumbled away. I looked for her for a long time in the surrounding forest, but I couldn't find her. She's a very observant and capable girl, and she's used to being outdoors, so all I could do was hope that she made it home."

"She did not," Mr. Vanderbilt said, his hand pressed in worry to his mouth.

And then, for a long time, he just stood there thinking, absorbing all that she had told him.

"It's a terrible thing," he said as he stared at the floor, and then he lifted his eyes and looked at her. "But whatever happened out there, Serafina, we need to protect the occupants of this house. Mr. Doddman and Lieutenant Kinsley are organizing the men. They're going to find and kill whatever animal did this. And they'll be searching for Miss Braddick as well. But for now, you need to rest. You look exhausted. And then you'll rejoin us."

Serafina's heart lurched. She knew what *find and kill whatever animal did this* meant to the men out there. They were going to ride out into the forest and shoot whatever animal they saw—most especially her brother and sister.

"I can't rest," she was about to say to Mr. Vanderbilt, but at that moment, Lieutenant Kinsley strode abruptly into the house and walked up to them, his manner brusque and filled with purpose.

He was no longer in his dress uniform, but wearing rugged outdoor clothing for riding, and he had exchanged his long officer's dress sword for a sheathed knife and a holstered sidearm. He glanced at her, and his eyes seem to flicker with something—relief, concern, irritation, she wasn't sure what it was—but then he spoke directly to Mr. Vanderbilt.

"I took care of that first matter, sir," he said.

"Very good," Mr. Vanderbilt said.

"And the men are ready to go out. I will be leading one of the groups myself, sir."

"And the security manager?"

"Mr. Doddman will be leading the other group."

"You both have the same mission: kill whatever beast did this and find the Braddick girl."

"We will, sir. You can count on us." Lieutenant Kinsley nodded curtly, glanced at Serafina, and then exited as if he had just been given orders by his commanding officer.

After the lieutenant had gone and she left Mr. Vanderbilt, she headed quickly down to the basement to see her pa. She knew she didn't have much time—she had to make sure her brother and sister had fled the area—but she also knew her pa was going to be fretting about her.

"Come on over here," her pa said gently as he wrapped his arms around her. And she held him in return, just resting there in his arms for a few moments. After everything that had happened the night before, it was good to see her pa. It felt like she'd been gone for days. And she knew he must have been worried sick about her when he heard about the attack during the night. As he held her, there were no suspicions from her pa, no doubts, no uncertainty, no complications, not even any words for a long time. Just love.

"Come on," he said finally, "you're gonna need some breakfast in your belly."

"I can't, Pa, I gotta go back out."

"Understood," he said, nodding. "Go do what you need to do and get back safe."

She liked the way he didn't grill her with questions or demand that she stay clear of what was happening. Her rats had gotten bigger, and a whole lot nastier, but he knew she had a job to do.

After leaving her pa, she went straight upstairs to the second floor, knocked on the nursery door, and poked her head into the room.

"Come in, my dear," Mrs. Vanderbilt whispered as she set the blanketed bundle of baby Cornelia carefully into the rocking crib, which was stuffed with down pillows and white bedding.

"Is Cornelia all right?" Serafina asked as she came in.

"We had a difficult night, but she just fell asleep," Mrs. Vanderbilt replied.

The nursery was a newly finished room, with gold-and-maroon cut silk velvet wallpaper, and the delicate curves of fine French furniture.

"Did you see or hear anything strange in the night?" Serafina asked.

"There were a few creaks and bumps here and there, and then all the commotion of the men downstairs, but that was all," Mrs. Vanderbilt said.

"Good," Serafina said. "Does Baby Nell like her new crib?"

"Oh, yes, I think so," Mrs. Vanderbilt said. "But what about you? The maids said that when they went to make your bed this morning that it hadn't been slept in. Is it not to your liking?"

"I'm sorry, ma'am, I haven't had a chance to sleep," she replied, suddenly feeling terribly ungrateful for the kindness that Mrs. Vanderbilt had shown her.

"There's no need to apologize, my dear," Mrs. Vanderbilt said. "I understand that you must have been very busy with the shocking news about the hunting party, but I just want you to promise me that you'll rest as soon as you can. I'll make sure none of the servants disturb you."

"Thank you, ma'am, I will, as soon as I can," Serafina promised, but a moment later she headed outside.

As she stepped out into the cobblestoned courtyard at the front of the house, she saw that it was filled with the men preparing their horses and weapons. Lieutenant Kinsley stood nearby, loading the leather saddlebag on the side of his horse, a beautiful dappled gray mare.

"Bring plenty of ammunition!" the lieutenant was saying to the other men. "And make sure your girth straps are tight. We're going into some very steep terrain."

She marveled at how much he had changed in mood and action since she'd seen him at dinner.

The news of what had happened had brought the whole house up in arms. Country strolls and afternoon tea had given way to hunts for rabid beasts and searches for a lost child. Everyone was helping, servants and guests alike.

When Lieutenant Kinsley saw her standing there alone, he turned toward her in surprise. "Miss Serafina . . ."

"Hello, Lieutenant," she said.

"Have you come to join us?" he asked hopefully. "I'll have a horse brought up right away."

She hadn't expected the invitation. His gray eyes seemed to

flicker as he gazed at her, his face filled with not only the grim seriousness that it had possessed a few moments before, but a kind of encouragement as well. It was as if they were comrades-in-arms now, working together toward a common goal, the darkest of circumstances pushing them together.

"I wish I could," she said sincerely, "but I think it would be better if I went out on my own."

He gazed at her in surprise, as if trying to figure out exactly what kind of person she was.

"On your own?" he asked, his tone steady and respectful.

She didn't know how to tell him that she had never ridden a horse. Nor did she know how to tell him that while he and his men were hunting her feline kin, she'd be making sure they got away. She knew it must confuse him why a lone thirteen-year-old, seemingly with no weapon or steed, would venture out when a vicious animal was stalking the forest.

"In what direction will you be going?" she asked.

"Up to the North Ridge first," he said. "Where the attack took place and Jess was last seen."

"That sounds like a good idea," she said. "But stay on the lookout. It's very rocky and there are many gullies and cliffs. And if you end up going east, down into the low ground, stay well clear of the swamp. It would be treacherous terrain for your horses."

He nodded as he glanced toward his horse, seeming to take the advice to heart. "Arabella here is my pride and joy," he said, patting his horse's shoulder. "We've been together since I was a boy. We went through officer training together." And then he lifted his eyes and looked at Serafina. "And in which direction will you be going?"

"West to the river, then upstream. The last time I got lost up in those mountains, I used the river to find my way home. Jess may try the same thing."

"And you'll be careful, too . . ." he said, not with the forcefulness of a demand, or even a question, but with the softness of a request.

It amazed her how a man who was about to go out and shoot whatever moved could be so thoughtful, so gentle of heart toward her. She wondered, if Lieutenant Kinsley saw her out in the forest in her true form, how fast would he pull the trigger? Was there truly even a difference between a panther and a girl?

"I will be careful," she promised. "And don't worry. I'm a fast runner." And then, realizing she should change the subject, she asked, "So, you know Jess Braddick well, then?" She couldn't help but notice how seriously he was taking the responsibility of finding her.

"No," he said. "I met her at dinner, but that is all. But if she's still lost out there, we've got to help her. George Vanderbilt has been a friend and mentor to me since I was very young. He put me through school, and arranged my commission as an officer. I owe him a great debt. I just hope that when the moment comes, I can prove myself worthy of his trust in me."

Hearing the gravity in his voice, it was clear that he was expecting to come face-to-face with the man-killing beast they were all talking about. And for all she knew, it was out there, some sort of horrible creature she hadn't yet seen.

"Everybody mount up!" Lieutenant Kinsley shouted as he turned, and all the riders began to move in earnest, hurriedly tightening their saddle straps and making last-minute adjustments.

In the single, smooth motion of a well-trained young cavalry officer, the lieutenant vaulted deftly into his saddle. As he took up Arabella's reins, the horse shifted her hooves and tilted her head, raring to go.

"Please be careful out there, Lieutenant Kinsley," she said, looking up at him on his horse. "No one knows what we're dealing with."

"Whatever it is, we're going to find it, and we'll bring Miss Braddick home," he said, clearly trying to be brave and confident just as his training had taught him.

"But please keep yourself safe in the meantime," she said. "Dinners in the Banquet Hall wouldn't be the same without you."

He smiled, seeming pleased with her comment. "And you as well, Miss Serafina," he said. "I will see you at dinner."

And then he tipped his hat, turned forward, and spurred his horse away.

As the hunting party rode out, she watched him canter toward the front of the group.

"We need to cover as much ground as we can," he shouted to the other men. "And keep your rifles ready!"

She waited three beats of her heart and then ran for the line of trees, thankful that cats' paws were faster than horses' hooves.

The moment she was out of sight of the house, she shifted and ran, her panther legs taking her miles through the forest.

Nose to the ground, it didn't take her long to find her brother and sister. The two mountain lions were already wild-eyed and on the run. They had smelled the coming horses and heard the shouts of the men.

She had worried that because they had seen her in human form so many times, they had become too careless around humans. But it was clear that just as Kinsley only saw her as human, her brother and sister only saw her as cat, no matter what form she was in. It had been that way since she met them as spotted cubs just outside their mother's den more than a year before. She was relieved to see that their instinct to flee humans was still strong.

She got their attention with a rub of her shoulder, and signaled them to follow her, leading them deep into the very swamp she had warned Kinsley to avoid. They would need to stay there until the danger passed.

From there she traveled alone, upstream along the river for several hours, looking for any sign of Jess or the man-killing beast. She wasn't even sure it existed. But *something* had killed the hunters. Was it possible it was out here? It must have been large enough to shove a horse and deadly enough to slash a man right down the center of his chest. What could do such a thing? A hunger-crazed bear? A wolf? A man with a weapon? Could it truly have been her own claws? Or was there some sort of demon prowling through the forest?

The night before, she had already scoured the North Ridge where the hunting party was going, but she still hoped they might somehow find Jess. And she prayed that Lieutenant Kinsley and the other members of the hunting party would stay safe. There was no doubt in her mind that they'd try to kill any large animal they encountered, but they didn't deserve to die.

After searching all day and into the night to no avail, she finally turned and headed back toward Biltmore, totally exhausted. She'd been up for far too long.

As she traveled through the forest, she heard the sound of horses. Still in panther form, she climbed a tree and watched from a safe distance as the hunting party moved past her.

Their enthusiasm for the kill had waned, their heads and their rifles hanging down. Wet and tired, they were heading home, just as she was. It was clear that they hadn't found what they were looking for. But then she realized that one of the men was missing. Lieutenant Kinsley was no longer with them.

Her heart tightened. Had he been killed? Lost? Or had he decided to continue the search for Jess even after sending his exhausted men back home?

When she finally got back to Biltmore, she checked in on her sleeping pa in the workshop, then headed upstairs to the second floor. Both of the hunting parties had returned hours before. The house was dark and still, everyone asleep after a long and difficult day.

As she went into her room, Smoke and Ember both purred gently, as if pleased to see that she'd made it home. And she was pleased to see them as well, especially little Ember, whom she'd been worried about after seeing her outside.

Ember seemed content to sleep, but Smoke studied her with watchful eyes.

"Are you all right?" she asked him gently as she petted his neck. With his gray eyes watching her, he seemed more worried than usual.

She lit a small fire in the bedroom fireplace, casting the room in a soft flickering light and filling it with a gentle warmth, then took off her dress and crawled between the silky sheets to get some much-needed rest. The down padding of the bed and the comforting weight of the blanket over her body made her feel warm and protected.

Her two apprentices joined her on the bed, snuggling up with her, Ember actively purring and kneading her chest with her little paws, and Smoke sitting quietly behind her calves, looking out into the rest of the room, ever on guard. There was nothing in the world quite as comforting as taking a long nap on a soft bed with two cats.

Exhausted, she quickly slipped into a deep sleep.

Her plan had been to sleep for just a little while, but when she woke, the fire had died out and the room had gone cold and black.

Ember was upside down asleep beside her, her paws up in the air as if she were still kneading her chest.

Smoke's eyes were open and watchful, and she could swear the dark gray fur on his body was more puffed out than usual.

Glancing out the window as she rose from the bed, she could see that Jupiter had set, which meant it was probably well after two in the morning, and the moon was rising. The upper sky was clear, but isolated banks of fog were rolling down the sides of the mountains, enveloping the trees.

Remembering where she was, she glanced at the clock on the mantel, which confirmed that it was twenty past three in the morning.

She wasn't sure what had awoken her.

She looked out the window again and then crossed to the other side of her bedroom.

Everything appeared to be as it should be.

Then she heard the sound of running footsteps outside her door, the sharp scrape of furniture.

Her heart began to hammer in her chest.

Something crashed to the floor and shattered.

A man screamed in horror.

Serafina ran for the door.

She burst out of her bedroom and looked frantically around, expecting to come headlong into an attack. But there was nothing there.

She was sure that the scream she'd heard had come from the living hall right outside her door, but the large, open room was quiet and still.

Had she heard the scream in a nightmare and woken up suddenly, thinking that it was real?

A wash of moonlight was pouring through the windows, casting the room in ghostly light and holding it all perfectly still as if it were an image in a dream.

She scanned the room again, looking across the empty, ghost-lit chairs, and the dark shapes of Mr. Vanderbilt's animalier sculptures on the tables. The tall, wrought-iron floor lamps stood like wraiths in the night, casting long black shadows across the pale moon floor.

She could not see anything out of the ordinary, but she felt a crawling sensation on the back of her neck.

Standing very still, she moved her gaze from one empty chair to the next, into one dark corner and then the other, to the small black cave of the dead fireplace, to the murky voids beneath the tables, scanning every nook and cranny for any sort of danger lurking in the shadows.

Smoke and Ember padded slowly forward on either side of her, fanning out across the living hall floor.

"Go flush it out," she whispered as she searched the shadows.

She made her way carefully over to the Grand Staircase. Leaning over the railing, she peered up to the third and fourth floors above her, thinking that maybe the scream had come from up there, but she saw nothing out of place.

She gazed down the steps that flowed in a sweeping arc to the first floor. *Nothing.*

But when she looked straight down over the railing, through the spiral of the staircase, to the area of floor directly below her, she saw it.

A chill ran up her spine.

There was a dark shape lying on the floor.

She reflexively glanced behind her, filled with a sudden feeling that someone was creeping up on her.

She scanned the moonlit living hall once more, still sensing the presence of something. Smoke and Ember had disappeared, so she was alone.

Her instincts were telling her to go right back into her bedroom, shut the door, lock it, and hide. But she knew she couldn't do that.

We all have a job to do, she thought. *And this is mine.*

When she looked over the railing again, the dark shape was still there on the floor, exactly where it had been. No tricks of the mind this time.

Slowly pulling in a long, steady breath, she crept down the stairway, watching the slide of the shadows as she went. The moon shone through the windows of the Grand Staircase, casting everything in a bright silver light.

When she finally reached the bottom of the stairs, she saw the shape more clearly. It was lying on the floor. Very still. The body of a man.

Goose bumps rose up on her arms and her temples began to pound.

She glanced across the Main Hall toward the Winter Garden and down the corridor toward the Billiard Room.

There was no movement, no people, just the moonlight and the shadows, and the ticking of the grandfather clock in the Main Hall.

She made her way slowly toward the body.

The man was wearing a simple white cotton nightshift and she could see his bare feet. It was as if he had come running out of his room.

Carefully avoiding the pool of dark liquid that was seeping across the stone floor from his head, she moved closer and looked at his face.

It was Mr. Kettering, the gentleman who had come in late to the dinner, just as she had. She had not known him, but he had seemed like a kind and good man. And now he was dead.

She slowly tilted her head and looked up at the third floor some fifty feet above.

Had he come out of his guest room and fallen over the railing by accident?

And then she remembered the sound of commotion and the horrified scream, and the intense fear that she had felt when she stepped outside her room.

Had he seen something so frightening that he'd flung himself over the railing to get away from it?

Not wanting to look down at the gruesome sight of the dead Mr. Kettering again, she traced her eyes along the arc of the stairs. It had always disturbed her how on some nights the Grand Staircase looked so lovely and benevolent in spirit, but other nights, when the moonlight poured in, it seemed haunted with a pale, cold menace.

Tap-tap-tap . . .

She quickly tilted her head toward a sound in the distance.

Tap-tap-tap . . .

Coming closer. Tiny cloven hooves on the stone floor.

Tap-tap-tap . . .

Fear flooded into her limbs. Her body froze, unable to move. Suddenly, she felt as if she was being hunted again, like she was being tracked down. She was going to be killed. Was this the terror that had driven Mr. Kettering over the railing? Should she try to spin and fight? Should she try to flee?

Tap-tap-tap . . .

Whatever it was, it was right behind her now. Just a few feet away. But she was too frightened to turn and look.

25

A loud crashing noise exploded on the second floor above her, then the wailing caterwaul of a terrified cat. It was Ember!

As Serafina leapt to her feet, she glanced behind her, bracing herself for a startling fright. But to her surprise, there was nothing there.

What she thought had been there just a moment before was gone now.

She didn't have time to think about it. She sprinted up the stairway to help her cat.

She could hear the snarling, hissing little tabby fighting something, lamps getting knocked over, vases smashing onto the floor, like she was in a fierce, knock-down, drag-out battle to the death.

That ain't no rat, Serafina thought as she ran. And as she came up to the top of the stairway, she saw it. At first her brain couldn't comprehend what she was seeing. It appeared to be a hunched, lizardlike creature, about the size of a dog, but it had scaly skin, clawed feet, a long, writhing tail, leathery bat-like wings, and ugly bulging eyes. The sight of the unnatural beast jolted her with such intense fear that it almost paralyzed her. But she was desperate to save Ember. She charged forward.

The bizarre beast scurried away from her, running beneath a chair and then a sofa. Then it scuttled down into a ventilation shaft and disappeared, leaving her with nothing but a shudder down her spine.

Serafina ran back to help her wounded cat. "Poor little kitten," she whispered as she picked Ember up and held her. "I've got ya. We're all right now."

But Ember's body went limp in her hands.

"Are you all right, little one?" she cried.

But as Serafina held her, she could tell that Ember wasn't all right.

Her little legs hung loose, her eyes were closed, and her head was tilted down at an odd angle.

Her body was still warm, but Ember was dead.

Serafina's stomach churned.

Whatever that terrifying creature was, it had killed her cat.

Serafina held her in her hands.

"Good-bye, little one," she whispered as she looked down at her, stroking the fur on her cat's head and ears. She wanted Ember to open her eyes, to look at her, to purr like she used to.

Tap-tap-tap . . .

Serafina heard the sound coming up behind her, little hooves on the hardwood floor.

Tap-tap-tap . . .

She slowly set Ember's body back down, and then turned and looked behind her.

Her eyes widened.

Here, on the second floor of Biltmore, down at the end of the darkened corridor that led to the nursery and to Braeden's bedroom, stood the white deer.

And it was staring straight at her.

The white deer looked at her with the blackest eyes she had ever seen, filled not just with the darkness of the midnight sky, but the unsettling moonlike shimmer of *knowing*.

Serafina did not turn, but she knew that the moon was visible in the window behind her. And as she studied the deer, she could swear that she saw the reflection of herself and the moon in the deer's eyes.

She thought it must be the same white deer she had seen before. But now it was larger in size and it had a full set of antlers sticking up from its head like clusters of branches. She knew that normally only male deer had antlers, but this was a doe. It seemed to be changing every time she saw it, as if it wasn't just growing at a startling rate, but morphing its shape from one thing to another.

As she gazed at it, she kept thinking it was going to *do* something, run away or attack her, or even speak, but it just stared at her with those beady black eyes.

"What do you want?" Serafina asked the deer. "Why are you here?"

The deer made some sort of noise, but she could not tell what it meant.

When Serafina took a small step to the left to get a bit closer to the escape of the staircase, the deer took a small step to the right.

Feeling a creeping shiver run up the back of her neck, Serafina glanced into the shadows behind her, half expecting some horrible beast to lunge out at her, but there was nothing there.

When she turned back to the deer, it was gone.

She was left standing there in confusion.

What in the world? she wondered in exasperation. *What is going on in this place?*

And then she remembered Ember. She turned and saw Ember's body lying on the floor.

Her heart filled with aching pain as she slowly crumpled onto her knees next to her dead little cat. Her hands rose to her face and pressed against the bridge of her nose, and she breathed long, ragged breaths, pulling air in through her fingers. Ember's head was tucked in the way she used to when she was a little kitten, and her paws were curled tight.

Serafina remembered finding Smoke and Ember when they were just bundles of fuzz a few weeks old, and bringing them into the house, and feeding them, and letting them sleep curled up with her in bed, purring. She remembered teaching them how to hunt for mice and rats, and telling them that they had to make sure there were no vermin in the house.

No vermin in the house, Serafina thought now, her heart breaking. *That's exactly what Ember had been trying to do.*

"Poor Ember, you must have fought so hard," she said, crying. "This was a kind of vermin that you were too little to fight."

She just hoped that Smoke had somehow managed to escape.

Tears welling up in her eyes, Serafina lifted Ember's limp body in her cupped hands. The little cat's head hung down on one side of her hands and her long tail hung down on the other. Her fur was still so soft and her body still warm.

Serafina slowly carried her back into their bedroom and gently set her on the windowsill. She would bury her out in the garden by the azaleas. But right now, there were other things she knew she must do.

When she was younger, hunting rats down in the basement, she had crept through the shadows alone night after night, but over the last year she had learned many things, and one of them was that sometimes she needed to get help.

She crossed the living hall, went into the alcove, and knocked on the oak door of Mr. Vanderbilt's bedroom.

"It's me, sir. It's Serafina," she called through the door. "Something has happened. You need to get up."

Knowing that it would be difficult to rouse Mr. Vanderbilt from sleep in the middle of the night, she was just about to call out again, but the door suddenly opened and he stood before her. It startled her to see that he was not only wide-awake at this hour, but fully dressed.

"What is it? What's happened?" he asked.

"There's been an attack," she said. "Mr. Kettering is . . ." She had trouble saying the words. She knew he had been Mr. Vanderbilt's friend. But she had to tell him. "Mr. Kettering is dead, sir."

"What?" Mr. Vanderbilt said in dismay. "How?"

"There was some sort of creature . . ." she said. "Mr. Kettering fell over the railing of the stairs."

"Tell me what it looked like," he demanded.

It startled her that he didn't seem surprised by the news that there was a murderous creature in the house. He just wanted the specifics. As she did her best to describe it, she glanced into Mr. Vanderbilt's private bedchamber behind him, looking for some clue as to why he was up in the middle of the night.

She could make out the deep maroon curtains blocking out the night's moonlight, and the matching upholstery on the dark walnut furniture. With all the ancient Greek frescoes, oil paintings, and bronze sculptures in his room, it was like an art museum all in itself, so different from the sunlit velvet airiness of Mrs. Vanderbilt's suite, which was connected to his by the formal Oak Sitting Room where they shared their breakfast each morning.

When she was finished describing the creature to him, Mr.

Vanderbilt nodded. "I think that's what I saw the other night. It frightened me so badly that I couldn't even utter words to describe it. I didn't think it could be real. I prayed I had imagined it. For days now, I have been doubting my own sanity."

"I understand," she said, and she truly did. "But now we both know that it's very real. And I'm so sorry about Mr. Kettering. I know he was your friend."

Mr. Vanderbilt nodded appreciatively, and said, "You had better take me to him."

Serafina led him along the corridor, through the smashed-up living hall where Ember had died, and then down the Grand Staircase.

But when they got to the bottom of the stairs, she stopped abruptly in astonishment.

The floor was empty.

Mr. Kettering's body was gone.

"I don't understand," Mr. Vanderbilt said, looking at her.

"I heard him scream, I know I did," Serafina said, her voice shaking with uncertainty. "And I saw Mr. Kettering's body lying right here. I swear it. Right here."

But even as she said the words, the doubt began to creep into her mind.

Serafina watched Mr. Vanderbilt carefully as he stared down at the empty space on the floor.

She still didn't understand how it was possible that Mr. Kettering's body wasn't there. There wasn't even any blood. But she had heard the struggle from her bedroom and she had seen his body lying on the floor. Had that all been a bad dream?

She knew that Mr. Vanderbilt had already wondered how and why she'd been so close to the hunting party when it was attacked. Now what would he think of her? She'd gotten him up in the middle of the night with outlandish stories of dead bodies lying in the Main Hall.

When she saw the strained, uncertain expression on his face she was sure he was regretting his decision to move her up to the second floor. It was obvious now that she couldn't protect him and his family. She had no idea what was going on. She couldn't even tell the difference between real and unreal!

"This is indeed inexplicable," Mr. Vanderbilt said in confusion, his eyes still staring at the empty spot on the floor. "But I know you wouldn't make something like this up."

"I honestly don't understand where the body went . . ." she said in exasperation.

"It's possible that someone, or some*thing*, moved it," he said. "I will go and speak with the security manager. There has to be some kind of explanation."

It surprised her that he seemed so calm and logical about it all—she wasn't quite sure how he managed it—but there was something even more startling.

He believes me, she thought in wonder. *He actually believes me.*

It felt as if up to this moment she'd been buried in heavy stones, and now someone was lifting the stones away one by one. Finally, she had an ally, someone who truly trusted her, someone she could fight alongside. Maybe she wasn't losing her mind. It didn't seem possible that she had killed the hunters in the forest. And she was pretty sure she hadn't imagined Mr. Kettering's body lying on the floor. If someone as smart and honorable as Mr. Vanderbilt believed in her, then she should believe in herself.

She nodded in agreement with his plan, but Ember's death, and then Mr. Kettering's death, had shaken her badly, and her mind kept going back to the reason Mr. Vanderbilt had brought her up to the second floor. "I'm sure Baby Nell is fine, but I'm going to go back upstairs and make sure she's all right."

She quickly parted from him and hurried to the second floor. As she slipped into the darkened nursery and closed the door, she saw Baby Nell sleeping safely in her crib. A nursemaid usually attended to her, but Serafina was surprised to see that tonight Mrs. Vanderbilt was there, sound asleep in the moonlight, curled up on the settee beside the crib, her hair tumbling loosely around her shoulder. It was as if her mother's instinct had told her that something in the house was amiss.

Serafina could hear, beyond the closed nursery door, that the house had gone still and quiet again, and that suited her just fine. *We need some peace and quiet,* she thought.

She stepped over to the window and scanned the moonlit courtyard in front of the house, looking for any signs of trouble.

Pulling back from the window, she draped a blanket over her sleeping mistress, and stoked the embers in the fireplace to warm the room.

As she tiptoed back to the crib, she was expecting the baby to still be asleep, but little Nell looked up at her with her big beautiful eyes. The baby gazed at her for several seconds, then broke into a huge smile when she recognized her. Baby Nell began making little purring noises, imitating the sounds that Serafina had often made to her.

"Shh, shh," Serafina whispered gently, patting Nell before she woke up her mother.

Thonk-thonk.

Serafina jumped in surprise. Something had thudded against the nursery door. But then she realized what it was. When she opened the door a few inches, Smoke ran into the room.

"I'm glad to see you, my friend," she whispered, as she scooped him up into her arms and hugged him tight. But he was in no mood for cuddling. He jumped down from her arms and darted down the corridor, meowing. It wasn't like him to meow.

"What is it?" she asked as she closed the nursery door and went after him. "Show me."

She followed him around the corner, through the living hall, and down the Grand Staircase. She didn't want to leave Mrs. Vanderbilt and the baby, but it was clear that Smoke was on the trail of something.

"Where are you taking me?" she whispered, but Smoke just kept going, quiet and serious now.

As soon as he reached the first floor, he darted down the narrow servants' stairs into the basement and ran toward the kitchens.

"This better not be about getting a bowl of milk," she whispered.

Tap-tap-tap.

She stopped in the basement corridor and froze. It wasn't about a bowl of milk.

Tap-tap-tap.

The muscles in her back tightened.

Tap-tap-tap.

Her teeth clenched. *Not this again,* she thought.

Tap-tap-tap.

Fear pulsed through her veins, but she was sick of this! She wanted answers! She spun around, determined to confront her enemy once and for all.

28

In the split second it took her to turn, the corridor was already empty. She heard the *tap-tap-tap* of her enemy's feet trotting around the corner.

She dashed down the corridor and made the turn, only to catch a fleeting glimpse of something turning the next one.

She burst after it, rounding the next corner, but there was nothing there.

She paused and listened for any sort of sound coming from ahead of her. But then she heard the *tap-tap-tap* of the creature's footsteps immediately *behind* her.

That thing's wicked fast, she thought, but before she could even turn to see it, a clattering racket rose up from the kitchens, glass breaking, pots and pans crashing to the floor. A man screamed in horror. She charged toward the sound.

Her cat Smoke shot out of the Rotisserie Kitchen like a gray streak, his tail huge, his claws skittering across the tile floor in panic.

"Run, Smoke!" she shouted as they passed each other.

The moment she reached the doorway of the kitchen, she lurched back in confusion. Mr. Vanderbilt was there! And he was charging straight at Mr. Cobere, Biltmore's butcher and rotisserie cook.

Mr. Cobere tripped backward, trying desperately to escape him. "Stop! Please! No!" he begged as he threw up his shaking hands to defend himself. But Mr. Vanderbilt attacked, filled with a violence she had never seen in him.

Mr. Vanderbilt grabbed Mr. Cobere and shoved him back until the poor man crashed against the butcher block. He lost his balance and fell against the large black iron rotisserie spit where he had been roasting a haunch of venison on the cook fire.

As the two men grappled, Serafina froze in shock. Who was she supposed to fight, the attacker or the attacked?

"No! Please!" Mr. Cobere begged as Mr. Vanderbilt struck him repeatedly with his fist. Mr. Cobere tried to struggle away, tried to fight back, but he was a small man and there was little he could do. And then Mr. Vanderbilt grabbed one of the wrought-iron fire pokers and slammed it hard against his head. Poor Mr. Cobere toppled to the tiled floor.

Serafina gasped in horror.

Mr. Vanderbilt turned and saw her for the first time. His face looked bronze-colored in the dim, flickering glow of the rotisserie fire, and his eyes were filled with terrifying wildness. He dropped the iron poker to the floor with a ringing clatter and ran from the room, fleeing down the corridor.

She knew she should go after him, fight him, capture him, *something*, but she was too stunned by what she had just seen to even move.

A bout of black-haze dizziness swept through her like a sickening wave. She pressed her hand to the wall to steady herself. *How could it be?*

Her mind swirled in anguish and confusion, her temples pounding. It felt like everything she had ever counted on in the world was crashing down around her head. But she knew she had to stay focused, she had to stay sane.

Just get your wits, girl, she told herself fiercely.

She grabbed a rag from the counter, fell to her knees, and tried to stanch the blood oozing from Mr. Cobere's head.

His eyes were open, and he gazed up at her in utter shock of what had happened to him. "Why, Serafina?" he asked in a weak, raspy voice. "Why did he do that?"

"Just hold on, Mr. Cobere, hold on . . ." she cried, but even as he looked at her, his body went limp and his eyes went glassy.

Mr. Cobere was dead.

And Mr. Vanderbilt was the murderer.

She stumbled down the corridor away from the scene of the crime, every step she took pounding in her head, the walls of the passageway undulating with darkened colors. The floor felt slanted beneath her feet.

All she could see in her clouded mind was the sight of Mr. Cobere raising his arms to cover his head as Mr. Vanderbilt struck him down.

In all her dealings with him over the last year, Mr. Vanderbilt had always seemed like a fair and gentle man. She just couldn't understand how he could possibly have murdered Mr. Cobere. But she had seen it with her own eyes!

And she knew Mr. Cobere was a good man. He wasn't

some kind of criminal or demon or a treacherous fiend that Mr. Vanderbilt had to defend himself against.

As she made her way down the basement corridor, she could still hear the echo of Mr. Cobere's screams in her mind.

What was she going to do now? She had no place to go. No place was safe. If the master of Biltmore was a murderer, what was he going to do next? He had *seen* her watching him. He knew she had witnessed him killing Mr. Cobere.

She didn't want it to be true. She didn't want it to be real. But she knew it was.

There must be some dark, violent part of Mr. Vanderbilt that I didn't know about, she thought. *Did everyone have some sort of black panther living inside them?*

If she couldn't trust Mr. Vanderbilt, then who could she trust? The pain of it seeped through her brain.

When she finally made it to the workshop, she stumbled to her sleeping pa and crawled into his cot with him, desperate for any kind of refuge.

She knew she had to keep moving, she had to figure out what to do, but her legs had stopped working and her mind couldn't think. How do you respond to something that's impossible? How do you move?

Her pa stirred and muttered as he pulled her close. "What's wrong, Sera?"

She buried her face in his arms.

"What's wrong?" he asked her again.

"Everything," she cried in despair, her voice wet and raspy.

"I want to help you, Sera. What I can do?"

"Nothing," she said miserably.

How could she tell him that the man he admired most in the world was a murderer? How could she tell him that heinous, winged beasts were slithering into Biltmore? How could she tell him that his daughter was a strange, shape-shifting creature of the night? It was just too much.

"All these bad things keep happening, all jumbled together, but I don't know how to stop them!" she cried.

"Listen, Sera," he said, holding her tight, "when you're down in the muck of the swamp and your feet are stuck in the mud and the weeds are so thick you can't see in front of you, then you *know* what you gotta do."

"I don't!" she cried.

"You do, Sera! You *know*."

"I don't!"

"Are ya gonna say that the swamp is too big and you can't get across it? Are ya gonna sink down into the water of the swamp and give up? Will that get you home?"

"No," she said.

"No, it won't," he said emphatically. "If you're stuck in the swamp and you give up, it's gonna get darker, you're gonna get hungrier, colder, more and more tired. There's an old saying: *The only way out is through.* Do you understand? When it feels like you're stuck in a swamp, you gotta keep goin', Sera, that's what ya gotta do. You might be tired, you might be runnin' blind, but you gotta keep pushing. You go on faith."

"Faith?" she said doubtfully. It felt like the whole world had broken, every part of it shattering. "Faith in what?"

"Faith in what you know is true," he said forcefully. "It might be hard to see, but you find it. Faith in yourself. Faith that there must be an end to the swamp, that it has another side. *The only way out is through.* Do you understand what I'm saying?"

"I understand," she said, opening her eyes and wiping her nose. "But I gotta tell ya, Pa, I'm right in the middle of a big ol' swamp, and it's a bad one."

"You'll find your way, Sera," he said. "Just keep pushing through."

As she felt the black darkness in her heart beginning to fill with something else, she wanted to tell him everything right then and there. She wanted to tell him who she truly was, not just a girl, not just his daughter, but a catamount, a panther, half human, half cat, a being with two halves to her soul, and she had fought battles against the darkest of enemies. But she knew she couldn't tell him. Deep down, she was just too scared. If he knew the truth, what would he think of her? How would he react? She wanted to tell him that the whole world was a lie and it was crumbling down around them. But she lay there, just holding him, too scared to tell him any of it.

She dreamed of Braeden coming to her on the terrace beneath the stars and saying her name. She dreamed of a white deer with a red stain. But she awoke to the sound of a woman screaming.

"Get up, Sera," her pa said, shaking her. "Something has happened."

She followed her father down the corridor toward the kitchens. It appeared that the servants had come in to begin their day. Twenty cooks, scullery maids, and other servants were gathered outside the Rotisserie Kitchen, gasping and whispering and asking questions no one had answers to.

"What's this all about?" her pa asked as he approached them.

But Serafina's stomach twisted. She already knew.

"Is someone hurt?" her pa asked them, trying to get through the crowd. Her father had known Mr. Cobere. They had been friends. And he was just about to see him dead.

But then the crowd of servants suddenly parted as someone else approached from the other direction.

Serafina's heart lurched when she saw Mr. Vanderbilt coming down the corridor.

"What is going on here?" the master of the house demanded in a firm voice.

"Mr. Cobere is dead!" one of the washerwomen cried out, sobbing.

Mr. Vanderbilt's face went grim and he shoved his way through the bystanders.

There he is, Serafina thought. *The murderer. Right there!*

Her pa pulled her back from the crowd of servants and the gruesome sight of what was lying on the kitchen floor, saying, "You don't need to see this."

She didn't have the heart to tell him that she'd already seen it, she'd seen it bad, the murder and the blood, and the great Mr. Vanderbilt, his friend and employer, was the one who had done it!

As her father led her away from the commotion, Serafina could hear many of the people in the crowd whispering about what might have happened to Mr. Cobere. And then, just as she and her pa turned the corner of the far corridor, Mr. Vanderbilt's voice rang out. "Has anyone seen Serafina? I need Serafina!"

Serafina ducked down, her heart accelerating in panic. Was he going to drag her away someplace and kill her? Imprison her?

Accuse her of something? She had no idea how she could face Mr. Vanderbilt after what she saw him do.

There was a part of her that wanted to point at him in front of everyone and scream out, *He's the murderer! He's the murderer!* But there was another part of her that remembered the horrific way he had killed Mr. Cobere. She imagined Mr. Vanderbilt charging toward her, striking her with the iron fire poker. She had seen everything he did, and now he was going to kill her!

"I'm sorry, Pa," she said, hurrying forward without him. "I'll come back later, but I've got to go."

She scampered up the servants' stairs to the main floor and fled the house through the side door, headlong into the pouring rain.

Her running legs took her across the courtyard through the storm, the blustering wind buffeting her body as thunder and lightning crashed overhead.

When she reached the cover of the trees, she lunged forward and landed on four clawed feet.

Snarling with frustration, she raced through the forest, the wind and the rain whipping her face.

She had such power with these muscles, such sharpness in her teeth and claws. She could fight any enemy. But how could she fight Mr. Vanderbilt, a man she admired and looked up to? And if not Mr. Vanderbilt, then who? Who could she fight?

She kept running, not even thinking about where she was going. She followed rocky, narrow ridges and crossed through thick stands of rain-dripping pines.

When she noticed fresh claw marks and scratches on the trunks of several trees, she brought herself to a stop. She had seen scratches like this before.

Even through the rain, she smelled the strong odor of blood, and saw its dark stains on the pine-needles. Then she saw the body.

A small black bear cub was lying dead on the ground.

At first she thought that the search party, the men hunting for the beast, had shot the cub. But it was clear that something had attacked and killed it in the most vicious manner.

It seemed like death was everywhere, coming faster and faster. And she had no idea what was causing it or how to stop it.

She continued on, running beyond the pines, through a deep forest of oak and hemlock, and then down into a thick, watery marsh.

It wasn't until she saw the gravestones that she knew where she was going.

Why here? she thought. *Why do I keep getting drawn back here?*

Longing for Braeden, for a friend, for anyone who would understand, she made her way through the graveyard to the Angel's Glade.

When she shifted back into human form, she wiped the rain from her face and squinted up at the stone angel. The angel stood tall above her, her wings aloft and her sword held strong.

Serafina read the familiar inscription on the pedestal.

OUR CHARACTER ISN'T DEFINED
BY THE BATTLES WE WIN OR LOSE,
BUT BY THE BATTLES WE DARE TO FIGHT.

Serafina thought about holding Ember in her hands as she died, and Mr. Kettering lying dead on the floor, and the sight of Mr. Vanderbilt murdering Mr. Cobere. And she thought about all the other things she had seen.

"How?" she screamed up at the angel's unmoving, tear-stained face. "How do I fight this?"

Serafina lifted her hands and shook them at the angel. "What good are these claws when there's nothing I can attack? What good are these teeth when there's nothing I can bite? Do you want me to kill Mr. Vanderbilt? This isn't a battle! It's chaos!"

But no matter how loud she screamed, the angel did not reply. Her face remained as stone and stoic as it always did.

In the past, Serafina had always imagined that the angel was on her side, speaking to her and guiding her, deep in her heart. The angel had seemed to possess a wondrous inner magic—her glade always green, her sword always sharp, and her presence filled with the power to hold life and death at bay. But now the Angel's Glade seemed dead and lifeless, and she felt a pang of doubt whether the spirit of the angel was even real.

And the more she sank into her thoughts, the angrier she became. What exactly was she fighting for? For Biltmore, the

174

place that hosted the hunters who had come to kill her kin? Was she fighting for Mr. Vanderbilt, a devious, two-faced rat of a man who had murdered Mr. Cobere? What was this ideal called Biltmore Estate?

"It's nothing!" she snarled. *"It's nothing!"*

As she gritted her teeth and turned from the statue, the torrent of the rain finally began to slow.

The rushing sound of the storm gradually fell away and all that remained was the rain dripping quietly from the bare branches of the trees and the mist rising from the ground.

As her mind cleared, and she began to calm, she thought about what her pa had told her.

The only way out is through.

But how?

There was no doubt she was stuck in the swamp just like he said—tired, lost, and losing hope.

How could she get through?

Over the last year, she'd come up out of the basement, found her claws, and learned to fight. She had defeated all her enemies in battle. But she couldn't claw her way out of this. She wasn't even sure what the *this* was. She wasn't even sure if she could trust what she had seen with her own eyes, what she had heard with her own ears, or even what she herself had done. How could any of it be true? She knew it couldn't be, but it was.

And what if what she was fighting for wasn't even worth fighting for? What if Biltmore itself was evil? What if Biltmore and the man who built it needed to be destroyed?

The more she thought about it, the more she realized that what scared her the most was that this time, she wasn't the hunter. She was the hunted. There was something a-prowl, killing them off one by one. She wasn't thinking—she was reacting. She was running. She'd been desperate to catch someone, to fight someone, but she was flailing. She was blind.

She had to figure out what her enemy was doing, what was driving him, what he wanted, and then maybe she could anticipate his next move. It was no good finding poor Mr. Kettering lying dead on the stone floor at the bottom of the Grand Staircase. He had already fallen. It was no good watching Mr. Vanderbilt kill Mr. Cobere. Before she could figure out what to do, the killing blow was already struck.

One of the things her pa had taught her from a young age was that when it seemed like everything was coming at her, when life was just too confusing and overwhelming to bear, then she should stop, sit down, and ask herself one question: What is the most important thing? What is the one thing that I *must* do? And then focus on doing it.

What is the one thing? she wondered. *What must I make sure I do no matter what?*

It did not take long for the answer to form clearly in her mind.

I must protect the good and innocent people of Biltmore.

That meant her pa, and Essie, and Mrs. Vanderbilt, and poor Jess, who she'd abandoned in the forest, and so many others. And most of all, it meant little Baby Nell.

She couldn't just sit here in the graveyard feeling sorry for herself, scared and shaking, a little mouse among other mice, all getting hunted one by one.

No matter how frightening it was, no matter how confusing, she had to do her job the best she could.

She had to protect them.

As she finally made her way back to Biltmore, the sun was setting and she found herself slipping through the foggy cover of a coming night, the clouds hanging so low that it was impossible to tell if she was below them or inside them.

She approached the house quietly and unseen, trusting no one.

Avoiding the front doors and the Main Hall of the house, where she feared there could be footmen, guests, or even Mr. Vanderbilt himself, she circled through the woods, down into the valley, and snuck along the back side, where the mansion's massive stone foundation rose up out of the steep slope like the wall of a castle.

She followed closely along the wall until she came to a small rectangular pit at its base, then wriggled her body down through its iron cover-grate. When she reached the bottom of the pit, she shinnied up a brick-lined vertical shaft some thirty feet, her back pressed against one side of the shaft and her feet pressed against the other, inching her way up like a little crevice-dwelling caterpillar.

She had used this method to enter Biltmore many times when her life in the basement had been unknown to the fancy folk above, and that was the secrecy she needed once again.

Thanks to the house's architect, Mr. Richard Morris Hunt, this well-hidden shaft fed fresh air to the giant boilers in the subbasement, like the windpipes of a gargantuan stone-and-steel beast, and established the central spine of the mansion's vast ventilation system.

When she reached the top of the shaft, she pushed up the metal grate, crawled out, and arrived in one of the subbasement storage rooms. Making her way through the piles of long, criss-crossing, storm-damaged copper gutters, she felt like she was crawling through the weathered bones of an ancient dinosaur in a dark, primordial cave.

She climbed up the narrow brick stairway to reach the basement level of the house. Then she darted from one shadow to the next, making sure that no one walking through the basement corridors late at night would see her, especially Mr. Vanderbilt or one of his men. Then she dashed up the back stairs to the second floor.

When she arrived in the back corridor near Mrs. Vanderbilt's suite of rooms, she crouched in a shadow, waiting and listening. The passageways of the second floor were dark and quiet. Everyone seemed asleep in their rooms.

She scurried forward and around the corner, slipping as quickly and quietly as she could past Mr. Vanderbilt's bedroom. He was the last person in the world she wanted to encounter in a dark, empty hallway.

As she passed the windows in the corridor, the arched glass roof of the Winter Garden was visible below. The white fog that she had traveled through to get home floated in the moonlight just outside the windows, like ghosts waiting to get inside.

But as she walked through the second floor living hall to get to the other side of the house, her pace faltered. She knew it wasn't possible, but when she looked across, she could swear the fog was now actually *inside* the room, floating over all the empty chairs and sofas, and around the cross-armed wrought-iron lamps standing like scarecrows in the pale, cold moonlight.

It felt as if she had been in this moment before.

But it's just a trick of the light, she told herself. *It's impossible for the fog to be inside the house.*

She ducked past the railing of the Grand Staircase and the doors of several bedrooms, and then paused uncertainly when she reached the T at the end of the corridor, everything so still and empty in the darkness. The right led down a dark hallway to Braeden's bedroom, closed and unused. The left led to the nursery.

She had walked down this corridor and turned this corner to the nursery a hundred times, but now her skin was crawling and she stopped cold, shrinking into the shadow along the wall.

There's something there, she thought as she stared at the corner and tried to keep her breathing steady.

It's right there.

She jumped violently when her cat Smoke burst toward her, his tail as thick as a feather duster. He ran straight to her and circled his body around her legs.

Crouching down, she held the frightened cat in her hands, and tried to listen to what was ahead.

Just around the corner, she heard a slithering, scratching noise.

Her lips went dry and her temples began to pound. There was definitely something there.

It sounded like the tips of sharp claws digging into wood, like something scratching incessantly at the nursery door.

She leaned down and whispered to Smoke, "Get downstairs and out of the house. Hide in the stables!"

As the cat scurried away behind her, she heard his feet pattering rapidly across the floor and down the back stairs. *Keep going, Smoke.*

When she was sure he was safely away, she turned back toward the corner.

She crept slowly forward, her heart pounding in her chest.

The scratching, scratching, scratching at the nursery door

continued incessantly. Something was trying to dig its way into Baby Nell's room.

She came to the edge of the wall and slowly, ever so quietly, peeked her head around the corner to see what it was.

32

What she saw scratching at the bottom of the nursery door was a sinewy, four-legged creature with a long, twisting body, almost like a large lizard, but squatting on all fours like a mammal, and it had bare, dark gray, leathery skin, bulging muscles, and visible protrusions of vertebrae along the length of its spine. Its neck was two or three times longer than any natural animal she had ever beheld. And its almost doglike, hairless head had long, sharply pointed ears, bulbous eyes, and a prodigious snout with rows of sharp, protruding teeth. In movement, it was fast, continuously scratching and sniffing as if it knew exactly what was on the other side of the door it was working desperately to dig through. In mind, it seemed obsessed, like a starved animal digging for a succulent piece of food.

She pulled back from the corner, her muscles pulsing, readying her for the fight.

This wasn't the exact beast that attacked Ember and Mr. Kettering. The other one had wings and its head was a different shape. But it was similar. She remembered the scratches in the Vestibule, and Ember running behind the planter and down into the hole. Then the sight of the dead bear cub in the forest flashed into her mind. Whatever these terrifying things were, they had a penchant for killing small animals. She didn't know exactly how she was going to fight this one, but she knew she couldn't let it get anywhere near Baby Nell.

She had always been very careful about showing people who she was. No one currently at Biltmore had ever seen her as a panther. But she wasn't sure she could kill this beast in her human form. It looked exceedingly dangerous.

She decided she had to risk being seen.

So right then and there, in the darkened corridor on the second floor, just outside the nursery, she shifted into her feline form.

Suddenly, the corridor felt so small and narrow. Her large, muscled panther body seemed as if it could barely fit. And the smells of the wood flooring and Persian rugs were so foreign to her panther nose.

But she knew she had no time to linger. Lowering her long, black-furred body nearly to the floor, she inched forward, and then slunk like a shadow around the corner.

She crept down the corridor toward the exposed, hunched back of the creature as it dug at the base of the door. She stalked so slowly, so quietly, that the creature did not detect her.

She crept closer and closer, sometimes stopping completely, so still that she was invisible in the darkness, just waiting, and then she continued slowly onward, inch by inch, foot by foot, until she was just a few steps away.

The instant the creature noticed her sneaking up behind it, it jerked back and hissed in alarm.

She lunged forward, striking at it with her claws. But the screeching thing scampered straight up the side of the wall, tearing into the wallpaper and clanging against one of the brass sconces. She pounced at it, heaving her body against the wall with a thump, but it scuttled upside down along the ceiling like a spider or a crab. She leapt at it again, swinging her paw at it, desperate to catch it or kill it, but it scurried out of reach, slipped into an air vent, and disappeared.

Gone, she thought angrily, panting through her fangs.

She quickly shifted back into human form before anyone spotted her, then pressed her back against the nursery door and looked down the darkened corridor, guarding the only way into the baby's room.

As she caught her breath, she tried to make sense of what she had just seen.

Was the master of Biltmore some kind of sorcerer who was controlling these creatures, or were they wild beasts crawling in from the forests hunting their prey? And what about the four men who had been killed on the North Ridge? Had that been Mr. Vanderbilt as well? Or did he have help to do all of this?

She knew Mr. Vanderbilt had many loyal employees at Biltmore, but would they murder Mr. Kettering on the Grand Staircase and then hide the body? Maybe it was more likely that one of these weird creatures had dragged the body away and then lapped up the blood from the floor.

But still, Mr. Vanderbilt must have had some sort of accomplice, maybe more than one.

Her first thought was Mr. Doddman, the security manager Mr. Vanderbilt had hired a few weeks before. She wasn't sure if the brutish man had been a police commander, an army sergeant, or a wretched crook before he came to Biltmore, but he seemed more than capable of violence.

And there was Mr. Pratt and the other footmen, and the head butler, and Mr. Vanderbilt's new valet, and the stablemen, and so many others. She didn't even know where to begin.

And then she remembered Lieutenant Kinsley. She thought about how he always said "sir" when he spoke to Mr. Vanderbilt, and the way he took orders from him like he was his commanding officer. *I owe him a great debt,* Kinsley had said.

Kinsley had seemed like such a good man. But could she trust what *seemed*?

As she gazed down the length of the corridor, watching and listening, she had to keep her flinchy mind from imagining that she could see traces of fog drifting in the shadows. She didn't trust shadows anymore, and especially didn't trust fog.

When she was out in the forest, she had seen that Kinsley hadn't returned to the house with the rest of the search party. That meant he was still out there someplace. But why? Had something happened to him or was he up to no good? Maybe he was the one who was controlling these strange creatures.

The truth was, she didn't know if Mr. Vanderbilt was working with accomplices or not. All she knew for sure was that he was a murderer and she had to do something about it. But what could she do? Who could she tell?

Good morning, Mrs. V, she imagined saying. *I hope Baby Nell is doing well today, and oh by the way, your husband is a murderer!*

The other thing she couldn't figure out was why Mr. Vanderbilt had asked her to move upstairs to the Louis XVI Room. Was it to get her out of the basement, away from the kitchens, so that he was free to murder Mr. Cobere?

Or did he ask her to move upstairs to protect his family? Did he know he was dangerous? A bizarre and startling thought sprang into her mind: What if he *wanted* her to kill him?

But what does the white deer have to do with this? she thought suddenly.

The more she wrangled with it all, the less any of it made sense.

It was like the entire Biltmore property was cursed in some way, like the house itself was murdering people.

But why? What was the rhyme and reason of it? Was there a pattern she wasn't seeing?

The first attack had been against the colonel, his daughter Jess, his friend Mr. Turner, the other hunter Mr. Suttleston, and the dog handler Isariah Mayfield.

And then she had found Mr. Kettering dead at the bottom of the stairs.

And then she had seen Mr. Vanderbilt murder Mr. Cobere in the kitchen.

She tried to think it through.

What did all of these victims have in common?

What was the pattern?

There is none, she thought in frustration as she pressed her back against the nursery door. *They're just random people who don't have anything in common at all. It's just death all around.*

How could she fight this? How could she defend against it?

Every day, every night, someone was dying. And it was getting worse.

At the far end of the corridor, she heard the sound of a claw scraping the wood wall.

She crouched, ready to spring.

The scratching noises moved toward her.

She peered into the darkness, looking for the source of the sound.

As the scratching came closer, she tried to figure out exactly where it was coming from, but then she realized it was actually coming from several different angles now, all moving toward her.

She readied herself for battle. Her heart pounded in her chest.

It sounded as if there were multiple creatures clawing their way toward her and the nursery door behind her.

They were surrounding her, *hunting* her.

Her eyes flitted from one shadow to the next, searching desperately for them, but she still couldn't see them.

It was impossible. How could she not see them?

The noises came even closer.

The creatures had to be just a few feet away from her now, but it was like they were invisible.

And then a thin stream of dust drifted down from above, the fine particles reflecting in the moonlight.

She snapped her eyes to the ceiling.

The creatures were above her!

They were in the air shafts!

While she was guarding the corridor, they had been crawling their way over her head. They were going to drop like clawed, leathery spiders into the nursery, right into the baby's crib.

Serafina charged into the room.

The moonlight was falling through the sheer white curtains of the bay window, casting the room in a haze of glowing fog.

She scanned the ceiling, looking for signs of the dangling creatures.

Mrs. Vanderbilt was asleep on the settee beside the crib, just as she had been the night before. Baby Nell was lying asleep in her crib, wearing her little sleeping outfit and a tiny cap on her head, all cuddled up, not too much bigger than Ember, and far smaller than a bear cub.

You have one job, Serafina, she thought fiercely as she scanned the ceiling again. *You've got to protect that baby! That's the one thing you absolutely must do.*

Bile rose in her throat as a desperate thought forced its way into her mind. She tried to swallow the bile down, but it burned.

Then she heard the scratching noises in the ceiling above her head. Fine lines of dust streamed down into the room.

The creatures were coming.

She didn't want to do what she was thinking. It was too horrible. But the more she thought about it, the more she knew she *had* to do it.

She glanced at the sleeping Mrs. Vanderbilt, and then leaned into the crib and lifted the baby into her arms.

She had to protect her.

She had to take her away from this place.

And she had to do it now, before it was too late.

Serafina clutched the whimpering baby to her chest and crept out of the room with her.

She scurried down the corridor, glancing this way and that as she ran, terrified that someone or some*thing* was going to catch them.

The thought that she was actually stealing Baby Nell from her mother made her sick to her stomach, and her vision blurred around the edges like she was running through a gray tunnel. But she had to protect the baby no matter what and she kept on running.

Every instinct in her body was telling her that the creatures were *hunting* the baby, that they'd follow her. The only consolation was that maybe they'd leave poor Mrs. Vanderbilt alone back in the nursery.

By the time Serafina made it to the second turn in the corridor, her chest hurt so bad she could barely breathe. She stopped at the corner, gasping and leaning her shoulder against the wall, Baby Nell cradled in her arms.

Just as she was about to continue and dash quickly past Mr. Vanderbilt's bedroom door, the door swung wide open.

Mr. Vanderbilt walked out of the room.

A burst of terror jolted through her body.

He seemed to be searching for something in the area outside his bedroom door.

She quickly stepped back from the corner and held the baby tight, praying she wouldn't squeal or cry.

Finally, she heard the sound of Mr. Vanderbilt's footsteps walking away from them, and then down the Grand Staircase.

As she began to breathe again, her skin prickled with the vestiges of fear still pulsating through her limbs.

Knowing it might be her only chance, she darted out and ran for the back stairs. She bounded up the steps two at a time until she reached the fourth floor, surprised by how much the baby in her arms slowed her down.

Running through the darkened corridor that led to the bedrooms of the sleeping maids and other female servants, she ducked through the tight passage beneath the North Tower, scuttled along the narrow arched hallway, and came to the third door on the right.

"Essie, I'm coming in," she whispered as she entered the

room and found the warm bundle of her friend covered in blankets in her bed. "Wake up, Essie," she said, touching her shoulder. "Please, I'm sorry, you've got to get up."

"What's goin' on?" Essie mumbled groggily, rubbing her face. "Am I late for my shift? Oh, miss, it's you! What are you doing up here? Is the house on fire?"

"I need your help," Serafina said.

"I'm ready," Essie said as she lurched out of bed and nearly tumbled to the floor. "Oh Lord, it's a baby!" Essie cried out when she saw Cornelia in Serafina's arms. "What are you doing with a baby? Is that—that's not—that's not Baby Nell, is it? What are you doing?"

"Something is wrong with Biltmore, Essie," she said. "We've got to get the baby out of here."

"Oh, Lord in heaven!" Essie said, her voice quaking.

"I need you to run down to the stables and get a carriage."

"Now, miss?" Essie said as she pulled on her cap. "Is it morning?"

"No, but we need it right away. The stable boy's name is Nolan. He sleeps by the horses. Tell him the carriage is for me and he'll do anything you say. I'll meet you in the Porte Cochere with the baby."

"I'm on my way, miss," Essie said as she pulled her coat over her nightgown and hurried out the door. Serafina heard her running down the corridor.

Once Essie was gone, and the darkened room went quiet and still again, Serafina looked down at Baby Nell in her arms and saw that her eyes were open and she was staring at her. It was then that she realized the true magnitude of what she was doing, how irreversible it was. Once she did this, that would be it. She could not take it back. The people of Biltmore weren't going to understand. They weren't going to forgive her. They were going to hate her. They'd kill her if they had to.

She wished she could somehow reach her pa and tell him what she doing and why, but she knew there was no time for that. It was far too dangerous. She had to get out.

As she snuck down the back stairs with the baby, now gurgling away in her arms, she began to hear the noises that she had prayed she wouldn't hear. A rushing wave of hissing and scratching was coming down the stairway behind them.

She hurried more quickly down the stairs, glancing over her shoulder into the blackness of the shadows above her.

She couldn't fight the creatures here, not like this, with the baby in her arms. And she knew there were at least two of the creatures pursuing them.

Then she heard the sounds of claws scrabbling through the walls around her.

There were more of them.

When she finally reached the first floor, she ran through the shadows toward the Porte Cochere, where she prayed the carriage would be waiting.

She desperately wished she could stop all this. She wished she could go back upstairs and convince Mrs. Vanderbilt to flee in the middle of the night with her and the baby. But the creatures were everywhere and there was death all around. If she couldn't trust Mr. Vanderbilt, then who could she trust? And she knew that she'd never be able to convince the mistress that her husband was the killer. Serafina barely believed it herself and she had seen him do it!

Just as she was about to reach the Porte Cochere, Baby Nell began to wriggle and squawk, as if she suddenly realized that some vile creature of the night had filched her from her mother's crib and was thieving her out into the cold.

At the same moment, Serafina heard a man's footsteps coming down the corridor toward her. She peered past the black shadows to where faint rays of moonlight were slicing in through the narrow windows. The bars of light and darkness flickered as the silhouette of the man moved through them. The murky shape of Mr. Vanderbilt came into view, walking straight at her, his expression grim, his eyes cast toward her, and a long iron fire poker clenched in his fist.

Serafina gasped and ran, gripping the squirming baby tighter to her chest. Nothing but the wind of movement now, pulling her hair, pressing against her cheeks, the baby's little fingers reaching up and grasping her face as she raced toward the door. Shifting the bawling baby to her left arm, she slammed her right shoulder against the door, working frantically at the lever until it flew open and she stumbled out.

"Go, Nolan, go!" she screamed to the skinny ten-year-old stable boy sitting atop the carriage as she sprinted toward it with the screeching bundle in her arms.

The startled Nolan snapped the reins of the four black horses, jolting them to attention, and his hollering shout drove them into a bolting gallop that lurched the carriage away.

"Here!" Essie called as she threw open the carriage door from the inside, and Serafina leapt in, tumbling onto the carriage floor with her arms still wrapped around the crying baby.

"Fly, Nolan, fly!" she shouted as she clambered to her feet in the swaying carriage, the baby in her arms.

Nolan drove the running horses with wild shouts and snapping reins, their steel-shod hooves clattering on the cobblestones of the courtyard, rising up into the night and filling the house with ominous, echoing sound.

As the galloping horses charged out through the main gate, Serafina peered through the small window at the back of the carriage. The last thing she saw was the lights on Biltmore's second floor coming on. And the last thing she heard was a terrifying sound rising up into the night, a shriek that could only be one thing: a mother screaming for her missing child.

The carriage swayed back and forth as the horses traveled down the road at a fast, steady clip. The baby was quiet now, but looking up at her with uncertain, worried eyes.

"I've got you, Nell," Serafina whispered to her reassuringly, and the baby replied to her with soft cooing, babbling noises.

"What are we doing, miss?" Essie asked, her voice strained and anxious as she stared wide-eyed at her from the opposite seat.

"We're keeping the baby safe," Serafina said.

They were traveling down the Approach Road, which wound its way through the forest for three miles toward Biltmore Village, where there was a collection of small houses, shops, and a train station. She thought that if they could just get through Biltmore's outer gate and reach the village, then they'd somehow be safe.

"I don't know my way around the village, Essie," she said. "I'm going to need your help when we get there."

"But why isn't the mistress with us?" Essie asked. "Did she tell you to do this?"

"The truth is, she didn't, but it needed to be done to protect the baby."

"Who was that man coming out of the house behind you with that stick? It looked like Mr. Vanderbilt."

"Yes, it was him," Serafina said soberly, knowing that it wasn't going to settle well with her companion.

Essie swallowed hard as she gazed at her, and then said, "Are you sure we're doin' the right thing, miss?"

"I don't understand it all, either," she admitted. "But there was no time to talk to anyone. We just needed to get out of there."

"But we're goin' back, right?" Essie asked. "I mean, we ain't really leavin'."

It was hard to imagine, but once they reached the village, she might have to keep going, as far away from Biltmore as she could get, all the way to Asheville and beyond if she had to.

As she and Essie were talking, Serafina saw something through the back window of the carriage. She leaned forward and peered through the glass. In the distance, a group of dark shapes were coming up behind them on the road.

It took her several seconds to make out that ten or twenty

men on horseback were following them, whipping their running horses mercilessly.

Serafina threw open the side window and screamed up at Nolan, "Riders behind us! We can't let them catch us!"

"Got it, miss!" Nolan called back to her.

He snapped the reins and shouted "Yee-haa!" to his team of horses. The carriage lurched forward as the horses accelerated into a canter, pulling the carriage at great speed, thundering down the road, Nolan's wild shouts driving them on.

But when Serafina looked back behind them, she saw that the riders were still coming.

Their carriage crossed stone bridges over rushing creeks, and rounded tight curves that snaked through the hilly terrain, but their pursuers did not relent. The men behind them were closing the distance between them, spurring their horses on, striking them with their crops, coming closer and closer.

"We need to go faster, Nolan!" Serafina shouted again.

"I'm trying, Miss!" Nolan cried out. With the next snap of the reins the four black horses bent their necks and broke into a full-out gallop, yanking the carriage forward at startling speed. Serafina held Baby Nell tight as the carriage was buffeted back and forth, the baby's bright, wide eyes gazing up at her in bewilderment.

"Oh Lord, please don't let us die!" Essie screamed.

"Faster, Nolan!" Serafina screamed. Hearing the turmoil in her voice, Baby Nell began to wail for her mother.

"There's another carriage!" Nolan shouted.

Had she misheard him? How could another carriage have caught up with them so quickly? And then she realized that it wasn't *behind* them.

She peered out ahead of them. A black coach was barreling down the road toward them. Nolan pulled the reins, steering their carriage around a sharp bend in the narrow road, the whole carriage careening wildly. Essie screamed and pressed her outstretched hands to the inner walls as the carriage tilted dangerously to the side.

"Hang on, everybody!" Nolan shouted.

Serafina tucked her knees, wrapped her arms around the baby, and held on tight.

The wheels of the carriage skittered off the edge of the road, biting into the gravel, throwing dirt and rocks in all directions until the wheels collapsed into the ditch and the whole carriage toppled over with a terrific crash, and then scraped along its side, tearing itself apart as the horses neighed and battled against their twisting harnesses.

The crashing carriage heaved her and banged her body, one blow after another as she tumbled against the walls and the roof, holding Baby Nell tight in her arms.

When they finally came to a stop, she found herself upside down, crumpled on top of herself, cradling the baby to her chest. She quickly hugged the baby close and cuddled her reassuringly. "Don't worry," she whispered to the little one. "We're gonna make it out of here just fine. You watch."

But the truth was that the roof of the carriage had come

down on top of them, and the walls had collapsed like an accordion with them inside.

She heard the movements and gasping breaths of someone digging them out of the wreckage, frantically pulling the debris away.

"Come on, we've got to get them out!" the voice shouted, and a second person joined in the effort.

But who was it? It couldn't be Nolan or Essie. They were undoubtedly just as buried as she and Nell were.

"Are you hurt?" the voice asked in a shaking, worried tone. "Take my hand."

Serafina reached up to the boy's outstretched hand and grasped it in astonishment. The moment they touched she knew exactly who it was.

35

It felt like it was impossible, but her eyes were telling her that Braeden was right in front of her.

"Are you hurt?" he asked again as he helped her to her feet. "Is Cornelia all right?" He examined the baby, running his hands over the little one's head and body with the anxious concern of an older cousin.

"I think she's all right," Serafina said, cradling the baby.

As Serafina glanced at the wreckage of the pulverized carriage, a coachman in a long greatcoat and tall hat was helping Nolan scramble out of a tangle of horse reins and busted-up boards. And closer to her, a second pile of the wreckage began to move.

"Are we all dead and gone?" Essie asked loudly as she pushed aside the debris and crawled out.

"Oh, Essie, are you hurt?" Serafina gasped, hurrying toward her.

"My head took a wallop," Essie said, as she rubbed her temple and squinted her eye, "but I ain't no worse for it."

Braeden looked around at all of them, and then brought his gaze back to Serafina. "What were you all doing out here at this time of night with the baby?"

"And why were you going so fast around that turn?" the coachman challenged.

As if in reply, the thundering sound of running horses came barreling around the bend in the road.

"Stop right there!" one of the riders shouted as a dozen grim-faced men surrounded them and aimed their rifles at Serafina.

She sucked in a sudden breath and froze. With the baby in her arms, and Braeden and the others around her, she could not fight them or run.

The riders dismounted and surrounded her, pointing their rifles directly at her head.

"What are you doing?" Braeden shouted at them, shocked by their behavior.

"Do not try to move!" Mr. Doddman ordered Serafina, ignoring Braeden.

The security manager was a heavyset, thick-necked man with massive hands and callused knuckles, aiming the long black barrel of his rifle straight at her, just inches from her face, as if he was trying to make sure that when he pulled the trigger he wouldn't hit the baby in her arms.

Knowing she was a single finger-twitch from death, Serafina remained perfectly still. In all her life, she had never had the muzzle of a gun pointed at her. Now there were twelve. If any one of these men decided to pull the trigger, or even sneezed, she was dead.

"Stop this!" Braeden shouted at them.

"Step away, Master Braeden," Mr. Doddman ordered him.

"What do you think you're doing?" Braeden asked angrily.

In the distance, beyond the men who surrounded her, Serafina saw two more riders approaching.

Mr. and Mrs. Vanderbilt rode up on their cantering horses and came to a sudden stop. Serafina's stomach knotted at the sight of them.

The master and mistress of Biltmore quickly dismounted, handed their reins to one of the men, and hurried toward her and the baby.

"Serafina, what are you doing?" Mrs. Vanderbilt demanded, her voice roiling with dismay.

"I was trying to help—" Serafina cried, the anguish ripping through her body.

"But why did you take Cornelia?" Mrs. Vanderbilt shouted at her.

Braeden watched all of this in confusion.

"I swear I would never do anything to hurt the baby," Serafina pleaded with Mrs. Vanderbilt. "I was trying to protect her!"

Mr. Vanderbilt strode straight at her, pulling off his leather riding gloves as he came, his dark eyes glaring with fury. Surrounded by his men, she was defenseless against him.

"Get the baby," Mr. Vanderbilt ordered, the tenor of his voice vibrating with harshness.

Mr. Doddman immediately shouldered his rifle and stomped forward. He ripped Cornelia from her arms and thrust the now crying baby at her mother.

Serafina didn't try to resist him as his giant hand shoved her brutally to the ground. "Down! Now!" he shouted at her, his spittle hitting her in the face.

"Stop this!" Braeden screamed, charging forward and trying to hold Mr. Doddman back from hurting her.

But Serafina didn't cry out or fight back. She knew she couldn't, not here, not like this.

She lay on the ground where Mr. Doddman pushed her. As she looked up at Braeden, and Mr. and Mrs. Vanderbilt, and all the surrounding men, she knew she couldn't explain everything she'd seen and she couldn't accuse Mr. Vanderbilt of murder. No one would believe anything she said.

The physical pain of the carriage crash and being shoved down to the rocky ground at the side of the road began to radiate through her body, the aches and bruises, but worse than that was the sickening feeling of what she had done to poor Mrs. Vanderbilt and how it must look to all of them.

"Aunt Edith, why are you treating Serafina like this?" Braeden beseeched Mrs. Vanderbilt.

"She kidnapped Cornelia, Braeden!" Mrs. Vanderbilt screamed at him.

"If she took the baby from the house," Braeden said firmly, "then Cornelia's life must have been in danger. Don't you see that?"

As Serafina gazed up at Braeden, her heart began to swell. He *believed* in her.

He had seen for himself that she had been fleeing the house with the baby in the middle of the night. And now they were all shouting at her and pointing their guns at her, accusing her of a most heinous crime. All the evidence in front of Braeden's eyes was clearly and obviously against her. But it didn't seem to matter to him. He *believed* in her, without doubt, without question.

"Uncle," Braeden said, moving toward him. "You *know* Serafina is the Guardian of Biltmore, the protector of our family. Why would you ever doubt this? Why?"

"You don't understand what's been happening here, Braeden," Mr. Vanderbilt told him.

"Look at her," Braeden said, gesturing toward her on the ground. "You don't think she could just flee from you right now and disappear into the darkness if she wanted to? You don't think she could fight all of you? She was obviously trying to protect the baby, and she still is!"

"But where were you taking her?" Mrs. Vanderbilt cried out at Serafina.

Away from your husband, the murderer! Serafina wanted to scream in reply, but she knew she couldn't.

"If Serafina thought Cornelia was in danger, then she was in danger," Braeden said bluntly, the force rising in his voice.

"How many times does she have to save all of your lives for you to know this?"

"But she snatched Cornelia out of her crib and skulked away with her in the middle of the night!" Mrs. Vanderbilt said, straining with shaking emotion as she spoke. "She should have spoken to me!"

"She obviously had to act quickly. So now you chase her down and aim guns at her?" Braeden said, boiling with frustration.

Mr. Doddman, provoked by Braeden's insolent tone, pushed toward him and shouted at him in his gruff, commanding voice, "Tell us, boy, just how did you get here anyway?"

Braeden turned toward him and faced him head-on. "How did I get here?" he replied, his voice edged with sharpness.

"The trains do not arrive at the station in the middle of the night," Mr. Doddman challenged him.

"They do if your family owns the railroad and all the trains on it, Mr. Doddman," Braeden said fiercely as he stepped toward Serafina and pulled her up onto her feet. "Now put down your guns. This is foolish."

It was at that moment that she realized that it wasn't just luck that Braeden was here. He didn't just happen to be traveling down the road for no reason. He had come from New York with great speed and purpose. And she could see that Braeden's confidence in her was wearing down the resolve of her accusers.

"But what happened to you, Serafina?" Mrs. Vanderbilt asked, looking at her. "What did you see that made you do this? Why did you not speak to me first?"

Serafina stared back at her, trying not to glance over at Mr. Vanderbilt standing a few feet away.

"Tell us what you saw, girl," Mr. Doddman demanded, shoving her with his hand.

She felt an overwhelming urge to bite him with her long panther fangs. But she had to get out of this. She had to get these men away from her so that she could talk to Braeden alone and tell him what was really going on.

As she looked around at Mr. Doddman and all of the other men surrounding her, an idea came into her mind. It wasn't the whole truth, but it might be just the right amount of it.

"I saw two wickedly unnatural creatures," she said, purposefully putting a tremor of fear into her voice. "They were lizardlike, but with sharp teeth and long, nasty claws. One killed a bear in the forest. Another killed my cat. Then I saw the creatures trying to scratch their way into Baby Nell's bedroom."

Everyone around her stared at her in shock. Several of the men couldn't help but glance into the darkness of the forest behind them.

She lowered her voice to a barely audible whisper. "Mr. Vanderbilt saw the creatures, too."

"What did you say, girl?" Mr. Doddman said, shaking her by the shoulder.

"I said that Mr. Vanderbilt saw the creatures."

Everyone turned and looked at Mr. Vanderbilt.

The master of Biltmore studied her for several seconds. It was clear he didn't want to talk about strange creatures crawling through the house. But now he had no choice. He looked around at the others. "It is true," he admitted finally. "I did see some sort of unnatural beast."

"One of the creatures attacked and killed Mr. Kettering," Serafina said, hoping to stir a little more fear among her accusers, and sure enough, they all began looking out into the surrounding forest.

"And Mr. Cobere was killed as well," Mr. Vanderbilt said.

Serafina gasped, shocked by the deviousness of his lie. *He* had killed Mr. Cobere, not the creatures!

She didn't even know how to respond to what he had said, but she continued with her plan, turning to look at Mrs. Vanderbilt. "When I saw the creatures crawling into Baby Nell's room, I had to get her out of there as fast as I could. I'm so, so sorry I took her like that, but I had to!"

Mrs. Vanderbilt stared back at her, speechless.

Serafina could see in her mistress's eyes that maybe her anger and suspicion were finally beginning to subside.

Seeing the opportunity, Braeden stepped forward and spoke to everyone. "If there are nasty creatures prowling around, then we better all get to safety," he said, and many of the men immediately agreed with the young master.

"Let's mount up and get home," Mr. Vanderbilt ordered the men. "I want four guards around my wife and daughter on the way back."

"Yes, sir," several of the men said in unison.

"Mr. Doddman," Mr. Vanderbilt said as he turned toward the security manager. "When we get back to Biltmore, my family will be spending the rest of the night in my chambers instead of the nursery. Post additional guards around the room and throughout the second floor."

"Yes, sir. I'll see to it," Mr. Doddman said.

As she heard Mr. Vanderbilt's orders, Serafina's mind raced with suspicion. It made sense for all of them to get out of the forest, but the creatures were in the house as well. No place was safe. And Mr. Vanderbilt knew that. But Mr. Vanderbilt and the others were all so used to Biltmore being a place of refuge that their minds couldn't think in any other way.

Or maybe that wasn't it at all. Maybe Mr. Vanderbilt had a more sinister, hidden plan. Maybe it wasn't about safety, but entrapment. How could she convince them all that Biltmore itself was the danger, that the man in charge was the one they should be most frightened of?

All she knew for sure was that she still had to do her job, still had to protect little Cornelia and the other innocent people of Biltmore.

She watched as Mrs. Vanderbilt handed Cornelia to Essie, mounted her horse, and then took Cornelia back into her arms. There was only one way Mrs. V was returning to Biltmore, and that was with her baby. One of the men helped Essie up onto his horse, and they all began the journey home.

"Braeden," Mr. Vanderbilt said, looking at his nephew with harsh, troubled eyes. "I don't know what you're doing back here at Biltmore when you should be in New York, but you need to come with me now and explain yourself."

"I will, sir, I'll come right away, I'll explain everything," Braeden said quickly. "But I need to attend to the horses that may have been injured by the crash." He gestured toward Nolan and the coachman trying to disentangle the four black thoroughbreds from the wreckage of the carriage.

"Get yourself and the horses home as quickly as you can," Mr. Vanderbilt said as he climbed up into his saddle.

"I will, sir," Braeden said, nodding.

"And *you*," Mr. Vanderbilt said sternly as he turned toward Serafina and locked his black searing eyes on to hers. "I will see you at Biltmore as well."

Serafina stared at him, her heart pounding, but she did not reply and she did not look away.

Finally, Mr. Vanderbilt turned his horse and followed the other riders back up the road to Biltmore.

She knew there would come a time very soon that she would meet that man alone, face-to-face, and there would be no place for either of them to go.

The moment his uncle was gone, Braeden looked over at Serafina in relief, and then hurried on to help the entangled horses.

Nolan and the coachman used knives to cut the horses out of the hopelessly twisted harnesses as Braeden steadied the horses' heads.

"We're all right," Braeden whispered to the horses in quiet, reassuring tones. "We're all together."

She knew that years before, these four fine thoroughbreds had carried the caskets of Braeden's mother, father, brothers, and sisters during the funeral in New York City after a catastrophic fire burned down the family home. Braeden and these four horses had been companions ever since. When he moved to Biltmore to live with his uncle, he came with no possessions other than his black dog Gidean, who had saved him from the fire, and these four black horses, who had saved him from the devastating sorrow that followed.

As Nolan and the coachman finally got the harnesses cut away, they led the horses out of the ditch and up onto the road.

"I'll take them on up to Biltmore, master," Nolan said, jumping onto the bare back of one of the horses.

"We'll be right behind you," Braeden said. "Be careful on the road."

As she and Braeden watched Nolan ride off with the horses, she said, "I'm very sorry I put them in danger."

"I know. Come on, let's get home," he said, gesturing toward the carriage he had arrived in.

"Do you think you can get us around all this wreckage, John?" he asked as the coachman climbed up into the driver's seat.

"I can manage it," the coachman said with a quick nod.

Serafina thought it was kind of Braeden to open the carriage's door for her and hold her hand as she stepped up into it. He was always a gentleman, even to a girl who was more often a prowling cat than a fancy young lady.

It wasn't until Braeden climbed into the closed space of the carriage, sat in the seat across from her, and let out a long sigh that she realized how nervous he'd been about standing up to his uncle and all those other men. He had seemed so brave, so resolute, but she realized now that his heart had probably been pounding just as hard as hers.

"Thank you for believing in me back there," she said, her voice quavering.

"You would have done the same for me," he said, nodding. Again, there was no doubt in him.

Sitting alone with him in the carriage as it traveled down the road reminded her of the first carriage they had ever been in together, a year before, traveling through a dark forest, not that different from this one.

"I'm very glad to see you," she said, and then, in as soft a voice as she could, she asked him the question that she couldn't help from asking. "After the night by the lake . . . what happened to you?"

Braeden dropped his eyes to the floor and slowly shook his head. "I'm so sorry, Serafina," he said, his voice rife with shame. "I left for New York early the next morning. I couldn't face you to say good-bye. After everything I said by the campfire, I didn't know how to tell you that I still had to go . . . I still had to leave. . . . The whole thing made me sick."

As she listened to his words, and heard the remorse in his voice, she could feel her heart opening up to him. She nodded, trying to show him that she understood. "I thought that you must have gone back, but I didn't know for sure," she said, more disappointed in her own confused, frightened, flinchy mind than in him, but he still took her words hard.

"I shouldn't have done it," he said, shaking his head. "I should have faced you. I should have come to you and said good-bye. I'm a total coward sometimes."

She looked at him and tilted her head in surprise. "You're

not a *total* coward," she said. "You're just a plain old, regular coward, a typical horseback-riding, train-jumping, animal-healing mountain boy. Nothing wrong with that. We seem to need those around here."

He smiled a little bit. "Thank you, but I *am* a coward, at least about some things."

"Maybe *some* things," she said. "But not where it counts. You stood up to those people. You were the only one who believed me."

"But tell me what's wrong," he said. "What happened to you after I left?"

"First, tell me about the white deer," she said.

He frowned in confusion. "Do you mean the little fawn?"

"Yes. What happened to it?"

"When I woke up, she looked like she was going to survive, so I released her back into the forest. I hope she's all right. Did you see her or something?"

She didn't even know where to begin. He had no idea what he had done or what had happened since.

"Tell me what you did after releasing the white deer."

"I cleaned up our camp so that no one would know that I snuck back home, and then I headed to the village to catch the next train to New York."

She nodded. All that made sense. She had been trying to tell herself that was definitely one of the possibilities. "But why are you here, Braeden?" she asked. "Your school must still be in session. Why did you come back now?"

He gazed at her without speaking; his eyes and face held

an expression that she could not fathom. Had her questions startled him? Was it embarrassment? Fear? It was a species of emotion she had never seen in him.

"Why did you come home, Braeden?" she asked him again.

He looked out the window of the moving carriage, and then down at the floor. "It was last night, or two nights ago, I don't even know anymore, I've been traveling so long," he said. "I was in my dorm room, and I was sleeping. It wasn't a dream and it wasn't a vision. It was more like a feeling. Like someone was calling out to me." Finally, he lifted his eyes and looked at her. "Like *you* were calling out to me, Serafina. I woke up. I listened for you. I didn't hear you again. But I could still *feel* you. And it was frightening. I didn't understand. But my heart was pounding. I could swear you were in trouble and you needed my help."

She listened to his story in amazement, remembering how she had lain in the Angel's Glade, her shoulder up against the pedestal of the statue as she cried out into the midnight sky.

"I *am* in trouble," she said finally. "And I *do* need your help."

"I came home as fast as I could," he said gently.

"You commandeered a train to do it," she said, smiling as she gazed at him.

"Well," he said, blushing. "One of the perks of being a Vanderbilt, I guess." And then he became far more serious. "But what's this all about? My uncle was so angry. And I've never seen my aunt so scared."

"She has good reason to be," Serafina said, glancing out the window into the darkness they were traveling through, then back at Braeden. "People have been dying ever since you left. I've been trying to figure out who the killer is and how I can stop him."

Braeden looked at her in surprise. "Why do you say 'him'? I thought you saw some sort of weird, unnatural creatures."

"There *are* creatures," she said. "But there is also a murderer, a man. I saw him."

"Did you get a good look at him?" Braeden asked, leaning toward her. "Who is it? We'll tell my uncle."

"This is going to be difficult for you to hear, Braeden. . . ."

"What do you mean? Why'd you say my name like that?" Braeden replied, his voice edged with a trace of fear. "What is it?"

"It's your uncle," she said, watching him carefully, trying to figure out how she could help him through this.

His brow furrowed. "I don't understand. What are you saying?"

"Your uncle killed Mr. Cobere."

"No, that can't be," Braeden said, shaking his head. "That's not possible."

"I saw him do it with my own eyes."

"My uncle would never kill someone. Or if he did, he must have been defending himself from an attack."

"No, he wasn't," she said firmly. "Mr. Cobere was begging him to stop. Your uncle struck him in the head with an iron fire poker and killed him."

Braeden stopped talking. His expression clouded as he tried to digest what she had told him. "But if that's true," he said finally, "then what does it all have to do with the white fawn and the strange creatures?"

"I don't know," she said. "That's exactly what we need to figure out."

As she and Braeden were talking, the carriage trundled along down the road, rocking gently back and forth. Despite everything that had happened and all there was yet to do, there was something invigorating about trying to solve a mystery with her old friend at her side.

She wasn't sure how much farther they had to go, but it looked as if they had left the forest and were now traveling past some of Biltmore's farm fields, which were bare for the coming winter.

Braeden's eyes narrowed as he looked out the window.

"What is that?" he asked.

She turned and looked.

"Stop the carriage!" she shouted to the driver.

The moon hung low and hazy in the night sky, casting the empty field in silver light as swirls of gray mist and fog drifted across it. Out in the distance, there was a man walking in the middle of the field. He looked like a young man, his blond hair almost white in the moonlight. He was carrying a rifle and something large draped over his shoulder. The man's face and arms were cut and bleeding. And by the way he was limping through the field, it was clear that he had been walking for a long time.

At first she thought he must be a hunter carrying the carcass of a deer he had shot. But as the man continued to trudge toward them, she realized that the body he was carrying was not a deer.

"Is that a person walking out there? Who is that?" Braeden asked.

"It's Lieutenant Kinsley . . ." Serafina said as she exited the carriage. "Come on, we've got to help him!"

As she ran across the field, the soft, tilled autumn earth pulled at her feet.

Lieutenant Kinsley's jacket was ripped and stained. One of his gloves was gone and the other torn and bloody. He looked like he barely had the strength to keep standing, let alone walking.

As he lifted his head and saw her coming toward him, his face filled with relief and he collapsed to his knees in exhaustion, gently laying the body he was carrying onto the ground.

"Kinsley," Serafina gasped as she held his shoulders to keep him upright.

ROBERT BEATTY

"I found her," he muttered, nearly out of his mind with fatigue.

Lying on the ground beside him there was the body of a girl, her neck smudged with mud, her hair tangled with sticks, and her fingers so curled from the cold that she looked dead. But she was tucked in on herself, her arms crossed over her chest, and she was visibly shivering. When the girl finally lifted her head, the first thing Serafina saw were her bright sapphire-blue eyes.

"Jess!" Serafina gasped, and threw her arms around her.

"Serafina . . ." Jess muttered.

It was only when Serafina heard the exhausted raggedness of her friend's voice that she truly began to realize what Jess and Kinsley had been through.

Braeden knelt down and gave them water from a leather skin he had retrieved from the carriage, and fed them pieces of leftover biscuits that he had stashed in his satchel during his long journey home.

"What happened to you out there, Jess?" Serafina asked.

"The dogs treed two mountain lions, and my father started shooting . . ." Jess said, her words so faltering that she almost seemed delirious. "But over the years my father taught me many things. . . ."

"What did he teach you?" Serafina asked, grasping her arm.

"How to adjust the sights of a rifle," Jess replied, looking up at her. "Before we went out that night, I set his sights three clicks to the right, and five clicks down. He got so angry and confused when his shots kept missing, but there was no way he was going to hit those cats. . . ."

Serafina's heart swelled. It had been Jess all along!

"But then the fog rolled in," Jess continued. "There were gunshots and flashes of . . . I don't know what it was. . . . I saw something metal . . . and then something black. . . ." Jess looked straight at her now, her eyes wide. "I shouldn't have tampered with my father's gun, Serafina. He was shooting, but he kept missing. He couldn't defend himself! My father died because of me!"

Serafina held Jess as she cried.

"But what attacked you, Jess?" Braeden asked, his voice shaking.

"Something black came at me from the side. My horse reared up. I was thrown. When I woke up, my head was bleeding, my leg twisted. I could see my father and the other men were dead. I knew I needed to get back to Biltmore, but my horse was long gone. I could kind of limp along on foot, and I thought I remembered the way home. But as I was going, I saw a white deer in the underbrush. It began to follow me. I saw it behind me, then tracking alongside, getting closer and closer, like it was hunting me. I thought for sure I remembered how to get back to Biltmore, but I got hopelessly lost. I was so cold. I was sure I was going to die. But Lieutenant Kinsley found me. He gave me all his food and water, and he wrapped me in his coat. We rode together on his horse, but then we started seeing the white deer again. . . ."

"We need to stop talking," Kinsley said forcefully as he got himself up onto his feet. "There's no time for this." He scanned the line of trees in the distance. "We need to get out of here."

"You're safe now," Serafina said, putting her hand on his shoulder to reassure him. "We're almost home. We'll take you the rest of the way."

"I can help you to the carriage," Braeden said to the lieutenant, trying to hold Kinsley's arm to help him walk.

"You don't understand!" Kinsley snapped, pulling away from him. "It's still out there!"

He peered out across the field toward the forest, his trembling white fingers gripping his rifle. "It's not going to give up! It's coming for us!"

As she gazed at the panicking lieutenant, Serafina recognized the same fear and confusion she had felt, a sense that the world wasn't just coming apart at the seams in some random way, but that she was actually being tracked down. And she remembered seeing it in Mr. Vanderbilt's eyes the morning he arrived unexpectedly in the workshop.

"We've got to go!" Lieutenant Kinsley said, glancing frantically all around.

"You're right, let's go, right away," Serafina said, and pulled Jess to her feet.

The four of them trekked as quickly as they could across the field toward the carriage.

"How did you get back to Biltmore?" Serafina asked as she helped Jess along.

"We were crossing through a swamp, and the white deer came again," Jess said.

"I took a shot at it to scare it off, but it just kept coming," Kinsley said, looking over his shoulder. "Every time we shifted direction, it reflected our movements."

"Our horse panicked and ran," Jess said, gasping for breath as they moved quickly across the field. They were nearly to the carriage now. "One of its hooves went down into some kind of hole and it broke its leg. Kinsley had to put the poor animal out of its misery."

"My sweet Arabella is dead," Kinsley said, "and I was the one who killed her!"

"I'm so sorry, Kinsley," Serafina said as they finally arrived at the carriage.

"It's going to be all right now," Braeden assured them as he opened the carriage door and helped Jess inside. "We'll get you in front of a warm fire, with a hot cup of tea, and—"

Braeden stopped midsentence.

He froze right where he was standing, his eyes locked on something in the distance.

"She's back . . ." he said.

Serafina turned and saw the white deer standing at the top of the nearest hill, its antlers sticking up around its head.

"There it is!" Kinsley shouted. "Everybody go! I'll hold it off!"

Standing suddenly strong and fierce, he swung his rifle and aimed at the deer.

"No," Braeden said, lurching forward and pushing the rifle down, a reflex to protect any animal from harm. "Don't shoot her."

Kinsley pushed him away. "You don't understand, Braeden. It's been hunting us!"

And then he retook his aim at the deer and pulled the trigger. His rifle flashed in the night with a startling *crack*. But even more startling, Serafina heard the bullet whiz past her ear and smash through the window of the carriage behind her.

"We can't let it get any closer!" Kinsley screamed as he levered his rifle and shot again. The bullet hit the dirt at their feet.

The bullets are being deflected, Serafina thought suddenly, *like reflected light splintering from a diamond.*

Kinsley levered another cartridge and fired again.

"No, Kinsley, stop shooting!" she screamed as she lunged toward him, but it was too late. He pulled the trigger.

"Aaagh!" Kinsley shouted out in pain and surprise as the bullet ripped through his arm. He dropped his rifle and clasped his hand against the bloody wound, stumbling back against the wheel of the carriage, and then collapsing to the ground.

"What in tarnation is going on?" the coachman asked as he hurried down from the driver's seat in a panic and pulled a knife from his belt. "What is that thing out there?"

The white deer began walking toward them.

Serafina's heart hammered in her chest. The moment she began to move, she could feel the deep, soft soil clinging to her feet.

And then she caught something out of the corner of her eye and turned.

"Braeden, what is that coming toward us?"

A cold, moonlit fog had risen from the moist soil of the farm field, and there were three shapes rushing toward them out of the trees from the direction of the house.

"It . . . I . . ." Braeden stammered.

"Run!" Kinsley shouted as he struggled back up onto his feet despite his bleeding wound.

Serafina gazed in astonishment at the three shapes coming toward them, unable to believe what she was seeing.

A living, flesh-and-blood medieval warrior—a young woman clad in full plate armor and brandishing a long, steel-tipped spear—was charging toward them. And there were two huge male African lions charging with her.

"All of you, run!" Kinsley shouted again.

But Serafina did not run.

She didn't understand what she was seeing. But she knew she couldn't let herself and her friends die.

"Into the carriage, now!" she shouted at Braeden and Jess as she pushed them inside and closed the door behind them.

Then she turned toward the oncoming attackers and shifted into a black panther.

The knife-wielding coachman standing nearby screamed at the sight of her. A medieval warrior, a pair of African lions, and now a strange, black-haired thirteen-year-old girl changing into a black panther right before his eyes was all too much for him. He dropped his knife and bolted across the field in panic. She wanted to go after him, to show him that she didn't mean him any harm, but she knew she couldn't. She had to face the attackers charging toward her and Kinsley. Sticking together was their only hope.

As she turned to join the lieutenant, she bared her panther

fangs with a snarl of readiness and took her place at his side. Kinsley's eyes went wide in startled surprise as he said, "Well, that explains a lot!"

Then he pivoted his rifle and pointed it at the warrior and the lions bounding toward them.

He stood without fear or hesitation, and he aimed with perfect steadiness. But when he pulled the trigger, he shouted at the pain of the rifle's stock jamming into his wounded shoulder.

His first shot hit the warrior in the chest, but the bullet thudded against the slope of her fluted-steel breastplate. He immediately levered his rifle and shot again.

As their enemies charged toward them across the field, Serafina crouched, readying herself for the incoming attack.

Kinsley's second bullet hit the curve of the warrior's shoulder plate, but sparked away without doing her any harm. Despite the bullets striking her, the warrior kept coming, completely unafraid, thrusting her spear ahead of her.

And then one of the running lions spotted the coachman fleeing across the field in the distance and sped toward him. Serafina's heart lurched. She wanted to run to him, to protect him, but she knew it was too late.

The coachman screeched in horror as the great maned beast pounced onto his back and slammed him to the ground. The bleeding, screaming man scrambled away on all fours and got to his feet. But the lion lunged forward with incredible speed and struck him with its claws, knocking him down again.

Serafina couldn't believe the impossibility of what she was witnessing before her eyes. How could all this be happening?

How could a medieval warrior and two African lions even be here?

Kinsley fired again, their enemies seconds away now.

The wounded coachman punched and kicked, rolled through the dirt, and broke free, then sprang up and limped away, determined to stay alive. The lion hurled itself forward and tackled him, clamping its front paws around him, the full weight of its body dragging him down as it sank its massive fangs into his neck. When the screaming stopped, there was no doubt in Serafina's mind that the poor man was dead.

And then the lion was up and running again, sprinting to rejoin the other two attackers racing toward her and Kinsley. The sight of it startled her. A normal predator didn't immediately abandon its kill to join another fight, but here it came, straight at them.

Her powerful panther heart pounded in her chest. Her muscles tightened. At the last second, as the two big cats burst ahead of the armored warrior, Serafina leapt forward, her long black body speeding across the ground to meet them head-on.

39

Knowing she couldn't fight both lions at the same time, she attacked the closest one with everything she had. Her plan was to kill it quickly and move on to the next before they could gang up on her.

But the first of the five-hundred-pound beasts reared up on its hind legs and slammed into her, chest-to-chest. The lion wrapped its front legs around her in a violent, bearlike embrace, then dug its claws deep into her back and threw her to the ground. The heavy blow immediately stunned and knocked the wind out of her. And then the lion held her down by the neck, its massive jaws clenched tight, pinning her on her back, her legs flailing helplessly in the air.

Any thought that the attackers were figments of her jittery

imagination or ghosts in the autumn mist was instantly gone now. She was seconds from suffocation.

Pinned upside down by the lion's colossal weight, she twisted her long, feline spine, bent herself in half, and snagged all four of her clawed paws onto the lion's face. Then she pushed. The lion roared with the pain of her claws tearing through its skin and muscles, scratching against the bone, as it tried to wrench itself free.

She burst upward, spinning in midair, and landed on top of it, clawing into its sides. But with a deafening, guttural growl, the lion twisted away, ripping into her and trying to clamp on to her head with its long fangs.

Serafina spun again, clawing the lion's back. Then the lion twisted and turned and threw her off, lunging at her with a fierce triple swipe of its claws as it charged. Serafina sprang back, and back again, dodging the swipes, then threw herself into the lion with a snarling, biting counterattack.

The second lion lunged at her at the same time, sending spasms of pain through her legs as it ripped four streaks of blood across her haunch. And she caught a glimpse of Kinsley striking at the armored warrior with a mighty swing of his rifle. It would have been a killing blow, but the warrior blocked the strike with the steel vambrace of her raised arm, then used her other hand to thrust the tip of her spear into Kinsley's stomach. Kinsley cried out in pain as he clutched at the shaft of the spear.

Outnumbered and outmatched, speed and agility were Serafina's only weapons against the two lions, her only means of survival. She clawed at one lion, then sprang at the other.

She bit the head of an incoming attacker, then dodged to the side, spun, and swatted the face of another. Back and forth, bite and claw, lunging and leaping, twisting and darting, she was everywhere, all the time.

But these lions would not give up. She had scratched them, pierced them, torn at their faces, but they would not retreat like normal cats would. They weren't *lions*, they were mindless killing machines.

She dashed away, ran twenty strides, and then pivoted. The two lions charged toward her. She lunged at the closest one just as she had done before. And just as before, it reared up onto its hind legs and wrapped its front legs around her, trying to throw her to the ground with the weight of its shoulders.

But this time, she didn't try to fight against its weight and strength. She didn't try to overpower it. She could not battle a male African lion in the way male African lions fought. Instead, she folded her body straight to the ground, dragging her claws down the entire length of the lion's exposed underside.

She felt her claws tearing into it, the blood coming down.

Just as the first lion collapsed and died, the second lion slammed into her. The two of them tumbled across the ground in a ball of snarling teeth and ripping claws.

Instead of trying to fight against it, she twisted herself upside down, turned underside-out, and sprang free. She leapt upward, spinning in midair, and came down hard on its back.

As her fangs clamped onto its spine, its body jolted and went still.

The moment the second lion was dead, Serafina pivoted

toward the armored warrior, who was thrusting her spear into the wounded Kinsley for the third time.

Snarling with anger, Serafina sprang toward her, flying through the air.

She pounced onto the warrior's back and tore her clanking, metal-clad body tumbling to the ground.

Leaping on top of her, Serafina clawed her and bit her, but she couldn't get through the warrior's armor plates. She scraped and scratched to no avail as the warrior pummeled her sides with her gauntleted fists.

Realizing that brute force wasn't going to work, Serafina extended the claws of her right paw, hooked them on to the warrior's uppermost shoulder plate, and pulled it back to expose the warrior's neck. Then she slammed her fangs into the warrior's throat and clenched her panther jaws.

With her full weight holding the warrior down, and her teeth clamping the warrior's throat, she sensed her enemy's death was near. Even as the warrior began to die, she kept fighting Serafina, kept trying to do as much damage as she could. But the truly disturbing thing was that she wasn't fighting to *live*. She wasn't fighting to *breathe*. There was no last-second burst of strength to escape, no all-consuming instinct to survive. Just as with the lions, it was as if killing was primary, and living was secondary.

As Serafina held the warrior's windpipe clamped shut, she felt the warrior's lungs begin to deflate, her heart stop beating, and her blood stop flowing.

Finally, the warrior was dead.

But it was as if, in some ways, she had never been truly alive.

Serafina crouched low over Kinsley's fallen body, growling as she protected him, her claws still out as she scanned the field for the next attack. When she looked over her shoulder to make sure Braeden and Jess were still safely inside the carriage, she saw their blanched faces peering out of the window at her and Kinsley. And then she searched the top of the distant hill and the forest beyond. But there were no more attackers, and the white deer was gone.

She shifted into human form and dropped to her knees beside Kinsley, staring at him in dismay.

He was lying on the ground flat on his back, sunk deep into the soil of the field, gasping desperately for breath. The skin of his face was white with deathly pallor as he gazed up at her in shock. It seemed so *wrong*! They had fought hard, they had stuck together, they had done everything right, but he was still down, still wounded, and there was nothing she could do!

"Just hold on, Kinsley," she cried. "We're gonna get you through this!"

But the truth was, she didn't know how to help him. She didn't know how to save him.

And as she pressed her hands against his wounds to stanch the bleeding, a lake of warm blood welled up between her fingers.

She tried to stop the bleeding, to hold him, to talk to him and give him hope. But Kinsley looked up at her one last time, and then his eyes drifted shut. A long, ragged breath escaped from his struggling body, and he went still.

She wasn't sure if he was dead or alive, but her chest filled with aching pain. All Kinsley wanted was to be a brave and worthy friend to Mr. Vanderbilt. All he wanted to do was lend a hand to the people around him. *I'll see you at dinner,* he had said to her the last time they parted.

"Braeden, Jess, come quickly!" she shouted toward the carriage.

Braeden came running out, Jess stumbling behind him.

"Kinsley's been stabbed," Serafina said, her eyes tearing up, as Braeden knelt down and put two of his fingers to the lieutenant's neck. She knew Braeden couldn't heal humans the way he could animals, but she desperately hoped he could help in some way.

"I can't feel a pulse," Braeden said, shaking his head.

Serafina's heart sank at the discouraged sound of his voice.

"He's not dead," Jess said from behind them.

They both turned in surprise.

"Look carefully at the bullet wound at his shoulder," she said. "The blood is welling up in the hole. If he were dead, his heart would be stopped, and the blood would sink to the lower part of his body."

Serafina felt a surge of relief and nodded to Jess: her eagle-eyed friend was back.

"We've got to get him to a doctor right away," Braeden said as they got to their feet and worked together to drag Kinsley's unconscious body.

As they pulled him toward the carriage, Serafina gazed sadly out across the field at the body of the coachman in the distance. They would need to return for him later.

"Get back to Biltmore as fast as you can," Serafina said as Braeden climbed up into the driver's seat of the carriage and took up the reins of the horses.

"What about you?" Braeden asked, clearly startled that she wasn't coming.

"I'll catch up," she said.

As Braeden snapped the reins and the team of horses sped

the carriage away, Serafina ran back to where Kinsley had been wounded.

She gazed at the dead body of the medieval warrior lying on the ground. The girl looked about seventeen or eighteen years old, tall and strong, and she had a handsome face with white alabaster skin. The triangular white-and-gold battle standard attached to her spear lay crumpled around her, unusually long, as if it was designed to be seen across the murky chaos of a battlefield filled with the peasants, knights, and kings of old. There was nothing about her that seemed fake or conjured. There was even what looked like a gold cross hanging around her neck. And beneath the plates of her armor, she wore a tunic of chain mail.

And there Serafina paused.

Chain mail, she thought.

She slowly crouched down.

She reached out her hand, and touched her trembling fingers to the skin of the dead girl's cheek.

Her face felt cold.

But also *hard*.

Moments before, this girl's face had been flush with life. But now her cheek didn't feel warm. It didn't even feel like *skin*. More and more, it felt disturbingly like *stone*.

And not just stone, Serafina thought. *Limestone.* She knew limestone very well. Biltmore was constructed out of it.

A notion so strange that it could barely be believed crept into her mind.

She ran over to the two dead lions and reached out her hand.

Their bodies weren't limestone. But they weren't lion, either. They were cold and hard, smooth to the touch, and reddish in color.

"Italian rose marble," Serafina whispered in amazement.

As she said the words it felt as if a dam was breaking and a rushing flow of thoughts poured through her mind.

She shifted into panther form and ran for the carriage.

41

A thirteen-year-old human girl could not run as fast as cantering horses. But a panther could.

She streaked down the Approach Road and came up behind the moving carriage. The horses must not have had blinders on their harness that night, because they soon spotted her with their rear vision. Panicking, they broke into a full-on gallop to escape the vicious black predator charging up behind them.

It was just the burst of speed she wanted from them. The faster they got Kinsley home, the better.

She accelerated toward them and leapt onto the roof of the hurtling carriage. Then she shifted into human form and sat down in the driver's seat next to Braeden.

"Glad you made it," he said, glancing at her as he steered the carriage at barreling speed through Biltmore's main gate and into the courtyard.

"Mr. Pratt!" he called as he brought the carriage to a fast stop at the main doors. "Lieutenant Kinsley is badly hurt. Get him into the house right away and get the doctor."

"Yes, sir," Mr. Pratt replied, shouting for the assistance of several other footmen as he opened the carriage door to retrieve the lieutenant.

"Miss Serafina," Mr. Pratt said as she climbed down from the carriage roof. "Mr. Vanderbilt wants to see both you and the young master in his office immediately."

"I understand," she said as she helped Jess out of the carriage. "Please make sure you take care of Miss Braddick as well, Mr. Pratt. She needs food and water, and she needs to get warm."

"Yes, miss, right away," Mr. Pratt said as several of the footmen took Jess's arms and helped her into the house. "Don't worry, we'll attend to her."

It felt good to have their help, to be working together with the other servants of Biltmore, to be able to depend on them.

The moment she saw that Jess and Kinsley were in good hands, she looked at Braeden.

"Come on, we have things to do," she said and walked across the front terrace.

"But what about my uncle?" Braeden asked, the strain in his voice making it clear that he didn't want to see Mr. Vanderbilt any more than she did.

"We've got to figure this out," she said, pulling him along, and then she stopped him with her hand and pointed to the empty area of the terrace just to the side of Biltmore's front steps. "Look! Do you see? They're gone. The lion statues. They're actually gone!"

It felt as if all the planets were finally coming into alignment. The two lion statues that normally sat on either side of Biltmore's front doors were no longer there.

Braeden looked back toward the fields where the battle had just taken place. "But they're not just gone . . ." he said in amazement. "They're dead."

Serafina felt a wave of recognition crashing through her as the connections came together in her mind. Finally, things were beginning to make sense.

"Come on," she said, and they headed farther along the front terrace.

She gazed up toward the external wall of the Grand Staircase, where the spiral of slanted windows and intricate carvings rose up with each floor of the house.

Biltmore's front facade was so vast, and so ornate with statues, gargoyles, and châteauesque decoration, that few people even noticed the details of it, but what she saw now astounded her.

"That's it!" she said triumphantly, pointing up toward the corner of the tower.

Braeden gazed up in the direction she was pointing.

High above, between the second and third floor of the Grand Staircase's external wall, the carved limestone statue of Joan of Arc was gone.

The statue had been a grand and romantic representation of the French heroine, dressed in full battle armor.

"I just killed Joan of Arc," Serafina said in disbelief.

"Saint Louis is gone as well!" Braeden said, pointing to the adjacent alcove where the statue of the ancient French king was supposed to be standing.

She remembered that Saint Louis had been depicted with a helmet, full chain mail armor, and his famous longsword.

"A longsword," she said, remembering the battle on the North Ridge and the sight of Mr. Turner lying dead on the ground in the forest, a long, straight slash across his chest. And she remembered the clanking metal sounds that she had heard in the fog that night.

"It's the *house*," she said in astonishment. *"It's coming alive. . . ."*

Braeden's eyes widened as he gazed up at the two empty alcoves where the statues had been, and his mouth opened as he tried to gather words. "How can . . ." he stammered, and then he paused and looked at her. "Is it just the lions and these two statues, or are there more?"

She stepped back and looked up toward the front walls of Biltmore looming above them. Her lips went dry with nervousness as she slowly scanned the details of the facade. There were many graven ogres, griffons, harpies, minotaurs, satyrs, and other mythical creatures covering the wall.

And then she saw it.

High above.

An empty spot where there had once been a stone gargoyle.

It had been a nasty-looking, grotesque creature, with a hunched back, four reptilian legs, large bat-like wings, bulging eyes, and snarling teeth.

And then she turned and looked out across the Esplanade, up toward the top of Diana Hill, which rose directly in front of the house.

"Come on," she said.

"What's up there?" Braeden asked as he followed.

"If I'm right," she said, "it's more a question of what's *not* up there."

As they reached the top of the hill, she and Braeden gazed at the white statue of Diana, goddess of the hunt.

"She's still here," Braeden said, confused. "I thought she was going to be gone."

"Look more closely," Serafina said, "at the base of the statue."

"There's a part missing," Braeden said as he examined it.

"Diana was standing next to a deer," Serafina said.

"The *white* deer," Braeden said in amazement.

"Exactly," Serafina said.

"But what does this mean?" Braeden asked.

"Everything," Serafina said, a tremendous wave of relief surging through her body. It felt as if she was waking up from

a dark and awful nightmare and realizing that it wasn't true. "Let's go," she said excitedly. "There's one more place to check. The most important of all."

The two of them ran back down the hill and down the length of the Esplanade. By the time they reached the front door, they were gasping for breath.

"Miss Serafina," Mr. Pratt said as he came out to meet them. "Mr. Vanderbilt is demanding your presence immediately."

"Thank you, I'll be there as soon as I can," she told him.

She went in through the Vestibule, entered the Main Hall, and turned to the right. Following the corridor that ran along the Winter Garden, she passed the door to the Billiard Room, and walked toward the Banquet Hall.

And there, in the corner, she saw the spot where it had always been.

The bronze statue of Mr. George Washington Vanderbilt, the grandson of the famous Commodore Cornelius Vanderbilt, and the master of Biltmore Estate.

Mr. V.

And just as she had hoped, it was gone.

Serafina couldn't help but smile. Now she knew for sure that Mr. Vanderbilt hadn't killed anyone. She wanted to cheer. She wanted to hug him. She wanted to shout to the heavens that something finally made sense in the world.

Have faith in what you know, her pa had told her, and she should have, but her faith had been mightily shaken. She kept thinking about poor, wounded Kinsley and all the people who had died. But despite how strange and almost inconceivable it was that the statues were doing all this, she felt a swell of excitement that she was finally starting to put some of the pieces of the puzzle together.

"I don't get it," Braeden said bluntly. "Why are the statues coming to life now after all this time? What's the cause of it all?"

"It might be a sorcerer or a spell," Serafina said, "some sort of evil intruder."

"But why? Why would a sorcerer want to kill all these random innocent people?"

"There must be some connection between them, some kind of pattern," Serafina said.

"It all started on the night Colonel Braddick died, didn't it?" Braeden asked. "He was the first one attacked."

"Along with Mr. Turner, Mr. Suttleston, Isariah Mayfield, and Jess," she said.

"Who was next?" Braeden asked.

"Mr. Kettering at the bottom of the stairs," she said. "And then Mr. Cobere in the kitchen."

She thought about the people on their list. What was the pattern, the motivation?

And then she asked the same question she had asked herself before and not been able to answer. "What do all these victims have in common?"

"Maybe the key is that they don't have anything in common," Braeden said.

"What do you mean?"

"Maybe there's an important difference between them, and we're not seeing it."

"Colonel Braddick, Mr. Turner, Mr. Suttleston, Isariah Mayfield, Jess Braddick, Mr. Kettering, Mr. Cobere . . ." Serafina listed off.

"Rich and poor . . ."

"Male and female . . ."

"Northerner and Southerner . . ."

"Biltmore resident and Biltmore guest . . ."

"How they died . . ."

And then she paused.

"Dead," Serafina said.

"They aren't all dead!" Braeden said.

"That's right," Serafina said. "Jess wasn't killed that first night."

"Was she just lucky?" Braeden asked.

"There's a pattern," Serafina said, feeling the surge of realization in her chest. "At least at the beginning of it all, there was definitely a pattern. . . ."

Keen on the trail, she and Braeden hurried down the corridor.

"In those first few nights, what did all the *dead* victims have in common with each other, and how were they different from the one victim who wasn't killed?"

As they crossed through the Banquet Hall and into the back corridor known as the Bachelors' Wing, she went through the list of questions in her mind. Rich or poor. Male or female. Northerner or Southerner. Resident or guest . . .

"The victims were all so different from one another," Braeden said.

"But something connected them," Serafina said.

Pausing in the corridor, she thought about Colonel Braddick at dinner bragging about his gun. And she heard the baying of the hounds as they chased down the mountain lions. And she remembered looking out the window of her new bedroom and seeing Mr. Kettering returning from a hunt.

A shiver ran down her spine. She remembered searching through the fog and darkness for Jess after the battle on the North Ridge, the feeling of being hunted. And she remembered how Kinsley had been in such a panic right before the battle with the lions in the field. He, too, had said it felt as if something were hunting him.

When she looked up, she realized that they were standing in front of the Gun Room.

As she and Braeden stepped into the room, she gazed at the glass-fronted cabinets that encased the long rows of rifles and shotguns. And then she looked up at the hunting trophies lining the walls—the heads and antlers of many deer.

She knew that Mr. Vanderbilt was not a hunter. When he built the house he purchased these mounted animal heads as decor to create what was supposed to look like the gun room of a proper country gentleman.

She thought again about the people who had died. "The pattern is right here. . . ."

"But what about Mr. Cobere?" Braeden said, clearly following her train of thought. "Mr. Cobere wasn't a hunter. He had no connection to the hunters at all."

"He was the butcher and meat cook . . ." she said, remembering the sight of him lying on the tiled floor of the Rotisserie Kitchen. "He was in charge of preparing and cooking the fish and game brought in by the hunters and fishermen. The trout, the wild turkey, the rabbit—"

"And the deer," Braeden finished.

"Exactly," Serafina said. "In those first few nights, the

difference between the ones who were killed, and the one who wasn't, was simple."

"Hunting," Braeden said.

"That's right," Serafina said, feeling the excitement of the discovery scintillating in her mind. "Jess had tried to work against the hunters. It wasn't a coincidence that she was the only one who survived that night. The connection to hunting was right in front of my eyes all along, but I didn't see it."

"But if someone is murdering people connected with hunting, then that's all of us," Braeden said. "We all live here!"

Serafina's brow furrowed as she wiped her mouth. Did the acceptance of an act mean you were guilty of the act? She wasn't sure. But it was clear that they were still missing pieces of the puzzle. The pattern seemed to be breaking down, the violence getting worse and worse, more random, like it was spiraling out of control now. Baby Nell's nursery had been attacked. And the bear cub and the coachman had been killed. . . .

"When did all the trouble begin?" she asked.

"The night Colonel Braddick and the other mountain lion hunters were attacked."

Serafina paused, wondering. "Or did the violence truly begin the night before that, the night the white deer was shot?"

"Are you saying . . ." he began uncertainly, "the white deer is the *cause* of all this, or she's trying to help us?"

And then a thought that she'd had earlier came back into her mind. "It's the *house*," she said. "The house itself is bringing its statues to life. The white deer was just the first one."

"But why now?" he asked. "My uncle has been hosting the hunting season here for years."

"Did it begin the day the thirteen carriages arrived?" Serafina asked. "Could one of those guests be the cause of all this?"

As they were talking, a series of images began to flow through her mind. She remembered standing on the terrace the night Braeden came to her like a ghost. And she remembered them lying on the shore of the lake with all the stars above them. That was the first time they saw the white deer. It had seemed as if it was a beautiful young fawn, running through the forest, glowing in the light of the stars, almost magical in its appearance. It had brought her such a sense of peace and joy to see it.

But Colonel Braddick and his hunting companions saw this same magnificent, rare, magical creature and they shot it. They tried to kill it so that they could add the unusual specimen to their collection of trophies. Or maybe it was just boredom, or a bit of sport to see who could hit such a small, moving target. But in the end, whatever the reason, they shot it.

As she thought again about lying beside the lake with Braeden, she began to feel something tingling in her mind. *That's it,* she thought. *That was the moment it all began.*

She sensed she was getting closer and closer to the answer.

But then she heard the rushing sound of many footsteps coming down the corridor. Mr. Doddman and six other armed men stormed into the Gun Room and surrounded her and Braeden.

44

r. Vanderbilt walked into the Gun Room immediately behind Mr. Doddman and the other men.

When Serafina saw him, she felt a rush of glorious emotion. It was startling how dramatically one's opinion of someone improved when you realized they weren't actually the heinous murderer you thought they were.

She walked straight up to the master of Biltmore and embraced him.

Mr. Vanderbilt was clearly taken aback, but he did not reject her embrace.

"I'm very sorry about taking Cornelia. I was so confused about what we were fighting," she explained as they separated and faced each other. "But not anymore."

"What are you talking about?" Mr. Vanderbilt asked.

"If there is anyone still out hunting for the beast or searching for Jess, we need to bring them back immediately," Serafina said. "And if anyone sees a white deer, they should run."

She knew what she was telling Mr. Vanderbilt and his men sounded ridiculous, but she said it firmly and with confidence.

"A white deer . . ." Mr. Doddman repeated suspiciously.

Serafina looked at the security manager and the other men. "If anyone sees an animal or someone they don't know, they should immediately get away from it."

The master of Biltmore studied her for a moment, and then looked at Mr. Doddman. "Send out word that no more search parties should go out, and all hunting must stop immediately. And everyone should stay clear of this white deer creature. Get everyone safely into the house."

"Sir, if I may," Serafina interrupted. "Please don't bring everyone into the house. Get everyone *out*. Load the carriages and send them away, the guests, the servants, your family. A great danger is upon us and only those who have skills to fight should remain."

All the men stared at her in utter shock.

"There is absolutely no cause for such drastic action," Mr. Doddman said forcefully.

But Mr. Vanderbilt said, "You want to actually abandon Biltmore?"

"Yes, sir. We must."

"She's right, Uncle," Braeden said. "Everyone is in danger here."

"If this so-called white deer is so dangerous," Mr. Doddman said, "then we should hunt it down and kill it."

"No," Serafina said, shaking her head. "That's going to make it worse. This whole thing started small, but now it's getting much, much larger. Do you see? The violence is bringing violence. Bullets aren't going to hurt the white deer anymore. Its magic has grown too strong. Your guns will be effective against the newer creatures at first, but not the white deer. That's how Kinsley was hurt. In his attempts to protect Jess, he tried to fight it."

The men listened to her with blanched faces, as if they weren't quite able to believe or comprehend what she was saying.

She had gone many days and nights without knowing what was going on, without knowing what to do, but now she did know, at least some of it, and she had to tell them as plainly and bluntly as she could.

Mr. Vanderbilt had listened intently to everything she said, but she could still see the hesitation in his eyes.

"It's the statues, sir," she said finally.

"I don't understand what you're saying," he said. "What's the statues?"

"They're coming to life and they're killing us," she said, her voice as steady and serious as she could hold it, her eyes locked on his.

His expression tightened and his brow furrowed. She knew that what she had just told him was so foolishly impossible that it barely warranted serious thought. And yet . . . And yet there was *something* she was telling him that caught him. She could see him thinking it through.

"It was a gargoyle . . ." he said in amazement.

"That's right," she said.

"And there's a statue of me in the house . . ." he said, his voice so low and uncertain that it was barely audible. "That's what scared you so badly . . . why you didn't come to me . . . why you took Cornelia. . . ."

Serafina let out a long breath, relieved that Mr. Vanderbilt was beginning to realize why she acted the way she did. "I saw a person who looked like you kill Mr. Cobere," she told him. "I couldn't understand it. It seemed impossible! But there have been many others, and there's going to be more."

At that moment, the pressure in the room seemed to immediately change. Mr. Vanderbilt turned to his dumbfounded men, who had been listening to all of this, and gave them new orders.

"Now listen carefully," he told them in a strong, firm voice. "We're going to do exactly what Serafina says. Get everyone into the carriages, women and children first, including my wife and daughter, and send two armed men with each and every carriage to make sure everyone gets out safely."

"Yes, sir," Mr. Doddman and the other men said together, and immediately moved into action.

"We're doing what needs to be done, sir," Serafina said. "I'm sure of it."

"I've been so frustrated that there was nothing I could do

about all these terrible things that were happening," he said. "I'm no marksman or soldier, but this is one way I can lend a hand."

Lend a hand, she thought, the same expression that her pa had used. And it surprised her to hear the same dismay in Mr. Vanderbilt's voice that she had felt in herself just days before. This man of power and experience had been caught in the same roiling sense of worthlessness that she had suffered.

As Mr. Vanderbilt hurried away to organize the evacuation of Biltmore, Serafina grabbed Braeden's arm.

"We need to figure out specifically what's causing all this," she said.

"What's your plan?"

"Down by the lake, when everything started," she said, "do you remember how we could see all those stars that night? You were telling me what they meant. And then we saw the white deer running through the forest—"

"You think it was a constellation . . ." Braeden said in amazement. "You want to use Biltmore's Library. . . ."

"Unless you already know what we're looking for, I think it's our only hope."

Seconds later, as they ran through the Main Hall, dozens of guests were hurrying toward their rooms to grab what belongings they could. Others had abandoned their belongings entirely and were now fleeing directly for the carriages that were lining up at the front door.

As she and Braeden dashed down the length of the Tapestry Gallery, maids and footmen rushed to and fro around them, battening down the window shutters and closing up the piano, others trying to protect the gallery's fine furniture and its three hand-woven twenty-foot-wide silk and wool Flemish tapestries.

Serafina could hear Mr. Vanderbilt's voice in the distance behind her. "There's no time for all that," he ordered his staff. "Leave it and go!"

The whole house was erupting with activity. It would be the first time in her entire life that they would attempt to actually empty this vast house of nearly all of its inhabitants.

45

As she and Braeden entered the Library, the brass floor lamps glowed with amber light, reflecting on the gold-leaf titles of the books lining the shelves, and a gentle fire crackled in the marble fireplace. It was a peaceful sight, but the sounds of chaos filled the house behind them. She didn't know how much time they had, but she knew it wasn't much. And as she looked up at all the books, it just seemed so daunting. There were over ten thousand books on these shelves, and another twelve thousand scattered throughout the house. How could she find any answers in a place like this?

"Astronomy . . ." Braeden said as he quickly went over to one of the shelves near the wrought-iron spiral staircase that led up to the Library's second level. He tilted his head as he scanned the titles and then pulled out a dark leather-bound book.

As they leafed through the pages, Serafina caught glimpses of Greek gods and goddesses, great Titans and epic heroes.

"There are all kinds of myths and legends about the constellations," he said, "but I don't remember any stories about a white deer."

"What about the stars you were telling me about that night?"

"We saw Orion . . . and the star of Aldebaran . . . and Pleiades . . . and—"

"You were telling me about Pleiades," she said. "The Seven Stars. Do you remember? They were very bright."

"My uncle said that the Seven Sisters were the daughters of Pleione, some sort of nymph or something."

Serafina listened to what he was saying, but it didn't seem to have anything to do with what was happening at Biltmore. "You told me a story from the Bible where God says, 'Can you bind the chains of the Pleiades or loose the belt of Orion?' Do you remember that? You said that nearly every culture in the world had old stories about the Seven Stars."

Outside the Library, at the far end of the house, something glass smashed onto the floor. They both jumped at the sound of it, but Serafina was determined to stay focused on what they were doing.

Braeden hurried over to one of the shelves near the fireplace and pulled out a second book. "This one talks about how a

Māori god named Tāne collected seven stars and then threw them up into the heavens to adorn the god of the sky."

"I don't think that's it, either," Serafina said.

"Then let's try this one," Braeden said as he pulled out a much thicker black tome and began flipping through the paintings of constellations, Cygnus the Swan, Taurus the Bull, Orion the Hunter, page after page.

When she spotted a cluster of stars in a haze of glowing blue light, she stopped him. "That's the Seven Stars."

They leaned in and began reading the text, descriptions of Celtic myths and druid priests, of witchcraft and long-forgotten lore.

Now she could hear people shouting to one another in the distance. She wanted to go to them, to help them. *We don't have time for reading,* she thought frantically, but then she came to this:

There were seasons for all things, but autumn in particular was known as a time of change and calamitous events. Every fall, when the Seven Stars first rose high in the midnight sky, it was believed that the veil between the physical world and the magical world was at its thinnest. It was said that during this time if the Seven Stars were caught in a reflection, then they would reflect their magic into our world, while at the same time reflecting our world into their magic, like a mirror into a mirror. Whatever was occurring at the moment of the reflection—the good, the evil, the wondrous, and the vile—would become manifest in our world.

As she read the words, it felt as if her thoughts were glowing with heat in her mind.

"The reflection on the lake . . ." she whispered in astonishment.

"And the meteor storm . . ." Braeden gasped.

"It must have all started that night."

"But there's still nothing here about a white deer," Braeden said.

They quickly continued to the next paragraph.

It was generally believed, among the druid priests and the common people alike, that in some years the Seven Stars had the power to bring the dead into the realm of the living. This has long been thought by historians to be the origin of what we now observe as Halloween. It was also believed that in other years the Seven Stars had the power to bring spirit to that which did not have spirit. The exact stories varied from year to year, and from region to region, but they all had one aspect in common: Once the reflection of the Seven Stars faded, their magic faded with them, and the daylight world returned to normal.

"But this can't be right," Braeden said. "There's still nothing about a white deer. And if we were dealing with the magic of the Seven Stars, then it should have only lasted for a few minutes on that one night."

Gunshots split the air and echoed through the cavernous halls of Biltmore. She knew that people were in trouble, but she had to stay strong.

What Braeden had just said seemed to eliminate the Seven Stars as a possibility for what they were facing, but she remembered the ethereal sight of the white fawn running through the forest that first night, and Joan of Arc charging toward them a few nights later, and all the other creatures that had come alive.

"*The power to bring spirit to that which did not have spirit . . .*'" she whispered, trying to think it through. "It's like the magic of the Seven Stars has been entwined with Biltmore."

Braeden looked up at her. "But do you realize what that means? It's a reflection of ourselves at the moment when it occurred. The hunters shot the white fawn!"

"It bespelled the entire house, the grounds, *everything*!" she said. "And it's getting worse every night, twisting the stone of Biltmore with its own evil."

"No," Braeden said. "With *our* evil, you mean. *Our* evil! Don't you see? Like a mirror into a mirror. It's a reflection of *us*, all turned against us! It's the violence, the cruelty of that moment, turned against the hunters. It's the killing of small, defenseless animals. It's the terrifying feeling of being hunted. It's all of it!"

A bank of windows shattered in a nearby room.

"And it's reflecting into itself, spiraling out of control," she said.

"Especially when we try to fight against it, like Kinsley did."

"But it said that the magic would only last as long as the reflection."

"So why is it still here? Why is it still happening?" Braeden asked, his voice strained.

A sickening, sinking weight filled Serafina's stomach, and her face must have shown it, for Braeden's darkened immediately.

"What?" he said. "What's wrong?"

"The white fawn was meant to die," she said.

"What do you mean, *meant to die?*" he said, aghast.

"Not that the deer was meant to be shot by the hunters or that it *deserved* to die. But when the reflection of the stars in the lake faded, then the magic in the white fawn should have faded with it. The deer should have passed away or become stone again."

"Then why did she stay alive?" Braeden asked, but even as he said the words, she heard the hitch in his voice. "She stayed alive because I healed her," he said, his words laced with the realization of what he'd done. "I used my healing powers to help her, to infuse her with life. . . . I'm the cause of all this!"

"Braeden, you didn't know," she said. "It's not your fault. You didn't shoot the deer."

But what shocked her the most as she gazed up at the shelves of the vast library was that the answer to the puzzle had been here in these books all along. She'd been so close to it.

She had admired the beauty of the star-filled sky a thousand times, but until Braeden had told her about it, she had never heard of Pleiades, or the Seven Stars, or known much about the glistening objects sweeping through the darkness of space above her.

What if Colonel Braddick had known not to shoot the white deer? What if Braeden had known not to save it? What if Kinsley had known not to fight it during his heroic efforts to defend Jess?

Serafina stopped.

What if *she* had known *any* of it? She could have prevented this.

But they were all just doing what they always did. Killing and saving and defending and clawing.

A wave of screams rose up from the Main Hall, people running in panic. Serafina knew that they only had seconds left. But an idea sprang into her mind. "Braeden, did the Joan of Arc statue have any history behind it, any kind of dark past?"

"No, my uncle had it made for the house," Braeden said. "It was just a plain old stone statue."

"Was the real Joan of Arc a vicious fighter?"

"My uncle said that she wore armor and carried a sword into battle, but she was more of a spiritual leader, to boost the morale of the French troops. I think mainly she wanted peace."

"She sure didn't seem too peaceful when she was trying to kill us," Serafina said. "And the lions didn't act like real lions. They're all being brought into motion by the power of the reflection. . . . But how do we fight them?" As she tried to think it through, she knew that whatever they came up with, they had to act quickly. "We just saw that we can kill at least some of them with weapons and claws, but we've also seen what happens when the power of our world mixes with theirs."

Braeden nodded. "The white deer is darn near indestructible thanks to me."

The smell of smoke filled the air, the acrid stench of woolen tapestries on fire.

"I think we need to talk to her," Braeden said, his eyes solemn. "We need to somehow communicate with her, get her to stop doing this. I healed her, so she knows me. She knows I wouldn't hurt her. She'll trust me. If she's reflecting violence, then let's not give her any violence to reflect."

"I don't think that's going to work," Serafina said. "I already tried talking to it the night the hunters were killed and it didn't respond to me. And it's not just the white deer, it's statues all over the entire estate, the house, the gardens, the lake—"

A large vase just outside the Library smashed onto the floor. Whatever it was, it was coming and would soon be here.

"How do we fight the entire house?" Braeden asked in exasperation.

"We can't," Serafina said. "We've got to think of some other way to stop it."

"We just need more time," Braeden said, looking up at all the books. "The answer's got to be here somewhere!"

Tap-tap-tap.

The rap of cloven hooves moving across the hardwood floor drifted down the Tapestry Gallery toward the Library.

The hair on the back of Serafina's neck stood on end.

"What's that?" Braeden asked.

Experience was a peculiar thing. And reading books and asking questions and talking to one another . . . There were *many* teachers. But she feared that up to this moment, she had not been listening.

She turned to the door, knowing that the killing creature would soon be there, and she said, "We're out of time."

ap-tap-tap.

The sound of the tiny hooves grew louder.

"Get back," Serafina whispered to Braeden as she moved quickly forward to peek out through the archway of the Library's open double doors.

She looked down the length of the Tapestry Gallery, dark and full of shadows, the glow of the moon seeping through the sheer curtains on the tall, narrow windows.

The white deer stood at the far end of the long room, the creature's beady black eyes fixed on her. Its antlers rose above its head like a hovering crown of sharpened, deadly sticks.

Serafina stared straight into the eyes of the white deer, locking on to its gaze, and breathed as steadily as she could.

"Braeden . . ." she whispered without turning her head. "I want you to go out through the French doors behind us that lead to the South Terrace. I'll hold off the deer as long as I can."

"I'm going to try to talk to her," Braeden said, walking forward.

"Braeden, no!" Serafina screamed, but it was too late. He had already stepped into view of the white deer and was now walking down the Tapestry Gallery toward it.

Serafina wasn't sure if it was the bravest or stupidest thing she had ever seen him do, but Braeden was determined. He walked right toward the white deer, raising his open hands in a conciliatory manner as he went.

"There's nothing to fear from us," he said softly, his voice as smooth and soothing as when he talked to a spooked horse. "We welcome you here."

The deer pivoted its head and stared at Braeden. It made no sound. And its expression was utterly incomprehensible.

"It's not listening, Braeden," Serafina whispered. "It's not a true animal. You can't talk to it. Please come back now, don't frighten it, don't anger it, just come back. . . ."

But Braeden took another step forward.

"We mean you no harm," he said gently. "We can help you adjust to this world. Whatever we have done, we can make amends. We can live in peace together."

The deer gazed at Braeden and took a step closer to him.

"Yes, come . . ." Braeden whispered encouragingly.

The deer took another step forward, just staring at him.

It looks like it's actually working, Serafina thought in amazement.

But as she watched Braeden move slowly toward the white deer, it felt as if a snake were wrapping around her neck and tightening against her throat. She couldn't speak. She couldn't breathe.

It's a trick! she thought as she watched Braeden helplessly. *Don't go, Braeden. Come back!* She gritted her teeth in fury and frustration, trying to break free of the deer's gaze.

Suddenly, the deer's nostrils flared in anger. The deer raised one of its front hooves and slammed it down, sending a jagged ten-foot crack splintering through the hardwood floor.

Serafina wanted to charge at the deer, but she was frozen, like helpless prey, by the deer's spell.

"Braeden, it's not working!" she managed to hiss through the constriction of her throat, but Braeden took another step toward the deer.

"Don't worry, no one is going to hurt you . . ." Braeden said.

From the Main Hall, far behind the white deer, the sounds of shouting people rose up into the air.

Still staring at Braeden, the deer tilted its antlers down and shook its head once, then twice, and when its head came back up again the deer snorted loudly and stepped aggressively forward, a warning, a threat.

"It's going to be all right," Braeden said in his soothing tone, seemingly impervious to fear. "I won't let anyone hurt you. . . ."

A woman's bloodcurdling scream rose up from the Main Hall. The men, women, and children of Biltmore were rushing out through gaping front doors, fleeing for their lives. Something that sounded like a large wooden crate full of brass springs but was probably Biltmore's massive grandfather clock crashed down and shattered into pieces on the floor. Men were shouting to each other, as if coordinating some sort of counterattack. Others were running with shrieks of terror. The bellowing snarl of some sort of unearthly mythical creature echoed off the limestone walls of the house. The smell of singed furniture and acrid smoke filled the air. Baby Nell wailed. Her mother cried out. The clatter of horses' hooves stormed into the front hall.

Serafina wanted desperately to charge toward the chaos on the other side of the white deer and help those poor souls escape, but she knew she couldn't.

As the deer stared steadily at Braeden with its wicked eyes, Serafina saw something emerging from the shadows behind it. She heard the sound of coming footsteps, a gentleman's dress shoes, and then there he was, walking past the white deer and right toward her and Braeden. The walking man had black hair and mustache. It was Mr. Vanderbilt!

And then she saw the deadness in his eyes, and a surge of white-cold fear shot through her body, breaking the deer's spell.

The footman Mr. Pratt came running from the Main Hall to get Mr. Vanderbilt's attention.

"Watch out, Mr. Pratt, that's not him!" Serafina shouted, but it was too late.

As Mr. Pratt came up behind him and reached out to touch

his arm, the doppelgänger of Mr. Vanderbilt whirled around with a forceful, striking blow and slammed Mr. Pratt in the head with the iron fire poker clenched in its fist.

The stunned Mr. Pratt stumbled backward on his heels, his arms flailing as if trying to catch himself, blood streaming from his eyes. When the backs of his calves struck a coffee table, he crashed down into the splintering pieces of it and fell to the floor, blood pooling beneath his head.

Serafina desperately wanted to help Mr. Pratt, but even if she could find a way to break the spell and move, she couldn't abandon Braeden. As Braeden stood there face-to-face with the white deer, she kept thinking that maybe his idea would somehow work, that it *had* to work, that he'd find a way to communicate with it. But the deer stared at Braeden with its black, incomprehensible eyes, and Braeden stared back, frozen, as the doppelgänger pivoted and rushed toward him.

"Run, Braeden!" she screamed as the doppelgänger charged forward and raised its iron weapon.

But Braeden did not run. He stood completely immobile, caught in the white deer's bewildering, hypnotic power. He did not turn away. He did not raise his arms to block the blow from striking his head.

Instead, he took one last step forward, straight into his death.

Something ripped through the air past her ear and struck the doppelgänger in the forehead with a thud. It collapsed to the floor like a puppet with its strings cut.

"Will you two please get moving!" a young female voice shouted at her and Braeden, as if she was angry that they had just been standing there like a couple of deer caught in lantern light.

Serafina shook herself out of the mesmerized stupor, feeling the focus of her dilated eyes coming back to her.

She immediately grabbed Braeden by the arm and yanked him back into the Library, nearly pulling him off his feet but finally breaking the confounding power of the deer's stare.

Serafina was surprised to see that it was Jess who was

helping them. A jagged cut of dark crusted blood traced her forehead, but it looked like she had changed into a fresh dress, grabbed one of her rifles, and was ready to go.

"You're a sight for sore eyes, Jess," Serafina said as they took cover behind a set of bookcases. "I was afraid we lost you for good."

"Mr. Vanderbilt sent Kinsley and the other wounded to the hospital in Asheville, but I thought I should come and lend a hand."

"We're glad to have you," Braeden said, looking mighty relieved to be out of the deer's spell.

But there was no time to linger. The screaming chaos of the people trying to escape through the Main Hall's front doors, and the snarling viciousness of whatever creatures were attacking them, came roiling down the length of the gallery.

The priceless Flemish tapestries that covered the walls of the gallery were on fire, the flames licking up toward the exquisitely painted wood beams on the ceiling, its gold leaf flickering in the light of the flames.

Amid all the violence and destruction, Serafina looked up to see a large white swan flying down the length of the Tapestry Gallery toward her, flapping in deep, graceful pulls that curled the plumes of smoke at the tips of its outstretched wings. The swan was so white that its feathers seemed to scintillate with the incandescence of the brightest stars.

Serafina couldn't do anything but gasp at the sight of it. As it flew over her head, the rushing air of its wings brushed her cheeks and lifted her hair.

But in the same instant, a snarling griffin with the back legs and body of an African lion and the front legs, head, and wings of an eagle came charging into the Library and straight toward her. The mythical beast knocked her off her feet, took flight with a mighty heave of its wings, and slammed into Braeden, dragging him brutally to the floor with its savage talons.

Jess swung her rifle and fired, the sharp report of the shot buffeting the ceiling.

Forgetting about the boy it had pinned to the floor, the beast lunged viciously at Jess, screeching and hissing. She retreated rapidly, but never stopped firing, *bang, bang, bang* at point-blank range, until the griffin finally went down.

"Two more!" Serafina shouted, ducking as a pair of griffins came diving into the Library with great sweeps of their wings, books and papers whirling in all directions.

She pulled Braeden to his feet and dragged him toward the French doors that led out to the South Terrace. But even as they reached the doors, she saw through the panes of glass that dozens of large, lizardlike gargoyles from the rooftop were crawling and scraping there, looking for a way in.

She and her companions were trapped on both sides.

As the gargoyles smashed through the glass doors and slithered their way into the Library, Braeden wiped the blood from his face and shouted, "We're not getting out that way!"

Jess shot another griffin dead, levered her rifle, and shot again, trying to keep the snapping beasts at bay.

Braeden went deeper into the Library, shouting, "Everyone, this way!"

As they quickly followed him, Serafina could hear the screaming and crashing noises in the distance; she and her friends weren't the only ones fighting for their lives.

Another griffin stormed into the Library, its clenching claws shredding the Persian carpets and gouging the walnut woodwork as its slashing beak knocked the brass lamps to the floor, shattering their glass globes. The barrel-size, blue-and-white Ming vases rolled off their stands and smashed to pieces. A dozen writhing, black-skinned gargoyles broke through the French doors and poured into the room.

When she and her companions reached the far side of the fireplace, Braeden led them up the spiral staircase to the railed walkway that provided access to the books above.

"Through here," he said as he pushed open a hidden door behind the upper section of the massive fireplace.

It was a good way to reach Biltmore's upper floors, but as soon as she saw that Jess had a way to escape, Serafina knew what she had to do.

"Go and help the others," she told Jess. "I'm going to try to draw the creatures away from the house."

"Got it," Jess said, darting through the door.

"I'll go with *you*, Serafina," Braeden said.

"You're gonna need to hang on tight," Serafina said, nodding.

An instant later, she transformed into a massive black panther. Braeden leapt onto her back, and she dove claws-first, with a roaring growl, into the mass of gargoyles below her.

"Yee-haa!" Braeden shouted as they flew through the air and landed on the floor below. She knew he'd ridden plenty of horses, so he had the skill and balance to stay on, but judging by his whoop, he'd never experienced anything quite like riding a leaping panther.

She hit the ground and sprang through the gargoyles, across the Library, barreling straight into the griffin blocking the door. She slammed into it, exploding into a black ball of snapping teeth and slashing claws, battling with the eagle head and the talons, finally striking the beast down.

Spotting the white deer in the Tapestry Gallery, she ran straight at it, like a huge black bullet. She knew she probably couldn't truly hurt it, but she had to get its attention. As she leapt toward it, she lifted her paw and took a mighty swipe, striking it right across its flank. It was a strong, killing blow. But the tips of her claws scraped across the deer's side like she was striking glass, and a priceless painting on the wall behind her tore open and went spinning across the floor. The startled, snorting deer skittered aside, nearly toppling, then turning with a crack of its cloven hooves against the floor as if it expected another swipe. But instead of striking the deer, Serafina ran right past it.

Violence brings violence, so come and get me!

She sprinted down the length of the gallery, leaping over its damaged sofas and broken tables, darting around the splintered grand piano with its black and white keys spilled across the floor, and flying past the burning lamps and shattered windows.

When she reached the scorched walls and demolished remnants of the Main Hall, furniture and suitcases were strewn across the limestone floor.

Every sculpture and relief inside and outside the house was coming to terrifying life. Mr. Vanderbilt's visions of exquisite ancient art, grand operas, heroic journeys, beautiful ballets, and classic stories of literature had become a living nightmare.

Maids and footmen with lanterns were scurrying in all directions. Guests in nightshirts were calling to one another, trying to stay together in the smoke and darkness.

As Serafina ran toward the archway of the open front doors, she glanced over and was startled to see her pa and Essie hurrying down the Grand Staircase.

In all the turmoil and violence that had befallen the house, her pa must have stayed behind and run upstairs to the Louis XVI Room to find her. But he had found Essie instead, and they had become allies in the chaos, working together, helping each other, fighting to stay alive.

"It's not much farther, we're almost out," her pa was assuring Essie as they rushed down the stairs together. Their clothes were torn, their arms and bodies scratched and bruised. It was clear that they were fleeing some horrifying beast from the floor above.

When they reached the bottom of the stairs and looked up to see a massive, yellow-eyed black panther directly in front of them, both of their faces fell white with dread. It was as if they had been fighting and fighting to survive, but knew now, at this moment, that this was a fight they could not win.

They didn't seem to see or comprehend at first that there was actually a boy clinging to the panther's back. They were transfixed by the panther's black body, the massive head, the fangs, and the yellow eyes staring at them.

But Braeden rose from her shoulders and screamed, "Get down!"

Her pa pulled Essie to the ground just as Serafina sprang straight over their heads at the hellish winged lion charging down the stairway directly behind them. She and Braeden and the fighting lion went tumbling down the stairs, knocking her pa and Essie off their feet. The roaring growls of the two big cats exploded into violence as they battled with claws and teeth.

Braeden was flung from her back, but immediately sprang

to his feet and ran to help her pa and Essie scramble out of the way.

Her pa turned toward her, gazing in awe at the astounding sight of a black panther battling a winged lion. But high above them, Serafina heard the dome of the Grand Staircase crack under the weight of what sounded like a massive flying beast landing on the rooftop. As the bolt that held the four-story-tall wrought-iron chandelier was ripped from the dome, she suddenly remembered her pa's elaborate descriptions of how he had helped install the huge, seventeen-hundred-pound chandelier years before. Now it was falling, collapsing down through the center of the spiral staircase, *smash, smash, smash,* one level crashing into the next, with him standing right below it. She yanked herself away from the snarling battle with the winged lion and sprang toward her pa.

The full weight of her panther body slammed into her father, and they went tumbling across the floor as the wrought-iron chandelier crashed onto the charging winged lion and exploded into hundreds of clanging pieces.

Lying on the floor a few steps away, Serafina and her pa disentangled themselves and looked at each other face-to-face, the oak-brown eyes of a human being and the bright yellow eyes of a black panther.

She was expecting fear, horror, shock. But the first thing she saw in her father's expression at that moment was *recognition*.

He knew he was looking at his daughter.

Whenever she had thought of this moment, she had imagined her pa roiling with dismay, turning away from her in revulsion at the unnatural creature she was, and angry at how dishonest she had been to hide it from him all this time. But what she saw in her father's eyes was amazement, heartfelt pride and awe at what his little girl had become. She had gone for so long without him knowing who she was; she had felt so alone, so adrift. And now, in the midst of all this chaos and violence, a tremendous sense of relief poured into her body, a tremendous sense of love, to finally be seen by her father in her fullest and truest form.

"Come on, Serafina, the white deer's coming!" Braeden shouted as he ran toward her and leapt onto her back.

Serafina took one last look at her father and dashed out the front door of the house.

Several carriages had been split open at their doors by some great force. The wooden spokes and metal rims of their wheels had been smashed. The horses, still trapped in their harnesses, were dragging the broken carriages across the cobblestones, the bare axles throwing rooster-tails of sparks in all directions.

Mr. Doddman, the security manager, was cramming the elderly Mrs. Ascott and a half dozen other guests into one of the carriages that was still intact. But as he was shutting the carriage door and shouting instructions up to the terrified coachman, an arrow whizzed through the air and sank into Mr. Doddman's chest, stifling his shout.

He clutched at the shaft of the arrow desperately as his entire prodigious body crumpled downward and then fell dead to the ground.

Serafina looked out to see Diana, goddess of the hunt, charging toward them, firing arrows as she came.

Mr. Vanderbilt, bleeding from a wound to his neck and head, was frantically helping his wife and child into the next carriage.

Mrs. Vanderbilt held the crying baby Cornelia wrapped tightly to her chest as the barking, snapping Gidean and Cedric fought off a pack of gargoyles surrounding them.

The goddess Diana drew her second arrow, aimed straight at Mrs. Vanderbilt, and let the arrow fly.

51

Serafina threw herself at Mrs. Vanderbilt and slammed her against the side of a horse as the arrow whizzed by.

Then she charged straight at Diana, praying she could sprint faster than the goddess could nock another arrow.

Just as she made her final lunge at the goddess, the arrow shot past. Braeden screamed as it tore a gash out of his arm and struck a footman in the head behind them.

Mrs. Vanderbilt—stunned from being slammed against a horse by a huge cat, but still holding on to her baby—staggered forward, away from the wildly spooked horse, as her husband pulled her and their daughter into the carriage.

Nolan, the stable boy, scrambled up into the driver's seat

and grabbed the reins of Braeden's horses, harnessed at the front of the carriage.

"Go! Go!" Braeden shouted directly to the horses, and the horses charged forward, pulling the carriage away.

Two gargoyles leapt onto the carriage before it escaped and were now crawling across its roof toward Nolan's back as he concentrated on steering the galloping horses.

The remaining gargoyles turned on Gidean and Cedric with new viciousness. Serafina ran straight at the pack of them, swiping at the nasty beasts with her claws to give Gidean and Cedric enough time to break away and dash after the carriage. Nolan and the Vanderbilts were going to need all the protection they could get.

There were more carriages, more people trying to escape, but Braeden shouted, "We've got to keep running, Serafina!"

She turned to look behind her. The white deer was emerging through the front doors, its eyes scanning the chaos of the fleeing humans without emotion. It was looking for *her*, the panther that had charged toward it and clawed its side. And as soon as it saw her, it locked its powerful black eyes onto her.

"I think we've got her attention!" Braeden shouted.

Serafina wanted desperately to lunge at the deer, to claw it, to bite it. But fighting it was no use. Violence and attack made it stronger. It was as impervious to her claws as it was to Kinsley's bullets, and growing more and more powerful by the second.

Knowing what she had to do, Serafina pivoted and ran.

She didn't hide. She didn't go for cover. She ran *away*. Away from Biltmore. Away from her pa and Essie, and Mr. and Mrs. Vanderbilt and little Cornelia, away from all of them.

When she reached the flat, open area of the Esplanade she pushed herself harder, driving the force into her legs and blazing across the grass.

Come on, deer, she thought as she sped away. *Let's go for a little run!*

When she was sure she had put a good strong distance between her and the house, she glanced behind her, hoping to see the white deer following after her.

But what she saw struck cold, hard fear into her panther heart.

The white deer stood at the very front of Biltmore House, staring toward her and Braeden up on the hill. It was just standing there—with its all-white body, and its white antlers protruding from its head. For a moment, Serafina thought the bizarre creature had given up, that it had chosen to finally stop pursuing them. But then hundreds of gargoyles, chimeras, and other monstrous creatures poured from the facade of the house in an all-enveloping black wave. Thick channels of beasts streamed out of the front door and out through all the broken windows, like black swarms of hornets vomiting from an ungodly nest.

There were hissing, viper-headed fiends with burning eyes, grotesque humanlike ogres, hook-beaked hyenas, muscled wine gods with curved ram horns protruding from their chiseled heads, and hundreds of snarling, hunchbacked, razor-clawed gargoyles.

And they were all coming straight for her and Braeden.

"We better get out of here!" Braeden shouted.

Serafina turned and ran, sprinting as fast as she could up toward the top of Diana Hill. Her powerful panther heart pounded in her chest. Her great lungs pumped like bellows. Her feet drove against the ground, pushing her and Braeden forward.

She could run fast, *very fast*, but she couldn't run as fast as those wicked creatures could fly.

Halfway up the hill, two of the giant, bat-winged gargoyles bore down on her and Braeden. Braeden clung to her back with one hand and tried to fight them off with the other, swiping and punching at them as they came in for their attacks.

One of the gargoyles seized her back leg with its talons, dragging her to the ground, pulling her down the steep slope of the hill. Another gargoyle grabbed her front leg.

She roared with pain as a third gargoyle landed on her back, piercing her spine with its claws and snapping at Braeden with its teeth. Braeden kicked it in the snout and pushed the snarling, snapping creature back, but it lunged forward and closed its jaws around his shoulder, Braeden screaming in agony.

Serafina swiped her claws at one of the gargoyles, tearing it away with a powerful, roaring blow, but two more came in its place, biting her leg. She struggled to keep going, fought to keep pushing her way up the hill, but there were too many of them. She crashed to the ground under their weight. She tried to stumble forward, to press on, to keep running, but more and more of the winged beasts landed upon her.

52

A gunshot rang out. A splash of blood splattered across Serafina's shoulders and head. She sucked in a startled breath and craned her neck to look behind her, thinking Braeden had been struck, but he was still clinging to her back, his eyes white with astonishment as he wiped the blood from his face. The gargoyle that had been clutching his shoulder fell dead.

Another shot rang out. The creature holding Serafina's front leg slumped to the ground. She looked back toward the house and saw the flash of a third shot coming from the roof.

Someone was shooting at them.

But this third shot hit the gargoyle that was clamped on to her back leg.

Whoever was shooting wasn't shooting *at* them, but at the creatures all *around* them.

"It's Jess!" Braeden shouted in excitement.

The girl whose father thought she always missed wasn't missing anymore. She was hitting exactly what she wanted to hit.

Jess had taken a position high atop the front tower, looking out across the open grass of the Esplanade. And now she was firing shot after shot, bringing down gargoyle after gargoyle.

Another shot ripped past Serafina and thudded into the gargoyle charging toward her, toppling it to the ground.

Realizing that Jess was doing everything she could to give her and Braeden the chance they needed to escape, Serafina growled with new determination. She sloughed the dead gargoyle from her back, shook the dead gargoyles from her legs, and dragged herself to her feet.

"We can do it, Serafina!" Braeden shouted as he hunkered down on her back to prepare for her leap.

She took one last look at the horde of gargoyles coming behind them, and then, with all her power, ran forward and lunged into the woods.

As she hit the speed of her stride, she heard the shots behind her, knocking down one attacker after another. A running gargoyle charged up beside her. But just as it opened its fanged maw to bite her and drag her down, a bullet sent it rolling across the ground, falling dead in her wake.

As she ran deeper into the forest, the gargoyles, and the

sound of Jess's shots, fell long behind her. But she kept running.

When she finally slowed down enough to listen, she heard the sound of the white deer's hooves treading across the ground in the distance.

Perfect, Serafina thought.

But there were other sounds behind her, too, the footfalls of large cats, but with a pounding forcefulness rather than the soft grace of real cats.

What vile creatures have come to life now? she wondered.

She traveled down into a low river valley, then scrambled under the trunks of wind-toppled trees and through a bog of chokeberry and fetterbush.

She soon found herself wading through the green, swirling water of a swamp. Moss hung down from the craggy limbs of the tupelo trees, and thick coats of lichen grew on the ragged trunks of the old cedars. As she waded through a lagoon that was open to the glistening blackness of the night sky above them, thousands of stars were reflecting on the flat surface of the water.

Glancing back over her shoulder, she saw that Braeden's face and body were scratched, bruised, and bleeding, his clothes stained and torn. He was as wet and bedraggled as a storm-drenched dog, droplets of gargoyle blood and swamp water scattered across his forehead. His arms and legs were shaking with fatigue. And she felt it, too. After the long stretch of running and fighting, her lungs ached and her muscles were giving out.

The only way out is through, she thought.

And as she pushed onward, it seemed as if the ground was finally sloping up toward the high ground. They crossed through an area of dense thicket and undergrowth. And then saw what she had come for.

Hundreds of weathered gravestones reached into the distance, their cracked, gray shapes overgrown with vines, many of them tilting or sunken down into the earth.

"Why here?" Braeden asked, his voice filled with trepidation as he climbed from her back. "Why the cemetery?"

She shifted into human form and stood beside him.

"We need to get to the Angel's Glade," she said. "It's not much farther."

She turned and looked behind them, back toward the swamp they'd just come through. They had traveled miles from Biltmore.

As she tilted her head, closed her eyes, and listened out into the darkness, Kinsley's eerie words drifted through her mind. *It started following us. It's not going to give up!*

And sure enough, she heard the faint sounds of four spindly little legs slowly swishing through the water toward them.

"It's still behind us," Serafina whispered to Braeden.

"Then we've got to get out of here," he said, peering through the vegetation for an escape, but she grabbed his arm.

"No, we've got to go deeper into the graveyard," she said, remembering her pa's words to have faith in herself and what she knew to be true. "We've got to get to the Angel's Glade."

But at that moment, the white deer emerged from the foliage.

She was expecting some sort of mythical, cat-footed animal to be with the white deer, maybe even two of them. But something else entirely arrived.

As she looked up at it, her first, split-second thought was, *So that's what landed on the rooftop and crashed the chandelier.*

And then she grabbed Braeden by the shoulders and threw him to the ground as the large, flying, dragon-like creature burst out of the upper trees and bore down on them with daggerlike claws.

The scaly beast had a long, chomping snout, two powerful hind legs, and large bat wings.

The corrupted magic of the Seven Stars had brought to life a *wyvern.*

The talons of the wyvern crashed down through the cover of the brush above them, tearing through the vegetation and knocking her and Braeden to the ground.

They scrambled frantically out of reach of the talons, the beast's claws ripping through the ground like plows and pulling up the roots of the trees.

"Run, Braeden!" she screamed as she rose to her feet and pulled him with her. "Into the graveyard!"

With a leap into the sky, and great, billowing flaps of its wings, the wyvern went airborne again, screeching as it pivoted in midair and came sweeping in low to the ground in pursuit of them. It was a fast and agile flyer, but the thickness of the forest helped them. Serafina leapt behind a large tree just as the wyvern's talons came slashing through the branches above. She thought she had escaped the attack, but the wyvern wheeled around with a mighty burst of its wings, and then its claws clenched right into her shoulder with a lightning bolt of piercing pain. The force of the blow lifted her off the ground. Screaming, she reached out and grabbed at the branch of a tree, yanked herself out of the wyvern's talons, and tumbled hard to the ground.

Her ribs reverberated with splintering pain as she crawled rapidly across the ground. *Stay low, stay low,* she thought as she scurried beneath a thicket of underbrush like a little weasel escaping the talons of a great horned owl. But where was Braeden?

As the wyvern circled overhead, Serafina hunkered down against the trunk of a gnarled old tree, caught her breath, and scanned the forest for him.

"I'm here!" Braeden said as he came crawling on his belly through the wet leaves toward her. Her heart surged with hope.

She thought they'd get a few seconds to figure out what to do, but then she heard something coming toward them through the underbrush. It was the sound of cat paws, moving fast and strong.

Two vile beasts emerged from the brush. They had the lower bodies of lions, but the upper bodies and heads of human women. They were the sphinxes that had adorned Biltmore's gate. These once beautiful feline sculptures had been transformed into vicious creatures with clawing feet and gnashing teeth.

The sphinxes crouched low and sinister, looking more like rabid hyenas than either lions or humans, growling and snapping, saliva dripping from their mouths.

The sphinxes lunged toward her and Braeden. She dodged the attack and sprang behind the trunk of a tree, but one of them got hold of Braeden and pulled him to the ground, biting at his throat as he grappled against it. Serafina leapt at the sphinx and knocked it away from him, but it immediately turned on her. Braeden picked up a large branch and slammed it into the sphinx.

And at that moment, the wyvern came crashing through the canopy of the forest and landed immediately in front of them, its great maw roaring as it drove toward them.

"I've got an idea," Braeden shouted as they scrambled away from the massive beast. He tilted up his head and made the strangest sound she'd ever heard a human make, a loud, croaking call up into the night sky. "Now go!" he shouted at her. "Run for it! Get to the Angel's Glade!" And then he sprang to his feet and charged straight at the wyvern.

"What are you doing? Braeden, no!" she screamed.

Suddenly thousands of flying black shapes came out of nowhere, seeming as if they were exploding from the trees themselves.

It looked like Braeden was intending to somehow battle the wyvern head-on. Surrounded by the black shapes that he'd called from the forest, he ran straight at it.

But with a great swoop of its wings, the flying beast leapt upward, and clutched him in its talons.

He screamed as the massive claws clenched around his body.

In a desperate panic, Serafina rushed forward to help him, but the wyvern flew upward and pulled him out of her reach.

"Braeden!" she screamed, her whole body filling with anguish.

The creature had grasped him in its claws and there was nothing she could do. It lifted his bleeding body up into the sky, Braeden screaming in pain, his arms and legs flailing.

The last she saw of him he was rising higher and higher away from her, dangling in the talons of the wyvern, until he disappeared into the darkness above the canopy of the forest.

54

"Braeden!" she screamed again, her throat straining with lacerating pain.

She tried to hold on to hope that he had somehow survived the attack of the wyvern and would call out to her.

But there was no reply.

Braeden was gone.

Her entire body throbbed with the ache of it. Her heart was shuddering in her chest.

How could she let this happen? Why did he run at the wyvern like that?

She could feel the sobs welling up inside her, ready to burst out. But there was no time to think or feel. The two growling sphinxes were moving toward her, forcing their way through the underbrush, and a thick horde of running, crawling, flying gargoyles were pouring through the forest straight at her.

She had to fight them. But she couldn't fight them.

She had to go after Braeden. But she couldn't go after him.

Her pa's advice came into her mind: What was the most important thing? What was the one thing she *must* do? She had to *run*, run for the Angel's Glade, and there she would confront the white deer in the only way she had left.

She turned and sprinted up the hill. She ran past grave after grave, darting between the broken headstones and tilting crosses.

When she finally looked behind her, the white deer was there, right with her, coming toward the Angel's Glade.

I hope this is gonna work, she thought as she scurried behind the pedestal of the stone angel.

The white deer moved toward her with unnerving speed, scuttling more like a scorpion than a deer. Every sphinx and gargoyle attacked. And every gravestone ripped out of the earth and flew at her.

A great, swirling maelstrom of wind and debris and flying gravestones rose up from the ground.

Serafina hunkered behind the pedestal, bracing herself for the barrage. But the first gargoyle flew past her. The second—a six-legged beast with no wings—ran straight at her, but then broke off to the side. The gravestones hurtling through the air tumbled to the ground behind her.

Not a blade of the perfect green grass was disturbed in the circle of the Angel's Glade.

All the sphinxes, gargoyles, and monstrous beasts converged

on her and attacked her. Hundreds of gravestones plunged through the air at her in a storm of violence. But she clung to the pedestal of the angel, unharmed by the attacks.

And yet she knew she could not stay in the glade for long. She was surrounded and there was no way out. She could not fight. She could not defeat her enemy.

The white deer, the sphinxes, and the gargoyles stood just outside the perimeter of the Angel's Glade staring straight at her. She knew they had probably already killed Braeden. And now they were going to kill her. They would not stop until they did.

"Come on!" Serafina screamed at the white deer and the other beasts. "You killed the hunters! You attacked Kinsley! Come on! Do it! Do it now!"

The white deer just stared at her with those malevolent black eyes.

You need to kill me, Serafina thought. *And I've left you only one way to do it.*

"Come on!" she screamed, spitting out the words. Then she picked up a fist-size rock and threw it at the deer, striking it in the side. *Violence brings violence.* "Come on!"

Finally, the white deer turned to the statue of the angel standing on the pedestal in the center of the glade.

That's it, do it, Serafina thought. *Do it!*

The stone angel began to move, coming alive just as the others had.

The white deer pivoted its head and looked directly at Serafina.

Despite all that Serafina had done to get to this exact moment, her chest seized in fear and her breathing stopped.

But the angel did not immediately attack. She gazed around her at the forest-choked graveyard and the storm of violence surrounding the glade. She gazed at the white deer, and the maelstrom of flying gravestones and attacking gargoyles. And then, finally, the angel tilted her head down and gazed at Serafina crouched at the base of the pedestal.

Serafina had looked up at this angel of stone so many times, had spoken to her, cried to her, and never once had the angel moved or made a sound. But now the living, flesh-and-blood angel was looking right at her, her eyes as alive as any human's eyes, as green as the moss that had once grown on her shoulders, and as powerful as any woman who had ever lived.

And Serafina saw in those eyes one thing: *understanding*. No one had ever looked at her and comprehended her more fully than in that moment. Everything she was now, everything she had ever been, and everything she wanted to be. The angel understood.

And then the angel looked at the white deer standing at the edge of the glade.

Unlike the inert, lifeless stone of Biltmore's statues, the angel in the glade was filled with a deep and powerful spirit all her own.

The white deer stared at the angel with those terrible, mesmerizing black eyes, as if trying to drive the angel with its will, trying to force her to attack.

But the angel did not bend to its will.

And the angel did not look away.

The angel raised the fullness of her great gray feathered wings up above her shoulders and her head, and she held them there, trembling, on the cusp of unimaginable transformation.

Serafina cowered behind the pedestal and covered her face with her arm as she peered out.

And then the angel brought her wings down.

The angel's wings came together in one blazing, swooping motion that sounded like a thunderstorm tearing the length of the sky. Her wings threw a hurricane of wind that snapped the trunks of the surrounding trees. Dirt and rocks flew from the earth. The gargoyles and sphinxes were thrown tumbling away, and the white deer was buffeted back.

The angel rose up, hovering above her pedestal, roaring with fury, her power engulfing everything around them.

Serafina clung to the base of the pedestal. She tried to suck in a breath, but there was no air to breathe, just wilding wind and clamorous noise.

As the white deer struggled to keep its footing against the terrific forces bashing against it, it used its powers to hurl massive rocks and gravestones at the angel, but the angel deflected them with gestures of her hand. And in her other hand, she held her long, straight, sharply pointed sword.

Still hovering, the angel glided forward through the air, then came slowly down to the grass of the glade and walked toward the white deer.

The white deer hurled rock after rock at her, and then entire gravestones and monuments, but it meant nothing to the angel.

The angel lifted her wings above her head once more, and stepped closer to the white deer.

With a deafening shout, the angel swung her sword, low to the ground and then upward toward the sky, in a great sweeping motion.

Serafina watched in amazement. The sword didn't cut through the white deer. Its tip sliced open the earth and sky, as if rending a seam in the fabric of the universe. The blade tore through space and time, creating a gaping split of blackness filled with nothing but stars.

For a fleeting moment, as if all time had come together in a great, swirling torrent, Serafina glimpsed the white deer as it had been the first time she saw it, a luminous magical creature springing through the forest.

And then the white deer and all the creatures around it exploded into bursts of blazing pieces. The painful blast of heat singed Serafina's skin, and the bright light burned her eyes.

With a great thunder crack of sound, the blinding rush of a meteor storm flew up into the sky, hundreds of fragments searing the air around her, ripping and smoking as they hurtled upward toward the Seven Stars.

55

The white deer was gone.

The fury of wind had stopped and the world had become still.

The snarling sphinxes and gargoyles had turned to stone where they stood.

And the screeching wyvern had gone silent and fallen from the sky.

All that remained of the battle in the Angel's Glade was the drifting, acrid smell of what Serafina thought must be the remnants of burning stars.

Her skin was still tingling, and her body still shaking, as she peeked slowly out from behind the pedestal.

The angel was walking toward her, calm and peaceful now.

She was tall, with long striding legs that moved in a fluid, graceful motion, and flowing silvery hair that seemed to be filled with light. Her gray feathered wings rose up from her shoulders like the wings of a swan. She was the most beautiful being Serafina had ever beheld.

When the angel stopped in front of her, Serafina could barely breathe.

The angel smiled, took Serafina's head gently into her hands, and kissed her forehead with a long, tender kiss that felt like the touch of a warm breeze against her skin. In this touch, in this moment, she felt a sense of acceptance more powerful than she had ever felt before, as if everything she had ever done right, everything she had ever done wrong, everything *she was*, was *perfect*. In this moment, she felt all that it meant to be loved.

For several seconds, Serafina was so overwhelmed by everything that had happened, and so stunned that the angel had actually looked at her and touched her, she could not move.

Finally, she gathered up her courage and, still trembling, rose to her feet and turned toward the angel. *Who are you?* she was about to ask. *What is your name? Why have you helped me?*

But the pedestal was empty.

The angel was gone.

I *need to find Braeden . . .*

She turned in the direction she'd seen the wyvern go down. *Was it possible that he had survived?*

She headed out into the forest to look for him, but immediately ran headlong into an obstacle. The ancient willow tree at the edge of the glade, which had once been the den of her mother, brother, and sister, had toppled to the ground, its trunk and branches a crisscross of broken destruction. She pushed into the fallen tree and clambered through its branches.

When she reached the other side, she got back onto her feet and tried to run, darting between the scattered, broken gravestones and the statues of gargoyles, but her feet sloshed through the inches of swamp water seeping out of the ground all around her. The gravestones and the trees and the fallen statues were sinking into the earth, the swamp engulfing everything, as if it had been only the Angel's Glade that had prevented it from doing so long before.

She climbed up and over the massive root ball of a fallen oak tree, and came down into two feet of green water.

Pushing through the swamp, she passed the stone bodies of the two sphinxes, with only their heads above the water now.

Her chest tightened as she gazed out at the dark and murky devastation of the flooding graveyard.

"Braeden!" she shouted desperately. "Braeden, can you hear me?"

She sloshed through the water in one direction and then the next, frantically looking for him. She could feel the heat of despair rising in her face. She had no idea which way to go. But she had to find him!

Frustrated, she stood in the waist-deep water and scanned in all directions, looking out across the drowning forest, trying to figure out what to do.

In the distance, she saw a single black shape circling above the canopy of the trees.

At first she thought it was the wyvern, flying way up in the sky, but then she realized that the wyvern had turned to stone and fallen.

Is it some kind of bird?

Still not sure, she moved toward it, her feet dragging and tripping on the rocks and branches beneath the water's surface.

Then she saw another dark shape similar to the first, and she began to make out the flapping of wings.

They definitely looked like birds, and they were circling.

It's the crows! she thought, pushing harder in that direction. *Braeden's crows!*

As she came closer to the spot over which the crows were circling, several other crows rose up from a branch and started flying around her. Soon there were dozens of crows, and then hundreds. The crows were everywhere, cawing raucously.

At first it seemed as if they were attacking her, but then she realized they were urging her on, guiding her where they wanted her to go.

She gasped in dismay when she spotted a pale white shriveled hand sticking up out of the swamp water.

57

Serafina shoved herself through the muck of the swamp. She could see the white limbs of Braeden's body down in the murky water, trapped under the large stone pieces of the broken wyvern. But one of his arms was sticking straight up out of the swamp, like he was raising his hand in class, as if he'd been trying to make sure she saw him there. It was as if he knew she would be coming for him. His other arm was under the surface, clinging desperately to a half-submerged toppled tree. And there, pressed against the trunk, was his head, his mouth just inches above the water.

"Braeden!" she shouted, lurching toward him and grasping his upraised hand.

His eyes opened suddenly. "You found me!" he said in relief. "I'm stuck, I can't get out!"

She reached under the water, grabbed on to him, and tried to pull him forcefully to his feet, but it was no use. A part of one of the wyvern's stone talons still gripped his leg, holding his lower body down into the water.

"The water level's rising fast," he said.

"Hold on," she said, as she looked hurriedly around for ideas. She needed some sort of leverage.

Then she spotted something gray sticking up out of the water nearby. She thought at first it was a gravestone. But it was actually a piece of the wyvern's stone wing. It wouldn't work as a pry bar, but she had another idea.

She gripped it in both hands and tried to lift it, but it was far heavier than she expected and it nearly pulled her off her feet.

Filled with anger now, she grabbed it again. With a heavy grunt, she raised it above her head. Her whole body tilted under the weight of it, leaning one way and then the other as she stumbled and splashed through the waist-deep water.

"Watch out, Braeden!" she yelled as she came barreling toward him.

"But I can't get out of the way!" he shouted up in panic as the stone came slamming down from above her head and smashed into the wyvern's talon, cracking it to pieces.

"You did it!" Braeden said, yanking his leg free.

Mighty relieved that she hadn't killed him, she pulled him to his feet. "Come on, we've got to get out of here."

"I couldn't agree with you more," he said, and they set off at a steady push. They waded through the swamp together, Braeden sometimes reaching out a hand to help her over the trunk of a fallen tree, other times Serafina leading the way through a particularly nasty thicket of bramble.

As they put the swamp behind them, Serafina glanced back over her shoulder. It was hard to believe, after all the time that she and Braeden and her feline kin had spent there, but the Angel's Glade and the old, abandoned graveyard that surrounded it had been destroyed.

"That was a good idea to use your crows to signal me," she said. "I would have never found you in time on my own."

"Some people send up rescue flares, I send up crows," he said, smiling. "They don't normally fly at night, but it was kind of them to help us."

Once they found their way out of the swamp, they traveled for several miles through the forest, back toward Biltmore.

When it was clear that they had left the battle well behind them, they rested for a few moments, climbing together into the shadowed hollow of an old tree that had been struck by lightning years before.

The space inside the tree was cramped, and the night air cold, so they huddled together, wrapping their arms around each other without saying a word.

They had meant to rest for just a moment to catch their breath, but once they were in the warmth of each other's arms, they stayed in the hollow of the tree for a long time, just holding each other.

Her heart stopped pounding so hard in her chest. Her body stopped shaking from the cold.

Braeden's panting breaths slowly quieted and his head tilted down, gently touching hers.

They had finally escaped.

Huddled there in the darkness, they did not move. They did not speak.

She could feel the pulse of her blood moving gently through her veins, her chest slowly pulling air into her lungs.

For a few moments, she simply *existed*, grateful to be alive.

58

Finally, Serafina said, "We'd better get on home."

"Yeah," Braeden said softly, and they reluctantly disentangled themselves from each other and crawled out of the tree.

As they headed home, she could sense that, like hers, Braeden's thoughts were turning to what lay ahead.

"What do you think happened at Biltmore after we left?" he asked.

"I don't know," she said, thinking about her pa and everyone else back at home.

As she and Braeden continued on their way through the forest, she asked, "Why did you run toward the wyvern like that?"

"The wyvern was preventing you from getting to the Angel's Glade."

"So you threw yourself into its talons?"

"I didn't throw myself!" he protested with a laugh. "I charged at the wyvern and tried to fight it, but it grabbed me! I didn't do it on purpose."

"What happened after it got you?"

"As it was flying, I kept fighting and kicking, trying to grab branches in the trees to hold myself closer to the ground. I knew I couldn't let it take me up too high or I was done for, so I called the crows. There wasn't much they could do against the wyvern, but they mobbed it and harassed it like it was a giant hawk in their territory. Crows don't like hawks. We weren't winning the fight, that's for sure, but at least we were distracting it and keeping it close to the ground."

"You were *distracting* it?" she said incredulously, remembering how her heart had lurched when she saw him dangling from its talons fifty feet in the air. "That was your plan, to throw yourself at the wyvern and distract it?"

"You make it sound like I tried to sacrifice myself in some sort of heroic, last-stand suicide attack or something."

"It looked an awful lot like a heroic, last-stand suicide attack to me," she said with a smile.

"Well, I think it was more of a flailing, screaming, hanging-upside-down sort of thing," he argued.

"But what were you thinking, doing something like that?"

"I told you, I wanted to give you time to get to the Angel's Glade."

"But you didn't even know why I wanted to get there," she said.

He walked on through the forest without saying anything for a few moments, as if her questions had stumped him a little bit, and then he said, "I knew you must have had some sort of plan."

"You *knew*," she repeated as she walked beside him, wondering about that word.

"I was right, wasn't I?" he said.

"Yeah," she said with a smile. "You were right."

"So what about you? How did you know the statue of the angel would do what it did?"

She wasn't sure she could give him an adequate answer, but she tried to explain it the best she could.

"From the books in the Library, we learned that people long ago thought that the magic of the Seven Stars had the ability to slip through the veil between the physical and the magical world, and that it had the power to bring spirit to that which did not have spirit."

"Like the statues at Biltmore," Braeden said.

"And that's the key. Unlike the statues at Biltmore, the angel in the glade already had a spirit."

Braeden took a few more steps, and then said, "So when the magic of the Seven Stars awoke the angel, it couldn't control her. . . ."

"That's right. The angel was far more powerful."

"But I don't understand. How did you know the angel had a spirit? How did you know she wasn't just plain old stone like all the other statues? Was that from a book, too?"

Serafina just kept walking.

Serafina and Braeden crept slowly out of the woods at the top of Diana Hill, near where the goddess of the hunt statue had been, the very place Serafina had been standing days before when the thirteen carriages arrived. She remembered she had been looking desperately for an evil intruder among those new arrivals. It never even occurred to her that the passengers of the carriages would be the *victims*.

She didn't know why the deer standing beside Diana had been the first of the statues to come to life. She had learned so much about what had happened, but there were so many things about the magic of the Seven Stars that she still didn't understand, and probably never would. She had come to realize that there would always be more mysteries. And there would always be more to learn.

"Was the white deer . . ." Braeden began to ask as he stared at the empty spot where the statue had been. "What would have happened if the hunters had never shot it that first night? Or if we hadn't tried to fight it? Was the white deer good or evil?"

She thought about it for several seconds.

Obviously, the white deer was evil: It had been killing people. So it had to be stopped.

She and the people of Biltmore were good. So *it* was evil. Right?

But the more she thought about it, the more she realized it wasn't that simple.

"I don't know," she admitted finally.

"I think maybe it was like the stories said, some kind of reflection of our world in the moment it came. And it splintered and bounced in all different directions, like light in a jewel."

"Or light on the water of a lake," she said.

"Right," he said.

"And there was something else, too," Serafina said. "The way it attacked mainly the hunters at first. That made sense to me. And even the spiraling out of control when we started trying to defend ourselves, when Kinsley was attacked and the others. But it took me a little longer to understand the rest of it."

"What do you mean?" he asked. "What rest of it?"

"When we confronted the deer in the Tapestry Gallery, did

316

you see the way it snorted at us and shook its antlers? It seemed so angry, so fierce, like it wanted to kill us."

"Yeah, I saw that all too close."

"But why did it do that? On that first night when we were down by the lake, the hunters didn't shoot the white deer out of anger. They shot it for sport, for the trophy of killing an unusual animal. Not out of rage or hatred. So, if it was reflection, where did the anger and fierceness come from, that drive for vengeance?"

"You're right," he said. "I never thought about it like that."

Serafina remembered that night by the lake, seeing the beautiful fawn and then hearing the gunshots. She remembered the way she had turned on those hunters, charging at them, her fangs snarling, her claws slashing.

"I think . . . I think maybe it came from me," she said, trying to absorb the meaning of what she was saying even as she was saying it. "A reflection of our world in that moment."

Braeden looked like he was about to open his mouth to argue with her. But then he paused and looked away, maybe beginning to realize that it was possible she was right.

"I don't know if that's what it was," he said finally.

"I don't, either," she admitted, and it was the truth, but it made her wonder.

It *all* made her wonder.

A s she and Braeden stood near the empty pedestal, she turned and gazed out across the expanse of the Esplanade toward the house. But instead of being a wide, flat open area of grass, the Esplanade was strewn with hundreds of stone statues—fallen gargoyles, slain ogres, and savage beasts of all descriptions.

The walls of Biltmore Estate looked as if they had been decayed by time, as if bits had fallen off and parts were missing—all the empty spots where the carven ornamentation had been.

It gave the house a gray, weathered look, and she imagined it was dead.

She had hoped to see people gathered outside, or perhaps in the windows or on the terraces, but there was no one there.

Her eyes darted from one area to the next, but she didn't see a single person.

Serafina knew that she and Braeden had been gone from Biltmore for far too long. They had to get home.

"Let's go down," Braeden said gravely, both of them sensing what awaited wasn't going to be good.

He led the way through the field of statues toward the house. She and Braeden moved quickly but warily, half expecting one of the statues to come back to life.

When they reached the front of the house, the doors were hanging wide open, broken off their hinges and tilting to the side. She was expecting to see a footman or someone else guarding the entrance, but no one was there. The house was eerily quiet and still.

"Let's go inside," Braeden said, sounding as nervous and uncertain as she was.

The stained-glass windows had been crushed in. The tall wrought-iron lamps had toppled and their glass globes broken. The magnificent grandfather clock had been knocked to the floor, its oak sides split, its springs sprung, and its gears in pieces. Vases that once held whimsical arrangements of flowers had crashed down and shattered across the floor. The carcass of the winged lion, now solid stone, lay among many other stone creatures.

Serafina swallowed hard and kept walking, Braeden quiet at her side.

As they made their way through the Tapestry Gallery, she could see that much of the furniture had been shredded by the claws of the gargoyles. Many of the Flemish tapestries had been burned or torn down and lay crumpled on the floor. But worst of all, the dead body of her friend, the footman Mr. Pratt, lay on the ground where he had been killed.

Serafina tried to keep breathing, tried to keep standing, but the sight of it was almost too much to bear.

As Braeden reached out and held her arm, he said, "We need to find my aunt and uncle. . . ."

"And my pa . . ." she said, her voice trembling.

As they went into the Library, they saw that it, too, had been severely damaged, but like the other rooms, it was empty of living souls.

"Where is everyone?" Braeden asked. "Did they all get away?"

"If they did, they should have been back by now."

"Let's try the other end of the house," he said unsteadily.

Staying close to each other, they walked back toward the Main Hall. They checked the Winter Garden, the Billiard Room, the Banquet Hall, the Gun Room, the Salon, the Breakfast Room, the Butler's Pantry, and all the other rooms on the first floor.

Normally filled with bustling maids, hurrying footmen, relaxing guests, and countless other people going about their business, it was so eerily peculiar to find it so quiet.

"In all the time I've been at Biltmore, I've never seen it empty before," Braeden said in a daze.

"Come on, let's check upstairs," she said. "There's got to be someone."

They moved quickly now, checking room after room, and they started calling out. "Hello, is anyone here?"

"Mr. Vanderbilt, are you here?" Serafina shouted, but her voice just echoed across the hard marble floors and limestone walls.

"What about the dogs?" Braeden said. "Gidean!" he shouted. "Come on, boy! Gidean!"

"Cedric!" Serafina shouted.

But no dogs came to their call.

"What about the stables?" Braeden asked.

They ran upstairs, out through the Porte Cochere, through the stable courtyard, and into the stable itself. The normally perfectly pristine brick floors were cracked in multiple places and scattered with hay, horse dung, and hurriedly discarded equipment. The cream porcelain-tile walls were scuffed with marks.

"It looks like there was a battle here, too," Braeden said gravely.

But what truly shocked her was that the sounds of their movement and their words echoed in the emptiness of the place.

Every coach, carriage, and cart was gone, and all the horse stalls were empty. Every last harness horse, sport horse, trail horse, draft horse, and pony had been taken.

Serafina heard a sound just ahead, a faint shuffling noise.

"Wait," Serafina said, touching Braeden's arm to keep him still. "Listen. . . ."

When she heard the shuffling again, she moved toward it.

"Be careful," Braeden whispered.

She stepped into the dark stall that it was coming from.

But as she moved through the darkness, she heard a single plaintive, desperate *meow*.

She found Smoke curled up in the hay in the back corner of the stall.

"It's all right, Smoke, I've got ya now," she said as she lifted the frightened gray cat into her arms.

"At least somebody's here," Braeden said in relief, and then a thought seemed to occur to him, and he said, "I'm going to check out back."

Serafina set Smoke down and followed Braeden to the rear of the stable, and then into the dry lot behind it.

There was a paddock there, with a single powerful black thoroughbred inside it.

The horse neighed when it saw them.

"It's good to see you, my friend," Braeden said happily as he walked toward his old companion.

Someone had left them a horse.

Braeden walked toward the horse and, in one quick, graceful motion, swung up onto its back.

"Come on," he said, extending his hand to her.

Serafina's eyes widened in surprise. Braeden knew full well that she had never ridden one of the great hoof-stompers, and he knew full well that she had always been frightened of them, but here he was offering his hand to her.

She hesitated a little, but then, feeling a rush of excitement, she grasped his hand and leapt up behind him. As she wrapped her arms around his torso, the horse lunged forward with startling speed.

"My uncle would never leave us behind, and neither would your pa," he shouted over the clattering of the horse's hooves as they crossed through the courtyard. "Now hang on!"

With the slightest nudge of Braeden's legs, the horse seemed to know exactly what he wanted and burst into a gallop. Serafina felt the push of the movement against her body, and the undulation of the horse's gait as it ran. She clung to Braeden, her hair whipping behind her, the wind brushing her cheeks as they sped across the fields.

The clear Southern sky glowed blue over the mountains as they rode, and the orange blaze of the rising sun began to come into view. More and more, she could feel the warmth of its rays on her cheeks.

She remembered the previous year, before she had become known to the Vanderbilts, watching the young master running across these fields on his horse. She remembered longing for a friend, someone to talk to, someone she could count on. And here she was, running across the very same fields with him.

"There!" Braeden shouted and pointed.

Way across the open land, on a distant hilltop, Serafina saw a mounted search party. It was a group of men on horseback, with the lean black shape of Gidean and the brown-and-white Cedric running with them. She could make out Mr. Vanderbilt and several other men. She even spotted Nolan, the young stable boy. And there, in the brightness of the sun, was Jess Braddick on a new horse, with her rifle in her hand. It brought Serafina such relief to see them all, to see them safe and fighting strong.

Then she spotted the figure of one more man, riding one of the estate's large, sorrel-coated Belgian draft horses. He was a stout and heavy man, more used to stomping through the machine rooms of the basement in his thick boots than sitting in a saddle atop a horse in the sunlight, but there he was.

Tears welled up in her eyes. After all that had happened, after all she had done, and after all he had seen, she was still his daughter. And he had come out in search of her.

61

In the days that followed, there were solemn funerals for Mr. Pratt, who had been killed by the doppelgänger, Mr. Doddman, who had been struck by one of Diana's deadly arrows, and for all the others who had passed away.

She had heard that Lieutenant Kinsley was recovering well at the hospital in Asheville, and she was looking forward to his return to Biltmore.

I'll see you at dinner, he had said, and she was going to make sure he kept that promise.

Over time, most of the servants who had escaped the attack returned to Biltmore, and the effort to clean up and restore the estate began, everyone working in their own way to bring life back to normal again.

Mrs. Vanderbilt returned with Baby Nell, and several additional members of her and her husband's family came down from New York for an extended visit. The autumn shooting had passed, but a few new guests began to arrive—a famous painter who hoped to capture the beauty of the Southern mountains, a naturalist who was studying species of trees, and a writer who needed a quiet place to work on his novel.

Colonel Braddick, Jess's father and her last living relative, had been killed at the estate, so with Mr. Vanderbilt's permission, Jess remained at Biltmore while the authorities determined what should become of her. There was talk of sending her to the orphanage in Asheville, or to an institution in the North. There was even talk that she might return to Africa, where she had spent much of her life. No one was quite sure where she should go. Serafina, for her part, just wanted her new friend to find a home.

Almost immediately after the patterns of life began to return to normal, Mr. Vanderbilt organized the destruction of the statues littering the Esplanade, and commissioned new sculptors, stonemasons, and craftsmen to come to Biltmore and restore the estate to its previous artistic glory. He replaced the Joan of Arc statue, the Saint Louis statue, the lions near the front doors, and many of his other favorites. But he did not replace the wyvern, the winged lion, the bronze statue of himself, or the nastiest of the gargoyles, saying, "I'm drawn to a friendlier sort of company these days."

But now, for reasons that Mr. Vanderbilt never spoke of, he had the new Diana statue made with a trusty dog at her side instead of a white deer. And although the new Diana did have a quiver of arrows on her back, she no longer held a bow in her hand with which to shoot them.

Serafina, for her part, began to settle in to her new life at Biltmore, enjoying the gentle routine of both the day and the night. She often ran through the forest with her brother and sister like she had before, leaping mountain streams and racing through the meadows. And she enjoyed her time in the house as well.

She had always loved her pa, and her pa had always loved her, but her pa knew her now in ways that he had never known her before—in all her forms—and it brought a great joy to her heart.

Jess, her comrade-in-arms during the battle against the Seven Stars, knew of her abilities as well. But Essie, Mr. and Mrs. Vanderbilt, and the other residents of the house thought of her as just a girl, and that was fine by her.

Late at night, she would often lie in her panther form on the balcony outside the nursery, her black silhouette nearly invisible in the darkness and her yellow eyes watching over the grounds. Sometimes, when no one else was around, she would play with little Baby Nell. She never told anyone, but Serafina was pretty sure that Cornelia's first word was *kitty*.

One afternoon, Serafina began pacing in her bedroom on the second floor, jumpy as an anxious cat. Essie had helped her wash her hair and laced her into the new dress that Mrs. Vanderbilt had given her. But Serafina still didn't feel ready.

"Don't fret, he'll be here soon," Essie said encouragingly, but Serafina wasn't so sure. She just kept pacing. Even Smoke meowed to her from his spot on the windowsill, wondering what had gotten into her.

Finally, there was a light rapping at the door.

"I told you, didn't I," Essie said happily. "Now you stay right there like a proper lady, and I'll get the door for you."

Essie opened the door, quickly bowed, and invited Braeden into the room. He was smartly dressed in one of his light brown jackets, with a high white collar and matching kerchief in his pocket.

"I hope I'm not too early," he said cheerfully.

"You're right on time, Master Braeden," Essie said, leading him into the center of the room, where a number of soft, comfortable chairs encircled a low table. Essie had set up a formal English-style tea, complete with a white tablecloth, fine porcelain cups, white cloth napkins, silver spoons, and a pyramid of scones and tea cakes with clotted cream and an assortment of jams alongside.

"This looks good," Braeden said, and then, glancing at Essie playfully, he added, "Eh, the battle in the house was pretty frightening, wasn't it?"

Essie narrowed her eyes at him, as if she was pretty sure he was up to some kind of mischief.

"Did you see that big black panther? Amazing, wasn't it?"

"Braeden Vanderbilt!" Essie scolded him, quite happily, using his name to his face for the first time in her life. "You stop that right now!"

"Why, what are you talking about?" Braeden said with exaggerated innocence, but laughing all the while.

"I've brushed that lovely black hair enough times that I would recognize it just about anywhere, so don't think you're foolin' anyone with this silly talk, pretending that I don't know! I didn't just fall off the turnip truck!"

When Essie glanced at Serafina, she winked and smiled, and Serafina smiled in return, happy that her friend had surmised the truth.

"Believe me, Essie," Braeden said, holding up his hands in a gesture of abject surrender. "I know I'm not fooling anyone."

Finally, Braeden turned to Serafina.

"Hello, Braeden," Serafina said quietly, stepping forward, and feeling oddly flushed at the sight of him. She'd seen this boy battling black cloaks and white deer, climbing into the attics of Biltmore's highest towers, crawling through the mud of the vilest swamps, digging graves in the pouring rain, riding his horse through forest fires, dangling from the talons of wyverns, and all manner of other activities. But for some reason, *this* moment made her heart thump in her chest.

She and Braeden slowly, almost awkwardly, took their seats at the table and tried not to look at each other for too long as Essie poured the tea into their cups, serving them in the manner of a proper English-style afternoon tea, just as she would for Biltmore's finest of guests.

As Serafina sipped her tea, she could feel Smoke lying on her feet beneath the table. And Gidean, Braeden's dog, sat at his side.

A boy and his dog, and a girl and her cat, she thought, and smiled a little.

"What's so funny?" Braeden asked as he slipped several of his tea cakes to Gidean, who gobbled them down appreciatively.

Noticing this, Smoke gave a little chirp of a purr and gazed up at her, making it clear he wouldn't mind a dab of the clotted cream.

Slowly, as she and Braeden began to relax, she came to realize that they were actually enjoying a lovely and delightful afternoon—the so-called "peace and quiet" that she had once scorned. It was unlike any they had ever spent together.

But near the end of it, when Essie stepped out of the room for a moment, Braeden brought up a subject that immediately darkened the mood.

"My uncle said he wants to talk to me tonight about New York," he said glumly.

"He's going to send you back," she said, feeling her heart sink as she said it.

"Yeah," he said. "I think you're right."

She raised her eyes and looked at him across the tea table. "But if you have to go," she said, trying to stay strong and positive for her own sake as much as his, "please know that I understand. I know it's important. I know it more than ever now."

"What do you mean?" he asked.

"I am a fighter, a warrior, a catamount, a black panther . . . but the truth is, I didn't defeat this enemy with my teeth and claws. And when I think about it, I didn't defeat the Man in the Black Cloak that way, either."

"I don't follow what you're saying."

"Last year, we only figured out who the Man in the Black Cloak was because of the Russian words we learned in the Library, do you remember? We only managed to survive against the sorcerer Uriah because of what we learned of Biltmore's past. And we only figured out how to defeat the magic of the Seven Stars by what we read in your uncle's books. It took *knowledge* to solve these mysteries and defeat these enemies.

Not just bravery and determination, not just sharp claws and muscled limbs, but *knowledge*. That's what made the difference. If we're going to succeed in whatever we set out to do with our lives, we need to *learn*, Braeden, we need to learn everything we can. For me, as the Guardian of Biltmore, it will literally be the difference between life and death. And the same is true for you. You've got to learn all you can."

Braeden nodded solemnly, as if he knew what she was saying was right, but he didn't like what it meant for the two of them. And then he looked up at her. "Do you remember that story from the Bible where God asks Job if he can bind the chains of Pleiades or loose the cords of Orion?"

"I guess it means that sometimes there are just things outside our control," Serafina said.

"Right," he said, "sometimes there are. But in this case, I keep thinking that maybe we *can* bind the chains of Pleiades and loose the cords of Orion."

Serafina smiled, not sure what he was talking about, but liking the sound of it.

"I think I might have an idea," he said.

63

The following morning, Mr. Vanderbilt asked Serafina and Braeden to join him in the Observatory at the top of the house's front tower, which he sometimes used as his private office.

"Have a seat," he said in a serious tone to Braeden, gesturing toward the leather chairs in front of his desk. "We need to talk about your schooling."

Serafina glanced at Braeden, encouraging him to say what he had come to say.

"I don't wish to be disrespectful, Uncle," Braeden said, "but I would like to present an idea to you."

"And what is it about?" Mr. Vanderbilt said, clearly unwilling to be derailed from the matter at hand.

"Three years ago, when my family passed away in the fire . . . I became my father's only living descendant."

"Yes, that's true," Mr. Vanderbilt said.

"So that means that I may have certain resources. . . ."

"You have *significant* resources," Mr. Vanderbilt said. "I am the executor of your father's estate, and you are its sole living beneficiary. It's being held in a trust for you until you reach the age of majority."

"Until I'm eighteen."

"That's right. It's my job as executor to make sure that you are safe and taken care of until that time. And I have been doing my best to do that. Although, sometimes, it feels suspiciously like you and your young companion here are taking care of me rather than the other way around."

"When I was on the train going up to New York, I had an idea."

"From what I've heard, it was to leap off the train and buy a horse with the money I gave you for school," Mr. Vanderbilt said, rather sternly.

"Yes, that's true," Braeden admitted, stuttering a little. "But first, I was thinking about Baby Nell."

"What about her?" Mr. Vanderbilt said.

"I was wondering where she will go to school."

"She's six months old," Mr. Vanderbilt said bluntly, as if he sensed that a challenge was being laid out before him.

"I mean when she's six or seven years old, and it's time for her to go to school," Braeden said. "Are you going to send her to New York?"

Serafina felt her throat go dry. She could only imagine how Braeden must feel at this moment, confronting his uncle in this way.

"Aunt Edith started a school here in Asheville for the local girls to learn weaving and sewing skills so that they can get jobs and earn their own money," Braeden said. "And at the church you built in Biltmore Village, you started a school for all of the local children to attend."

Mr. Vanderbilt listened intently to Braeden's words, but did not speak.

"Your library is one of the largest collections of books in the country," Braeden continued. "And you yourself are considered one of the best-read men in all of America."

"What is your point exactly?" Mr. Vanderbilt said, cutting him short.

"I was just wondering if maybe we could start a school here," Braeden said.

"You mean a school for you," Mr. Vanderbilt said flatly, "so that you can stay at Biltmore. Is that what this is all about?"

"A school for me, yes. But also for Cornelia in a few years. And for Serafina. And for Jess Braddick as well. We need to ask Jess to stay at Biltmore, Uncle. We can't just send her away. She saved our lives. Doesn't she deserve the best schooling we can give her? And what about the children of the servants? We'll call the school Carolina School, or Asheville School, or Biltmore School, or whatever you want to call it. We'll spend the money in my trust to do it. You've been assigning me books to read from your library, and I like that. We could keep doing more of that. And you could teach us about art and ballet and opera. The men at the Biltmore Forestry School that you set up could teach us about the trees and the mountains. Serafina's pa could teach us about electricity and machines. And we could bring in tutors and teachers from all over the country. We could build a very good school, something we could be proud of."

When Braeden finally stopped talking, his uncle did not speak. He just looked at him. And then, after a long time, he asked, "When exactly did you come up with all of this?"

"When I crossed the border into Tennessee."

"Why did Tennessee make you think of creating a school?"

"Because Vanderbilt University is in Tennessee," Braeden said.

Mr. Vanderbilt smiled, as if he was beginning to realize the extent to which his nephew had thought this through.

"Vanderbilt University is one of the most respected universities in the country," Mr. Vanderbilt said.

"And your grandfather founded it," Braeden said.

Mr. Vanderbilt nodded and smiled again, like a man who knows he's being checkmated, but isn't quite sure if he minds or not.

"I know that traditions are good, Uncle," Braeden continued. "It's how we pass down the good parts of our lives from one generation to the next. And I truly respect that my father wanted me to attend school in New York as he did. But sometimes, old traditions need to be changed and new traditions need to be made."

"I'm sensing this isn't the only tradition you're talking about," Mr. Vanderbilt said.

"There is one other," Braeden admitted. "It has been a tradition in our family for a long time to host the hunting season. And in the Blue Ridge Mountains it has been a tradition to hunt mountain lions, to kill off all the predators that live in these forests. But I think, in our family at least, we all agree now that, tradition or not, we're not going to do it anymore, we're not going to allow that kind of hunting on our land. We're going to protect our forests and our wildlife as much as we can."

Mr. Vanderbilt stared at Braeden in silence. At first Serafina thought that he must be angry. But then she realized that wasn't it at all. She could see in his eyes at that moment that Mr. Vanderbilt was immensely proud of his nephew.

"I couldn't agree more," Mr. Vanderbilt said. "I've been thinking the same thing."

"I think that some traditions need to be valued," Braeden said, "but others need to change. We shouldn't just follow the ways of the past. We should lead the way to a better future."

"If we move forward with this school idea of yours, it will require a considerable amount of work and commitment," Mr. Vanderbilt said as he studied Braeden. "It's obviously far more difficult to build an entirely new school than it is to go to an established school. Are you sure you want to do this?"

"Yes, I'm sure, Uncle," Braeden said, glancing over at Serafina. "I'm very sure."

"Once we start, you'll have to follow it through."

"I understand," Braeden said. "I'm ready."

And then the master of Biltmore turned and looked at her. "And what do you say about this idea?"

Serafina smiled excitedly. "When can we get started?"

64

That night, she sat with Braeden on the grass of a small hill nestled in the Biltmore gardens.

"Do you see that planet up there?" Braeden asked, pointing up into the star-filled sky.

Jupiter, Serafina thought wistfully. She had seen it nearly every night while he was gone, even on some of the cloudiest nights when no other planets or stars were visible. She could almost always see Jupiter shining through.

"When I was up in New York," he said, "I couldn't see most of the stars because of the lights of the city. But I could see Jupiter. And I always imagined it was you."

For a long time, she did not move or speak. She just let the moment flow around them and through them, his words, his tone of voice, his presence sitting beside her. She had never felt so deeply calm in all her life. And she wondered what could ever disturb that calm.

"It seems like we keep having to fight these battles to stay together," she said.

"And we'll keep fighting them," he said. A few more seconds passed, and then he added, "You *know* why I came back to Biltmore that night by the lake, right? And you know why I couldn't find the words I wanted to say before I left in the morning."

Serafina's heart began to pound in her chest.

"I think I do," she said, feeling as if her lips were suddenly going dry.

"I jumped off that train because I wanted to be with you, Serafina," he said. "I didn't care about anything else."

She smiled, letting the words soak down into her soul. And then she said, "Maybe next time wait until the train comes to a stop."

"Aw, that's no fun," he said, laughing softly. "Where's your sense of adventure?"

"Yeah, that's me," she said, "no sense of adventure," as she put her arm around him and rested her head gently against his chest.

And she knew, in that simple gesture of affection, that the great river of their lives had shifted course, and was pouring now across new ground, new worlds, places they had never seen or felt before.

"I love you, Braeden," she whispered.

"I love you, too, Serafina," he whispered in return.

About the Author

Robert Beatty is the #1 *New York Times* best-selling author of *Willa of the Wood* and the Serafina series. He lives in the mountains of Asheville, North Carolina, with his wife and three daughters. He writes full-time now, but in his past lives he was one of the pioneers of cloud computing, the founder/CEO of Plex Systems, the cofounder of Beatty Robotics, and the CTO and chairman of *Narrative* magazine.

Visit him online at www.robertbeattybooks.com.